Penguin Books
Joy in the Morning

Pelham Grenville Wodehouse was born in 1881 in Guildford, the son of a civil servant, and educated at Dulwich College. He spent a brief period working for the Hong Kong and Shanghai Bank before abandoning finance for writing, earning a living by journalism and selling stories to magazines.

An enormously popular and prolific writer, he produced about a hundred books. In Jeeves, the ever resourceful 'gentleman's personal gentleman', and the good-hearted young blunderer Bertie Wooster, he created two of the best-known and best-loved characters in twentieth-century literature. Their exploits, first collected in *Carry on, Jeeves*, were chronicled in fourteen books, and have been repeatedly adapted for television, radio and the stage. Wodehouse also created many other comic figures, notably Lord Emsworth, the Hon. Galahad Threepwood, Psmith and the numerous members of the Drones Club. He was part-author and writer of fifteen straight plays and of 250 lyrics for some thirty musical comedies. *The Times* hailed him as a 'comic genius recognized in his lifetime as a classic and an old master of farce'.

P. G. Wodehouse said, 'I believe there are two ways of writing novels. One is mine, making a sort of musical comedy without music and ignoring real life altogether; the other is going right deep down into life and not caring a damn.'

Wodehouse married in 1914 and took American citizenship in 1955. He was created a Knight of the British Empire in the 1975 New Year's Honours List. In a BBC interview he said that he had no ambitions left now that he had been knighted and there was a waxwork of him in Madame Tussaud's. He died on St Valentine's Day, 1975, at the age of ninety-three.

P. G. Wodehouse in Penguin

P. G. Wodehouse
Joy in the Morning

P.G.Wodehouse

Joy
in
the
Morning

PENGUIN BOOKS

PENGUIN BOOKS

Published by the Penguin Group
Penguin Books Ltd, 80 Strand, London WC2R 0RL, England
Penguin Putnam Inc., 375 Hudson Street, New York, New York 10014, USA
Penguin Books Australia Ltd, 250 Camberwell Road, Camberwell, Victoria 3124, Australia
Penguin Books Canada Ltd, 10 Alcorn Avenue, Toronto, Ontario, Canada M4V 3B2
Penguin Books India (P) Ltd, 11 Community Centre, Panchsheel Park, New Delhi – 110 017, India
Penguin Books (NZ) Ltd, Cnr Rosedale and Airborne Roads, Albany, Auckland, New Zealand
Penguin Books (South Africa) (Pty) Ltd, 24 Sturdee Avenue, Rosebank 2196, South Africa

Penguin Books Ltd, Registered Offices: 80 Strand, London WC2R 0RL, England

www.penguin.com

First published in Great Britain by Herbert Jenkins Ltd 1947
Published in Penguin Books 1999
9

Set in 9/11pt Monotype Trump
Typeset by Rowland Phototypesetting Ltd,
Bury St Edmunds, Suffolk
Printed in England by Clays Ltd, St Ives plc

Preface

The world of which I have been writing ever since I was so high, the world of the Drones Club and the lads who congregate there was always a small world – one of the smallest I ever met, as Bertie Wooster would say. It was bounded on the east by St James's Street, on the west by Hyde Park Corner, by Oxford Street on the north and by Piccadilly on the south. And now it is not even small, it is non-existent. It has gone with the wind and is one with Nineveh and Tyre. In a word, it has had it.

This is pointed out to me every time a new book of mine dealing with the Drones Club of Jeeves and Bertie is published in England. 'Edwardian!' the critics hiss at me. (It is not easy to hiss the word Edwardian, containing as it does no sibilant, but they manage it.) And I shuffle my feet and blush a good deal and say, 'Yes, I suppose you're right'. After all, I tell myself, there has been no generic term for the type of young man who figures in my stories since he used to be called a knut in the pre-first-war days, which certainly seems to suggest that the species has died out like the macaronis of the Regency and the whiskered mashers of the Victorian age.

But sometimes I am in more defiant mood. Mine, I protest, are historical novels. Nobody objects when an author writes the sort of things that begin, 'More skilled though I am at wielding the broadsword than the pen, I will set down for all to read the tale of how I, plain John Blunt, did follow my dear liege to the wars when Harry, yclept the Fifth, sat on our English throne'. Then why am I not to be allowed to set down for all to read the tale of how the Hon. J. Blunt got fined five pounds by the beak at Bosher Street Police Court for disorderly conduct on Boat Race Night? Unfair discrimination is the phrase that springs to the lips.

I suppose one thing that makes these drones of mine seem creatures of a dead past is that with the exception of Oofy Prosser, the club millionaire, they are genial and good tempered, friends of all the world. In these days when everybody hates everybody else, anyone who is not snarling at something – or at everything – is an anachronism. The Edwardian knut was never an angry young man. He would get a little cross, perhaps, if his man Meadowes sent him out some morning with odd spats on, but his normal outlook on life was sunny. He was a humble, kindly soul, who knew he was a silly ass but hoped you wouldn't mind. He liked everybody, and most people liked him. Portrayed on the stage by George Grossmith and G. P. Huntley, he was a lovable figure, warming the hearts of all. You might disapprove of him not being a world's worker, but you could not help being fond of him.

Though, as a matter of fact, many of the members of my Drones Club *are* world's workers. Freddie Threepwood is a vice-president at Donaldson's Dog Joy Inc. of Long Island City, U.S.A., and sells as smart a dog-biscuit as the best of them. Bingo Little edits *Wee Tots*, the popular journal for the nursery and the home, Catsmeat Potter-Pirbright has played the juvenile in a number of West End comedies, generally coming on early in Act One with a cheery 'Tennis, anyone?', and even Bertie Wooster once wrote an article on 'What the Well-Dressed Man is Wearing' for his Aunt Dahlia's weekly, *Milady's Boudoir*.

Two things caused the decline of the drone or knut, the first of which was that hard times hit younger sons. Most knuts were younger sons, and in the reign of good King Edward the position of the younger son in

aristocratic families was . . . what's the word, Jeeves?
Anomalous? You're sure? Right ho, anomalous. Thank
you, Jeeves. Putting it another way, he was a trifle on
the superfluous side, his standing about that of the litter
of kittens which the household cat deposits in the
drawer where you keep your clean shirts.

What generally happened was this. An Earl, let us say,
begat an heir. So far, so good. One can always do with an
heir. But then – these Earls never know when to stop –
he absent-mindedly, as it were, begat a second son and
this time was not any too pleased about the state of
affairs. It was difficult to see how to fit him in. But there
he was, requiring his calories just the same as if he had
been first in succession. It made the Earl feel that he was
up against something hard to handle.

'Can't let Algy starve,' he said to himself, and forked
out a monthly allowance. And so there came into being
a group of ornamental young men whom the ravens fed.
Like the lilies of the field, they toiled not neither did
they spin but lived quite contentedly on the paternal
dole. Their wants were few. Provided they could secure
the services of a tailor who was prepared to accept
charm of manner as a substitute for ready cash – and it
was extraordinary how full London was of altruistic
tailors in the early nineteen hundreds – they asked for
little more. In short, so long as the ravens continued to
do their stuff, they were in that blissful condition
known as sitting pretty.

Then the economic factor reared its ugly head.
Income tax and super-tax shot up like rocketing
pheasants, and the Earl found himself doing some
constructive thinking. A bright idea occurred to him and
the more he turned it over in his mind, the better he
liked it.

'*Why* can't I?' he said to his Countess as they sat one
night trying to balance the budget.

'Why can't you what?' said the Countess.

'Let Algy starve.'

'Algy who?'

'Our Algy.'

'You mean our second son, the Hon. Algernon Blair Worthington ffinch-ffinch?'

'That's right. He's getting into my ribs to the tune of a cool thousand a year because I felt I couldn't let him starve. The point I'm making is why *not* let the young blighter starve?'

'It's a thought,' the Countess agreed. 'Yes, a very sound scheme. We all eat too much these days, anyway.'

So the ravens were retired from active duty, and Algy, faced with the prospect of not getting his three square meals a day unless he worked for them, hurried out and found a job, with the result that as of even date any poor hack like myself who, wishing to turn an honest penny, writes stories about him and all the other Algys, Freddies, Claudes and Berties, automatically becomes Edwardian.

The second thing that led to the elimination of the knut was the passing of the spat. In the brave old days spats were the hallmark of the young-feller-me-lad-about-town, the foundation stone on which his whole policy was based, and it is sad to reflect that a generation has arisen which does not know what spats were. I once wrote a book called *Young Men in Spats*. I could not use that title today.

Spatterdashes was, I believe, their full name, and they were made of white cloth and buttoned round the ankles, partly no doubt to protect the socks from getting dashed with spatter but principally because they lent a sort of gay *diablerie* to the wearer's appearance. The monocle might or might not be worn, according to taste, but spats, like the tightly rolled umbrella, were obligatory. I was never myself by knut standards really dressy as a young man (*circa* 1905), for a certain anaemia of the exchequer compelled me to go about my social duties in my brother's cast-off frock coat and trousers, neither of which fitted me, and a top hat bequeathed to me by an uncle with head some sizes larger than mine, but my umbrella was always rolled tight as a drum and though spats cost money I had mine all right. There they were, white and gleaming, fascinating the passers-by and causing seedy strangers who hoped for largesse to address me as 'Captain' and sometimes even as 'M'lord'. Many a butler at the turn of the century, opening the door to me and wincing visibly at the sight of my topper, would lower his eyes, see the spats and give a little sigh of relief, as much as to say, 'Not quite what we are accustomed to at the northern end, perhaps, but unexceptionable to the south'.

Naturally, if you cut off a fellow's allowance, he cannot afford spats, and without spats he is a spent force. Deprived of these indispensable adjuncts, the knut threw in the towel and called it a day.

But I have not altogether lost hope of a sensational revival of knuttery. Already one sees signs of a coming renaissance. To take but one instance, the butler is creeping back. Extinct, it seemed, only a few short years ago, he is now repeatedly seen in his old haunts like some shy bird which, driven from its native marshes by alarums and excursions, stiffens the sinews, summons up the blood and decides to give the old home another try. True, he wants a bit more than in the golden age, but pay his price and he will buttle. In hundreds of homes there is buttling going on just as of yore. Who can say that ere long spats and knuts and all the old bung-ho-ing will not be flourishing again?

When that happens, I shall look my critics in the eye and say, 'Edwardian? Where do you get that "Edwardian" stuff? I write of life as it is lived today.'

P. G. WODEHOUSE

Part 1

I

After the thing was over, when peril had ceased to loom and happy endings had been distributed in heaping handfuls and we were driving home with our hats on the side of our heads, having shaken the dust of Steeple Bumpleigh from our tyres, I confessed to Jeeves that there had been moments during the recent proceedings when Bertram Wooster, though no weakling, had come very near to despair.

'Within a toucher, Jeeves.'

'Unquestionably affairs had developed a certain menacing trend, sir.'

'I saw no ray of hope. It looked to me as if the blue bird had thrown in the towel and formally ceased to function. And yet here we are, all boomps-a-daisy. Makes one think a bit, that.'

'Yes, sir.'

'There's an expression on the tip of my tongue which seems to me to sum the whole thing up. Or, rather, when I say an expression, I mean a saying. A wheeze. A gag. What I believe, is called a saw. Something about Joy doing something.'

'Joy cometh in the mornings, sir?'

'That's the baby. Not one of your things, is it?'

'No, sir.'

'Well, it's dashed good,' I said.

And I still think that there can be no neater way of putting in a nutshell the outcome of the super-sticky affair of Nobby Hopwood, Stilton Cheesewright, Florence Craye, my Uncle Percy, J. Chichester Clam, Edwin the Boy Scout and old Boko Fittleworth – or, as

my biographers will probably call it, the Steeple
Bumpleigh Horror.

Even before the events occurred which I am about to
relate, the above hamlet had come high up on my list of
places to be steered sedulously clear of. I don't know if
you have ever seen one of those old maps where they
mark a spot with a cross and put 'Here be dragons' or
'Keep ye eye skinned for hippogriffs', but I had always
felt that some such kindly warning might well have
been given to pedestrians and traffic with regard to this
Steeple Bumpleigh.

A picturesque settlement, yes. None more so in all
Hampshire. It lay embowered, as I believe the expression
is, in the midst of smiling fields and leafy woods, hard
by a willow-fringed river, and you couldn't have thrown
a brick in it without hitting a honeysuckle-covered
cottage or beaning an apple-cheeked villager. But you
remember what the fellow said – it's not a bally bit of
use every prospect pleasing if man is vile, and the catch
about Steeple Bumpleigh was that it contained
Bumpleigh Hall, which in its turn contained my Aunt
Agatha and her second husband.

And when I tell you that this second h. was none
other than Percival, Lord Worplesdon, and that he had
with him his daughter Florence and his son Edwin, the
latter as pestilential a stripling as ever wore khaki shorts
and went spooring or whatever it is that these Boy
Scouts do, you will understand why I had always
declined my old pal Boko Fittleworth's invitations to
visit him at the bijou residence he maintained in those
parts.

I had also had to be similarly firm with Jeeves, who
had repeatedly hinted his wish that I should take a
cottage there for the summer months. There was, it
appeared, admirable fishing in the river, and he is a man
who dearly loves to flick the baited hook. 'No, Jeeves,' I

had been compelled to say, 'much though it pains me to put a stopper on your simple pleasures, I cannot take the risk of running into that gang of pluguglies. Safety first.' And he had replied, 'Very good, sir,' and there the matter had rested.

But all the while, unsuspected by Bertram, the shadow of Steeple Bumpleigh was creeping nearer and nearer, and came a day when it tore off its whiskers and pounced.

Oddly enough, the morning on which this major disaster occurred was one that found me completely, even exuberantly, in the pink. No inkling of the soup into which I was to be plunged came to mar my perfect *bien être*. I had slept well, shaved well and shower-bathed well, and it was with a merry cry that I greeted Jeeves as he brought in the coffee and kippers.

'Odd's boddikins, Jeeves,' I said, 'I am in rare fettle this a.m. Talk about exulting in my youth! I feel up and doing, with a heart for any fate, as Tennyson says.'

'Longfellow, sir.'

'Or, if you prefer it, Longfellow. I am in no mood to split hairs. Well, what's the news?'

'Miss Hopwood called while you were still asleep, sir.'

'No, really? I wish I'd seen her.'

'The young lady was desirous of entering your room and rousing you with a wet sponge, but I dissuaded her. I considered it best that your repose should not be disturbed.'

I applauded this watch-dog spirit, showing as it did both the kindly heart and the feudal outlook, but continued to tut-tut a bit at having missed the young pipsqueak, with whom my relations had always been of the matiest. This Zenobia ('Nobby') Hopwood was old Worplesdon's ward, as I believe it is called. A pal of his, just before he stopped ticking over some years previously, had left him in charge of his daughter. I don't know how these things are arranged – no doubt documents have to be drawn up and dotted lines signed on – but, whatever the procedure, the upshot was as I have stated. When all the smoke had cleared away, my Uncle Percy was Nobby's guardian.

'Young Nobby, eh? When did she blow into the great city?' I asked. For, on becoming Uncle Percy's ward, she had of course joined the strength at his Steeple Bumpleigh lair, and it was only rarely nowadays that she came to London.

'Last night, sir.'

'Making a long stay?'

'Only until to-morrow, sir.'

'Hardly worthwhile sweating up just for a day, I should have thought.'

'I understand that she came because her ladyship desired her company, sir.'

I quailed a bit.

'You don't mean Aunt Agatha's in London?'

'Merely passing through, sir,' replied the honest fellow, calming my apprehensions. 'Her ladyship is on her way to minister to Master Thomas, who has contracted mumps at his school.'

His allusion was to the old relative's son by her first marriage, one of our vilest citizens. Many good judges rank him even higher in England's Rogue Gallery than her step-son Edwin. I was rejoiced to learn that he had got mumps, and toyed for a moment with a hope that Aunt Agatha would catch them from him.

'And what had Nobby to say for herself?'

'She was regretting that she saw so little of you nowadays, sir.'

'Quite mutual, the agony, Jeeves. There are few better eggs than this Hopwood.'

'She expressed a hope that you might shortly see your way to visiting Steeple Bumpleigh.'

I shook the head.

'Out of the q., Jeeves.'

6

'The young lady tells me the fish are biting well there just now.'

'No, Jeeves. I'm sorry. Not even if they bite like serpents do I go near Steeple Bumpleigh.'

'Very good, sir.'

He spoke sombrely, and I endeavoured to ease the strain by asking for another cup of coffee.

'Was Nobby alone?'

'No, sir. There was a gentleman with her, who spoke as if he were acquainted with you. Miss Hopwood addressed him as Stilton.'

'Big chap?'

'Noticeably well developed, sir.'

'With a head like a pumpkin?'

'Yes, sir. There was a certain resemblance to the vegetable.'

'It must have been a companion of my earlier years named G. D'Arcy Cheesewright. In our whimsical way we used to call him Stilton. I haven't seen him for ages. He lives in the country somewhere, and to hobnob with Bertram Wooster it is imperative that you stick around the metropolis. Odd, him knowing Nobby.'

'I gathered from the young lady's remarks that Mr Cheesewright is also a resident of Steeple Bumpleigh, sir.'

'Really? It's a small world, Jeeves.'

'Yes, sir.'

'I don't know when I've seen a smaller,' I said, and would have gone more deeply into the subject, but at this juncture the telephone tinkled out a summons, and he shimmered off to answer it. Through the door, which he had chanced to leave ajar, the ear detected a good deal of Yes-my-lord-ing and Very-good-my-lord-ing, seeming to indicate that he had hooked one of the old nobility.

'Who was it?' I asked, as he filtered in again.

'Lord Worplesdon, sir.'

It seems almost incredible to me, looking back, that I

7

should have received this news item with nothing more than a mildly surprised 'Oh, ah?' Amazing, I mean, that I shouldn't have spotted the sinister way in which what you might call the Steeple Bumpleigh note had begun to intrude itself like some creeping fog or miasma, and trembled in every limb, asking myself what this portended. But so it was. The significance of the thing failed to penetrate and, as I say, I oh-ahed with merely a faint spot of surprise.

'The call was for me, sir. His lordship wishes me to go to his office immediately.'

'He wants to see you?'

'Such was the impression I gathered, sir.'

'Did he say why?'

'No, sir. Merely that the matter was of considerable urgency.'

I mused, thoughtfully champing a kipper. It seemed to me that there could be but one solution.

'Do you know what I think, Jeeves? He's in a spot of some kind and needs your counsel.'

'It may be so, sir.'

'I'll bet it's so. He must know all about your outstanding gifts. You can't go on as you have gone on so long, dishing out aid and comfort to all and sundry, without acquiring a certain reputation, if only in the family circle. Grab your hat and race along. I shall be all agog to learn the inside story. What sort of a day is it?'

'Extremely clement, sir.'

'Sunshine and all that?'

'Yes, sir.'

'I thought as much. That must by why I'm feeling so dashed fit. Then I think I'll take myself for an airing. Tell me,' I said, for I was a trifle remorseful at having had to adopt that firm attitude about going to Steeple Bumpleigh and wished to bring back into his life the joy which my refusal to allow him to get in among the local fish had excluded from it, 'is there any little thing I can do for you while I'm out?'

'Sir?'

'Any little gift you would like, I mean?'

'It is extremely kind of you, sir.'

'Not at all, Jeeves. The sky is the limit. State your desire.'

'Well, sir, there has recently been published a new and authoritatively annotated edition of the works of the philosopher Spinoza. Since you are so generous, I would appreciate that very much.'

'You shall have it. It shall be delivered to your door in a plain van without delay. You're sure you've got the name right? Spinoza?'

'Yes, sir.'

'It doesn't sound probable, but no doubt you know best. Spinoza, eh? Is he the Book Society's Choice of the Month?'

'I believe not, sir.'

'Well, he's the only fellow I ever heard of who wasn't. Right ho. I'll see to it instanter.'

And presently, having assembled the hat, the gloves and the neatly rolled u., I sauntered forth.

As I made my way to the bookery, I found my thoughts turning once more, as you may readily imagine, to this highly suggestive business of old Worplesdon. The thing intrigued me. I found it difficult to envisage what possible sort of jam a man like that could have got himself into.

When, about eighteen months before, news had reached me through well-informed channels that my Aunt Agatha, for many years a widow, or derelict, as I believe it is called, was about to take another pop at matrimony, my first emotion, as was natural in the circumstances, had been a gentle pity for the unfortunate goop slated to step up the aisle with her – she, as you are aware, being my tough aunt, the one who eats broken bottles and conducts human sacrifices by the light of the full moon.

But when the details began to come in, and I discovered that the bimbo who had drawn the short straw was Lord Worplesdon, the shipping magnate, this tender commiseration became sensibly diminished. The thing, I felt, would be no walkover. Even if in the fullness of time she wore him down and at length succeeded in making him jump through hoops, she would know she had been in a fight.

For he was hot stuff, this Worplesdon. I had known him all my life. It was he who at the age of fifteen – when I was fifteen, I mean, of course – found me smoking one of his special cigars in the stable yard and chased me a mile across difficult country with a hunting crop. And though with advancing years our relations had naturally grown more formal, I had never been able to think of him without getting goose pimples. Given the choice between him and a hippogriff as a companion for a walking tour, I would have picked the hippogriff every time.

It was not easy to see how such a man of blood and iron could have been reduced to sending out SOS's for Jeeves, and I was reflecting on the possibility of compromising letters in the possession of gold-digging blondes, when I reached my destination and started to lodge my order.

'Good morning, good morning,' I said. 'I want a book.'

Of course, I ought to have known that it's silly to try to buy a book when you go to a book shop. It merely startles and bewilders the inmates. The motheaten old bird who had stepped forward to attend to me ran true to form.

'A book, sir?' he replied, with ill-concealed astonishment.

'Spinoza,' I replied, specifying.

This had him rocking back on his heels.

'Did you say Spinoza, sir?'

'Spinoza was what I said.'

He seemed to be feeling that if we talked this thing out long enough as man to man, we might eventually hit upon a formula.

'You do not mean "The Spinning Wheel"?'

'No.'

'It would not be "The Poisoned Pin"?'

'It would not.'

'Or "With Gun and Camera in Little Known Borneo"?' he queried, trying a long shot.

'Spinoza,' I repeated firmly. That was my story, and I intended to stick to it.

He sighed a bit, like one who feels that the situation has got beyond him.

'I will go and see if we have it in stock, sir. But possibly this may be what you are requiring. Said to be very clever.'

He pushed off, Spinoza-ing under his breath in a hopeless sort of way, leaving me clutching a thing called 'Spindrift'.

It looked pretty foul. Its jacket showed a female with a green, oblong face sniffing at a purple lily, and I was just about to fling it from me and start a hunt for that 'Poisoned Pin' of which he had spoken, when I became aware of someone Good-gracious-Bertie-ing and, turning, found that the animal cries proceeded from a tall girl of commanding aspect who had oiled up behind me.

'Good gracious, Bertie! Is it really you?'

I emitted a sharp gurgle, and shied like a startled mustang. It was old Worplesdon's daughter, Florence Craye.

And I'll tell you why, on beholding her, I shied and gurgled as described. I mean, if there's one thing I bar, it's the sort of story where people stagger to and fro, clutching their foreheads and registering strong emotion, and not a word of explanation as to what it's all about till the detective sums up in the last chapter.

Briefly, then, the reason why this girl's popping up had got in amongst me in this fashion was that we had once been engaged to be married, and not so dashed long ago, either. And though it all came out all right in the end, the thing being broken off and self-saved from the scaffold at the eleventh hour, it had been an extraordinarily narrow squeak and the memory remained green. The mere mention of her name was still enough to make me call for a couple of quick ones, so you can readily appreciate my agitation at bumping into her like this absolutely in the flesh.

I swayed in the breeze, and found myself a bit stumped for the necessary dialogue.

'Oh, hullo,' I said.

Not good, of course, but the best I could do.

2

Scanning the roster of the females I've nearly got married to in my time, we find the names of some tough babies. The eye rests on that of Honoria Glossop, and a shudder passes through the frame. So it does when we turn to the B's and come upon Madeline Bassett. But, taking everything into consideration and weighing this and that, I have always been inclined to consider Florence Craye the top. In the face of admittedly stiff competition, it is to her that I would award the biscuit.

Honoria Glossop was hearty, yes. Her laugh was like a steam-riveting machine, and from a child she had been a confirmed back-slapper. Madeline Bassett was soppy, true. She had large, melting eyes and thought the stars were God's daisy chain. These are grave defects, but to do this revolting duo justice neither had tried to mould me, and that was what Florence Craye had done from the start, seeming to look on Bertram Wooster as a mere chunk of plasticine in the hands of the sculptor.

The root of the trouble was that she was one of those intellectual girls, steeped to the gills in serious purpose, who are unable to see a male soul without wanting to get behind it and shove. We had scarcely arranged the preliminaries before she was checking up on my reading, giving the bird to 'Blood On The Bannisters', which happened to be what I was studying at the moment, and substituting for it a thing called 'Types of Ethical Theory'. Nor did she attempt to conceal the fact that this was a mere pipe opener and that there was worse to come.

Have you ever dipped into 'Types Of Ethical Theory'?

The volume is still on my shelves. Let us open it and see what it has to offer. Yes, here we are.

Of the two antithetic terms in the Greek philosophy one only was real and selfsubsisting; that is to say, Ideal Thought as opposed to that which it has to penetrate and mould. The other, corresponding to our Nature, was in itself phenomenal, unreal, without any permanent footing, having no predicates that held true for two moments together; in short, redeemed from negation only by including indwelling realities appearing through.

Right. You will have got the idea, and will, I think, be able to understand why the sight of her made me give at the knees somewhat. Old wounds had been reopened.

None of the embarrassment which was causing the Wooster toes to curl up inside their neat suède shoes like the tendrils of some sensitive plant seemed to be affecting this chunk of the dead past. Her manner, as always, was brisk and aunt-like. Even at the time when I had fallen beneath the spell of that profile of hers, which was a considerable profile and tended to make a man commit himself to statements which he later regretted, I had always felt that she was like someone training on to be an aunt.

'And how are you, Bertie?'

'Oh, fine, thanks.'

'I have just run up to London to see my publisher. Fancy meeting you, and in a book shop, of all places. What are you buying? Some trash, I suppose?'

Her gaze, which had been resting on me in a rather critical and censorious way, as if she was wondering how she could ever have contemplated linking her lot to anything so subhuman, now transferred itself to the volume in my hand. She took it from me, her lip curling in faint disgust, as if she wished she had had a pair of tongs handy.

And then, as she looked at it, her whole aspect suddenly altered. She switched off the curling lip. She smiled a pleased smile. The eye softened. A blush mantled the features. She positively giggled.

'Oh, Bertie!'

The gist got past me. 'Oh, Bertie!' was a thing she had frequently said to me in the days when we had been affianced, but always with that sort of nasty ring in the voice which made you feel that she had been on the point of expressing her exasperation with something a good deal fruitier but had remembered her ancient lineage just in time. This current 'Oh, Bertie!' was quite different. Practically a coo. As it might have been one turtle dove addressing another turtle dove.

'Oh, *Bertie*!' she repeated. 'Well, of course, I must autograph it for you,' she said, and at the same moment all was suddenly made clear to me. I had missed it at first, because I had been concentrating on the girl with the green face, but I now perceived at the bottom of the jacket the words 'By Florence Craye'. They had been half hidden by a gummed-on label which said 'Book Society Choice Of The Month'. I saw all, and the thought of how near I had come to marrying a female novelist made everything go black for a bit.

She wrote in the book with a firm hand, thus dishing any prospect that the shop would take it back and putting me seven bob and a tanner down almost, as you might say, before the day had started. Then she said 'Well!' still with that turtle dove timbre in her voice.

'Fancy you buying "Spindrift"!'

Well, one has to say the civil thing, and it may be that in the agitation of the moment I overdid it a bit. I rather think that the impression I must have conveyed, when I assured her that I had made a bee-line for the beastly volume, was that I had been counting the minutes till I could get my hooks on it. At any rate, she came back with a gratified simper.

'I can't tell you how pleased I am. Not just because it's mine, but because I see that all the trouble I took training your mind was not wasted. You have grown to love good literature.'

It was at this point, as if he had entered on cue, that the motheaten bird returned and said they had not got old Pop Spinoza, but could get him for me. He seemed rather depressed about it all, but Florence's eyes lit up as if somebody had pressed a switch.

'Bertie! This is amazing! Do you really read Spinoza?'

It's extraordinary how one yields to that fatal temptation to swank. It undoes the best of us. Nothing, I mean, would have been simpler than to reply that she had got the data twisted and that the authoritatively annotated edition was a present for Jeeves. But, instead of doing the simple, manly, straightforward thing, I had to go and put on dog.

'Oh, rather,' I said, with an intellectual flick of the umbrella. 'When I have a leisure moment, you will generally find me curled up with Spinoza's latest.'

'*Well!*'

A simple word, but as she spoke it a shudder ran through me from brilliantined topknot to rubber shoe sole.

It was the look that accompanied the yip that caused this shudder. It was exactly the same sort of look that Madeline Bassett had given me, that time I went to Totleigh Towers to pinch old Bassett's cow-creamer and she thought I had come because I loved her so much that I couldn't stay away from her side. A frightful, tender, melting look that went through me like a red-hot bradawl through a pat of butter and filled me with a nameless fear.

I wished now I hadn't plugged Spinoza so heartily, and above all I wished I hadn't been caught in the act of apparently buying this blighted 'Spindrift'. I saw that unwittingly I had been giving myself a terrific build-up, causing this girl to see Bertram Wooster with new eyes and to get hep to his hidden depths. It might quite well happen that she would review the position in the light of this fresh evidence and decide that she had made a mistake in breaking off her engagement to so rare a spirit. And once she got thinking along those lines, who knew what the harvest might be?

An imperious urge came upon me to be elsewhere, before I could make a chump of myself further.

'Well, I'm afraid I must be popping,' I said. 'Most important appointment. Frightfully jolly, seeing you again.'

'We ought to see each other more,' she replied, still with that melting look. 'We ought to have some long talks.'

'Oh, rather.'

'A developing mind is so fascinating. Why don't you ever come to the Hall?'

'Oh, well, one gets a bit chained to the metropolis, you know.'

'I should like to show you the reviews of "Spindrift". They are wonderful. Edwin is pasting them in an album for me.'

'I'd love to see them some time. Later on, perhaps. Good-bye.'

'You're forgetting your book.'

'Oh, thanks. Well, toodle-oo,' I said, and fought my way out.

The appointment to which I had alluded was with the barman at the Bollinger. Seldom, if ever, had I felt in such sore need of a restorative. I headed for my destination like a hart streaking towards cooling streams, when heated in the chase, and was speedily in conference with the dispenser of life savers.

Ten minutes later, feeling considerably better, though

still shaken, I was standing in the doorway, twirling my umbrella and wondering what to do next, when my eye was arrested by an odd spectacle.

A certain rumminess had begun to manifest itself across the way.

3

The Bollinger bar conducts its beneficent activities about half-way up Bond Street, and on the other side of the thoroughfare, immediately opposite, there stands a courteous and popular jeweller's, where I generally make my purchases when the question of investing in *bijouterie* arises. In fact, the day being so fine, I was rather thinking of looking in there now and buying a new cigarette case.

It was outside this jeweller's that the odd spectacle was in progress. A bloke of furtive aspect was shimmering to and fro on the threshold of the emporium, his demeanour rather like that of the cat in the adage, which, according to Jeeves, and I suppose he knows, let 'I dare not' wait upon 'I would'. He seemed, that is to say, desirous of entering, but was experiencing some difficulty in making the grade. He would have a sudden dash at it, and then draw back and stand shooting quick glances right and left, as if fearing the scrutiny of the public eye. Over in New York, during the days of Prohibition, I have seen fellows doing the same sort of thing outside speakeasies.

He was a massive bloke, and there was something in his appearance that seemed familiar. Then, as I narrowed my gaze and scanned him more closely, memory did its stuff. That beefy frame . . . That pumpkin shaped head . . . The face that looked like a slab of pink dough . . . It was none other than my old friend, Stilton Cheesewright. And what he was doing, pirouetting outside jewellery bins, was more than I could understand.

I started across the road with the idea of instituting a probe or quiz, and at the same moment he seemed to summon up a sudden burst of resolution. As I paused to disentangle myself from a passing bus, he picked up his feet, tossed his head in a mettlesome sort of way, and was through the door like a man dashing into a railway-station buffet with only two minutes for a gin and tonic before his train goes.

When I entered the establishment, he was leaning over the counter, his gaze riveted on some species of merchandise which was being shown him by the gentlemanly assistant. To prod him in the hindquarters with my umbrella was with me the work of an instant.

'Ahoy, there, Stilton!' I cried.

He spun round with a sort of guilty bound, like an adagio dancer surprised while watering the cat's milk.

'Oh, hullo,' he said.

There was a pause. At a moment like this, with old boyhood friends meeting again after long separation, I mean to say, you might have expected a good deal of animated what-ho-ing and an immediate picking up of the threads. Of this, however, there was a marked absence. The Auld Lang Syne spirit was strong in me, but not, or I was mistaken, equally strong in G. D'Arcy Cheesewright. I have met so many people in my time who have wished that Bertram was elsewhere that I have come to recognize the signs. And it was these signs that this former playmate was now exhibiting.

He drew me away from the counter, shielding it from my gaze with his person, like somebody trying to hide the body.

'I wish you wouldn't go spiking people in the backside with your beastly umbrella,' he said, and one sensed the querulous note. 'Gave me a nasty shock.'

I apologized gracefully, explaining that if you have an

20

umbrella and are fortunate enough to catch an old acquaintance bending, you naturally do not let the opportunity slip, and endeavoured to set him at his ease with genial chit-chat. From the embarrassment he was displaying, I might have been some high official in the police force interrupting him in the middle of a smash and grab raid. His demeanour perplexed me.

'Well, well, well, Stilton,' I said. 'Quite a while since we met.'

'Yes,' he responded, his air that of a man who was a bit sorry it hadn't been longer.

'How's the boy?'

'Oh, all right. How are you?'

'Fine, thanks. As a matter of fact, I'm feeling unusually fizzy.'

'That's good.'

'I thought you'd be pleased.'

'Oh, I am. Well, good-bye, Bertie,' he said, shaking me by the hand. 'Nice to have seen you.'

I looked at him, amazed. Did he really imagine, I asked myself, that I was as easily got rid of as this? Why, experts have tried to get rid of Bertram Wooster and have been forced to admit defeat.

'I'm not leaving you yet,' I assured him.

'Aren't you?' he said, wistfully.

'No, no. Still here. Jeeves tells me you dropped in on me this morning.'

'Yes.'

'Accompanied by Nobby.'

'Yes.'

'You live at Steeple Bumpleigh, too, I hear.'

'Yes.'

'It's a small world.'

'Not so very.'

'Jeeves thinks it is.'

'Well, fairly small, perhaps,' he agreed, making a concession. 'You're sure I'm not keeping you, Bertie?'

'No, no.'

'I thought you might have some date somewhere.'

'Oh, no, not a thing.'

There was another pause. He hummed a few bars of a popular melody, but not rollickingly. He also shuffled his feet quite a bit.

'Been there long?'

'Where?'

'Steeple Bumpleigh.'

'Oh? No, not very long.'

'Like it?'

'Very much.'

'What do you do there?'

'Do?'

'Come, come, you know what I mean by "do". Boko Fittleworth, for instance, writes wholesome fiction for the masses there. My Uncle Percy relaxes there after the day's shipping magnating. What is your racket?'

A rather odd look came into his map, and he fixed me with a cold and challenging eye, as if daring me to start something. I remembered having seen the same defiant glitter behind the spectacles of a man I met in a country hotel once, just before he told me his name was Snodgrass. It was as if this old companion of mine were on the brink of some shameful confession.

Then he seemed to think better of it.

'Oh, I mess about.'

'Mess about?'

'Yes. Just mess about. Doing this and that, you know.'

There seemed nothing to be gained by pursuing this line of inquiry. It was obvious that he did not intend to loosen up. I passed on, accordingly, to the point which had been puzzling me so much.

'Well, flitting lightly over that,' I said, 'why were you hovering?'

'Hovering?'

'Yes.'

'When?'

'Just now. Outside the shop.'

'I wasn't hovering.'

'You were distinctly hovering. You reminded me of a girl Jeeves was speaking about the other day, who stood with reluctant feet where the brook and river met. And when I follow you in, I find you buzz-buzzing into the ear of the assistant, plainly making some furtive purchase. What are you buying, Stilton?'

Fixed by my penetrating eye, he came clean. I suppose he saw that further concealment was useless.

'A ring,' he said, in a low, hoarse voice.

'What sort of a ring?' I asked, pressing him.

'An engagement ring,' he muttered, twisting his fingers and in other ways showing that he was fully conscious of his position.

'Are you engaged?'

'Yes.'

'Well, well, well!'

I laughed heartily, as is my custom on these occasions, but on his inquiring in a throaty growl rather like the snarl of the Rocky Mountains timber wolf what the devil I was cackling about, cheesed the mirth. I had always found Stilton intimidating, when stirred. In a weak moment at Oxford, misled by my advisers, I once tried to do a bit of rowing, and Stilton was the bird who coached us from the towing path. I could still recall some of the things he had said about my stomach, which – rightly or wrongly – he considered that I was sticking out. It would seem that when you are a Volga boatman, you aren't supposed to stick your stomach out.

'I always laugh when people tell me they are engaged,' I explained, more soberly.

It did not seem to mollify him – if 'mollify' is the word I want. He continued to glower.

'You have no objection to my being engaged?'

'No, no.'

'Why shouldn't I be engaged?'

'Oh, quite.'

'What do you mean by "Oh, quite"?'

I didn't quite know what I had meant by 'Oh, quite', unless possibly 'Oh, quite'. I explained this, trying to infuse into my manner a soothing what-is-it, for he appeared to be hotting up.

'I hope you will be very, very happy,' I said.

He thanked me, though not effusively.

'Nice girl, I expect?'

'Yes.'

The response was not what you would call lyrical, but we Woosters can read between the lines. His eyes were rolling in their sockets, and his face had taken on the colour and expression of a devout tomato. I could see that he loved like a thousand of bricks.

A thought struck me.

'It isn't Nobby?'

'No. She's engaged to Boko Fittleworth.'

'What!'

'Yes.'

'I never knew that. He might have told me. Nobby and Boko have hitched up, have they?'

'Yes.'

'Well, well, well! The laughing Love God has been properly up on his toes in and around Steeple Bumpleigh of late, what?'

'Yes.'

'Never an idle moment. Day and night shifts. Your betrothed, I take it, is a resident?'

'Yes. Her name's Craye. Florence Craye.'

'What!'

The word escaped my lips in a sort of yowl, and he started and gave me the raised eyebrow. I suppose it always perplexes the young Romeo to some extent, when fellows begin yowling on being informed of the loved one's identity.

'What's the matter?' he asked, a rather strained note in his voice.

Well, of course, that yowl of mine, as you may well imagine, had been one of ecstasy and relief. I mean, if Florence was all tied up with him, the peril I had been envisaging could be considered to have blown a fuse and ceased to impend. Spinoza or no Spinoza, I felt, this let Bertram out. But I couldn't very well tell him that.

'Oh, nothing,' I said.

'You seem to know her.'

'Oh, yes, we've met.'

'I've never heard her speak of you.'

'No?'

'No. Have you known her long?'

'A certain time.'

'Do you know her well?'

'Pretty well.'

'When you say "Pretty well", you mean – ?'

'Fairly well. Tolerably well.'

'How did you come to know her?'

I was conscious of a growing embarrassment. A little more of this, I felt, and he would elicit the fact that his betrothed had once been very near to Bertram – a dashed sight nearer, as we have seen, than Bertram had liked: and no recently engaged bimbo cares to discover that he was not the little woman's first choice. It sort of rubs the bloom off the thing. What he wants to feel is that she spent her time gazing out of the turret window in a yearning spirit till he came galloping up on the white horse.

I temporized, accordingly. I believe the word is 'temporized'. I should have to check up with Jeeves.

'Her ghastly father married my frightful aunt.'

'Is Lady Worplesdon your aunt?'

'And how!'

'You didn't know her before that?'

'Well, yes. Slightly.'

'I see.'

He was still giving me that searching look, like a G-man hobnobbing with a suspect, and I am not ashamed to confess that I wiped a bead of persp. from the brow with the ferrule of my umbrella. That embarrassment, to which I have referred, was still up and doing – in fact, more so than ever.

I could see now what I had failed to spot before, that in thinking of him as a Romeo I had made an incorrect diagnosis. The bird whose name ought to have sprung to my mind was Othello. In this Cheesewright, it was plain, I had run up against one of those touchy lovers who go about the place in a suspicious and red-eyed spirit, eager to hammer the stuffing out of such of the citizenry as they suppose to be or to have been in any sense matey with the adored object. It would, in short, require but a sketchy outline of the facts relating to self and Florence to unleash the cave man within him.

'When I say "slightly",' I hastened to add, 'I mean, of course, that we were just acquaintances.'

'Just acquaintances, eh?'

'Just.'

'You simply happened to meet her once or twice?'

'That's right. You put it in a nutshell.'

'I see. The reason I ask is that it seemed to me, when I told you she was engaged to me, that your manner was peculiar –'

'It always is before lunch.'

'You started –'

'Touch of cramp.'

'And uttered an exclamation. As if the news had come as an unpleasant shock to you.'

'Oh, no.'

'You're sure it didn't?'

'Not a bit.'

'In fact, you were mere acquaintances?'

'Mere to the core.'

'Still, it's strange that she has never mentioned you.'

'Well, pip-pip,' I said, changing the subject, and withdrew.

4

It was a grave and thoughtful Bertram Wooster who
started to amble back to the old flat. I was feeling a bit
weak, too. During the recent scene I had run the gamut
of the emotions, as I believe it is called, and that always
takes it out of one.

My first reaction to Stilton's revelation had, as I have
indicated, been relief, and of course I was still rolling the
eyes up to Heaven in silent thankfulness a goodish bit.
But it is seldom that the Woosters think only of self, and
I now found the contemplation of the dreadful thing
which had come upon this man filling me almost to the
brim with pity and terror. It seemed to me that a Save
Stilton Cheesewright movement ought to be got under
way immediately. For though he wasn't what you would
call absolutely one of my bosom pals, like Boko
Fittleworth, one has one's human feelings. I remembered
how the iron had entered into my gizzard when I was
faced with the prospect of being led to the altar by
Florence Craye.

One could see, of course, how the tragedy had
occurred. It was the poor blister's pathetic desire to do
his soul a bit of good that had landed him in this awful
predicament. As is so often the case with these stolid,
beefy birds, he had always had a yearning for higher
things.

This whole business of jacking up the soul is one that
varies according to what Jeeves calls the psychology of
the individual, some being all for it, others not. You take
me, for instance. I don't say I've got much of a soul, but,
such as it is, I'm perfectly satisfied with the little chap. I

don't want people fooling about with it. 'Leave it alone,'
I say. 'Don't touch it. I like it the way it is.'

But with Stilton it was different. Buttonhole him and
offer to give his soul a shot in the arm, and you found in
him a receptive audience and a disciple ready to try
anything once. Florence must have seemed to him just
what the doctor ordered, and he had probably quite
enjoyed thumbing the pages of 'Types of Ethical Theory',
feeling, no doubt, that this was the stuff to give the
troops.

But – and this was the reflection that furrowed the
brow – how long would this last? I mean to say, he
might be liking the set-up, but, as I saw it, the time
would come when he would examine his soul, note how
it had sprouted and say, 'Fine. That's enough to be going
on with. Let's call it a day,' only to discover that he was
inextricably entangled with a girl who had merely
started. It was from this fate, which is sometimes called
the bitter awakening, that I wanted to rescue him.

How to do it was, of course, a problem, and many
chaps in my place would, I suppose, have been
nonplussed. But my brain was working like a buzz
saw this morning, and the two snifters at the Bollinger
had put a keen edge on it. By the time I was latch-keying
my way into the flat I had placed my finger on the
solution. The thing to do, I saw, was to write a strong
note to Nobby Hopwood, outlining the situation and
urging her to draw Stilton aside and make it quite clear
to him what he was up against. Nobby, I reasoned, had
known Florence since she was so high, and would
consequently be in a position to assemble all the talking
points.

Still, just in case she might have overlooked any of
them, I carefully pointed out in my communication all
Florence's defects, considered not only as a prospective
bride but as a human being. I put my whole heart into
the thing, and it was with an agreeable feeling of duty

done and a kindly act accomplished that I took it round the corner and dropped it in the pillar box.

When I got back, I found Jeeves once more in residence. He had returned from his mission and was fooling about at some domestic task in the dining-room. I gave him a hail, and he floated in.

'Jeeves,' I said, 'you remember Mr Cheesewright, who called this morning?'

'Yes, sir.'

'I ran into him just now, buying an engagement ring. He is betrothed.'

'Indeed, sir?'

'Yes. And do you know who to? Lady F. Craye.'

'Indeed, sir?'

We exchanged a meaningful glance. Or, rather, two meaning glances, I giving him one and he giving me the other. There was no need for words. Jeeves is familiar with every detail of the Wooster-Craye imbroglio, having been constantly at my side right through that critical period in my affairs. As a matter of fact, as I have recorded elsewhere in the archives, it was he who got me out of the thing.

'And what's so poignant, Jeeves, if that's the word I want, is that he seems to like it.'

'Indeed, sir?'

'Yes. Rather pleased about it all than otherwise, it struck me. It reminded me of those lines in the poem – "See how the little how-does-it-go tum tumty tiddly push". Perhaps you remember the passage?'

' "Alas, regardless of their fate, the little victims play", sir.'

'Quite. Sad, Jeeves.'

'Yes, sir.'

'He must be saved from himself, of course, and fortunately I have the situation well in hand. I have taken all the necessary steps, and anticipate a happy and successful issue. And now,' I said, turning to the other matter on the agenda paper, 'tell me about Uncle Percy. You saw him?'

'Yes, sir.'

'Was he in the market for aid and counsel?'

'Yes, sir.'

'I knew I was right. What was it? Blackmail? Does he want you to pinch damaging correspondence from the peroxided? Has some quick-thinking adventuress got him in her toils?'

'Oh, no, sir. I am sure his lordship's private life is above reproach.'

I weighed this in the light of the known facts.

'I'm not so dashed sure about that. It depends what you call above reproach. He once chased me over a measured mile, showing great accuracy with the hunting crop. At a moment, too, when, being half-way through my first cigar, I was in urgent need of quiet and repose. To my mind, a man capable of that would be capable of anything. Well, if it wasn't blackmail, what was the trouble?'

'His lordship finds himself in a somewhat difficult position, sir.'

'What's biting him?'

He did not reply for a space. A wooden expression had crept into his features, and his eyes had taken on the look of cautious reserve which you see in those of parrots, when offered half a banana by a stranger of whose *bona fides* they are not convinced. It meant that he had come over all discreet, as he sometimes does, and I hastened to assure him that he might speak freely.

'You know me, Jeeves. The silent tomb.'

'The matter is highly confidential, sir. It should not be allowed to go further.'

'Wild horses shall not drag it from me. Not that I suppose they'll try.'

'Well, then, sir, his lordship informs me that he is in

the process of concluding the final details of a business agreement of great delicacy and importance.'

'And he wanted you to vet the thing for snags?'

'Not precisely that, sir. But he desired my advice.'

'They all come to you, Jeeves, don't they – from the lowest to the highest?'

'It is kind of you to say so, sir.'

'Did he mention what the b. a. of great d. and i. was?'

'No, sir. But, of course, one has read the papers.'

'I haven't.'

'You do not study the financial pages, sir?'

'Never give them a glance.'

'They have been devoting considerable space of late to rumours of a merger or combination which is said to be impending between his lordship's Pink Funnel Line and an equally prominent shipping firm of the United States of America, sir. It is undoubtedly to this that his lordship was guardedly alluding.'

The information did not make me leap about to any extent.

'Going to team up, are they, these nautical tycoons?'

'So it is supposed, sir.'

'Well, God bless them.'

'Yes, sir.'

'I mean, why shouldn't they?'

'Exactly, sir.'

'Well, what's his difficulty?'

'A somewhat tense situation has arisen, sir. The negotiations would appear to have arrived at a point where it is essential that his lordship shall meet and confer with the gentleman conducting the pourparlers on behalf of the American organization. On the other hand, it is vital that he shall not be seen in the latter's society, for such a meeting would instantly be accepted in the City as conclusive proof that the fusion of interests was about to take place, with immediate reactions on the respective shares of the two concerns.'

I began to see daylight. There have been mornings after some rout or revel at the Drones, when this sort of thing would merely have caused the head to throb, but to-day, as I have said, I was feeling exceptionally bright.

'They would go up, you mean?'

'A sharp rise would be inevitable, sir.'

'And Uncle Percy views such a prospect with concern?'

'Yes, sir.'

'His idea being to collect a parcel cheap before the many-headed can horn in and spoil the market?'

'Precisely, sir. *Rem acu tetigisti*.'

'*Rem* – ?'

'*Acu tetigisti*, sir. A Latin expression. Literally, it means "You have touched the matter with a needle", but a more idiomatic rendering would be – '

'Put my finger on the nub?'

'Exactly, sir.'

'Yes, I get it now. You have clarified the situation. Getting right down to it, these two old buzzards have got to foregather in secret and require a hideout.'

'Precisely, sir. And, of course, the movements of both gentlemen are being closely watched by representatives of the financial press.'

'I suppose this mystic sort of stuff goes on all the time in the world of commerce?'

'Yes, sir.'

'One understands and sympathizes.'

'Yes, sir.'

'Though one dislikes the idea of Uncle Percy getting any richer. Already, he has the stuff in gobs. However, bearing in mind the fact that he is an uncle by marriage, I suppose one ought to espouse his cause. Had you anything to suggest?'

'Yes, sir.'

'I bet you had.'

'It occurred to me that such a meeting might well

take place unobserved, if the two parties were to arrange to come together beneath the roof of some remote country cottage.'

I mused.

'You mean a cottage in the country somewhere?'

'You have interpreted me exactly, sir.'

'I don't think much of that, Jeeves. You must be losing your grip.'

'Sir?'

'Well, to name but one objection, how can you go to the owner of a country cottage, whom you don't know from Adam, and ask him to let you and your pals plot in the parlour?'

'It would be necessary, of course, that the proprietor of the establishment should be no stranger to his lordship.'

'He would have to be somebody who knew Uncle Percy, you mean?'

'Precisely, sir.'

'But, Jeeves, my dear old soul, don't you see that that makes it still worse? Use the bean. In that case, the chap says to himself, "Hullo! Old Worplesdon having secret meetings with mystery men? Come, come, what's all this? I'll bet this means that the merger I've been reading about so much is going to come off". And he nips out and phones his broker to start buying those shares and to keep on buying till he's blue in the face. Thus wrecking all Uncle Percy's carefully laid plans and rendering him sicker than mud. You follow me, Jeeves?'

'Completely, sir. I had not overlooked that contingency. The occupant of the cottage would, of course, have to be some gentleman whom his lordship could trust.'

'Such as – ?'

'Well, yourself, sir.'

'But – sorry to have to rub it in like this, but it's only kind to remove the scales from your eyes – I haven't got a cottage.'

'Yes, sir.'

'I don't get you, Jeeves.'

'His lordship is placing one of his own at your disposal, sir. He instructed me to say that he wishes you to proceed to-morrow to Steeple Bumpleigh – '

'Steeple Bumpleigh!'

' – where you will find a small but compact residence awaiting you, in perfect condition for immediate occupation. It is delightfully situated not far from the river – '

It needed no more than that word 'river' to tell me what had occurred. On his good mornings, I don't suppose there are more than a handful of men in the W1 postal district of London swifter to spot oompus-boompus than Bertram Wooster, and this was one of my particularly good mornings. I saw the whole hideous plot.

'Jeeves,' I said, 'you have done the dirty on me.'

'I am sorry, sir. It seemed the only solution of his lordship's problem. I feel sure, sir, that when you see the residence in question, your prejudice against Steeple Bumpleigh will be overcome. I speak, of course, only from hearsay, but I understand from his lordship that it is replete with every modern convenience. It contains one large master's bedroom, a well-appointed sitting-room, water both hot and cold – '

'The usual domestic offices?' I said. And I meant it to sting.

'Yes, sir. Furthermore, you will be quite adjacent to Mr Fittleworth.'

'And you will be quite adjacent to your fish.'

'Why, yes, sir. The point had not occurred to me, but now that you mention it that is certainly so. I should find a little fishing most enjoyable, if you could spare me from time to time while we are at Wee Nooke.'

'Did you say "Wee Nooke"?'

'Yes, sir.'

'Spelled, I'll warrant, with an "e"?'

'Yes, sir.'

I breathed heavily through the nostrils.

'Well, listen to me, Jeeves. The thing's off. You understand? Off. Spelled with an o and two f's. I'm dashed if I'm going to be made a – what's the word?'

'Sir?'

'Catspaw. Though why catspaw? I mean, what have cats got to do with it?'

'The expression derives from the old story of the cat, the monkey and the chestnuts, sir. It appears –'

'Skip it, Jeeves. This is no time for chewing the fat about the animal kingdom. And if it's the story about where the monkey puts the nuts, I know it and it's very vulgar. Getting back to the *res*, I absolutely, positively and totally refuse to go to Steeple Bumpleigh.'

'Well, of course, sir, it is perfectly open to you to adopt the attitude you indicate, but –'

He paused, massaging the chin. I saw his point.

'Uncle Percy would look askance, you mean?'

'Yes, sir.'

'And might report the matter to Aunt Agatha?'

'Precisely, sir. And her ladyship, when incensed, can be noticeably unpleasant.'

'*Rem acu tetigisti*,' I said, moodily. 'All right, start packing.'

5

It has been well said of Bertram Wooster by those who enjoy his close acquaintance that if there is one quality more than another that distinguishes him, it is his ability to keep the lip stiff and upper and make the best of things. Though crushed to earth, as the expression is, he rises again – not absolutely in mid season form, perhaps, but perkier than you would expect and with an eye alert for silver linings.

Waking next morning to another day and thumbing the bell for the cup of tea, I found myself, though still viewing the future with concern, considerably less down among the wines and spirits than I had been yestreen. The flesh continued to creep briskly at the thought of entering the zone of influence of Uncle Percy and loved ones, but I was able to discern one reasonably brightish spot in the set up.

'You did say, Jeeves,' I said, touching on this as he entered with the steaming Bohea, 'that Aunt Agatha would not be at Steeple Bumpleigh to greet me on my arrival?'

'Yes, sir. Her ladyship expects to be absent for some little time.'

'If she's going to remain with young Thos till they've demumped him, it may well be that she will be away during the whole of my sojourn.'

'Quite conceivably, sir.'

'That is a substantial bit of goose.'

'Yes, sir. And I am happy to be able to indicate another. In the course of her visit yesterday, Miss Hopwood mentioned a fancy dress ball which, it appears, is to take place at East Wibley, the market town adjacent to Steeple Bumpleigh. You will enjoy that, sir.'

'I shall, indeed,' I assented, for as a dancer I out-Fred the nimblest Astaire, and fancy dress binges have always been my dish. 'When does it come to a head?'

'To-morrow night, I understand, sir.'

'Well, I must say this has brightened the horizon considerably. When I have breakfasted, I will go out and buy a costume. Sindbad the Sailor, don't you think?'

'That should prove most effective, sir.'

'Not forgetting the ginger whiskers that go with it.'

'Precisely, sir. They are of the essence.'

'If you've finished the packing, you can cram it into the small suitcase.'

'Very good, sir.'

'We'll drive down, of course.'

'Possibly it would be best, sir, if I were to make the journey by train.'

'A bit haughty, this exclusiveness, is it not, Jeeves?'

'I should have mentioned, sir, that Miss Hopwood rang up, hoping that you would be able to accommodate her in your car. Assuming that I should be falling in with your wishes in doing so, I took the responsibility of replying that you would be quite agreeable.'

'I see. Yes, that's all right.'

'Her ladyship has also telephoned.'

'Aunt Agatha?'

'Yes, sir.'

'No rot, I trust, about having changed her mind and decided not to rally round young Thos?'

'Oh, no, sir. It was merely to leave a message, saying that she wishes you to call in at Aspinall's in Bond Street before you leave, and secure a brooch which she purchased there yesterday.'

'She does, does she? Why me?' I asked, speaking with a touch of acerbity, for I rather resented this seeming inability on the relative's part to distinguish between a nephew and a district messenger boy.

'I understand that the trinket is a present for Lady Florence, sir, who is celebrating her birthday to-day. Her ladyship wishes you to convey it to its destination personally, realizing that, should she entrust it to the ordinary channels, the gift will be delayed in its arrival beyond the essential date.'

'You mean, if she posts it, it won't get there in time?'

'Precisely, sir.'

'I see. Yes, there's something in that.'

'Her ladyship appeared a little dubious as to your ability to carry through the commission without mishap –'

'Ho!'

' – but I assured her that it was well within your scope.'

'I should think so,' I said, piqued. I balanced a thoughtful lump of sugar on the teaspoon. 'So it's Lady Florence's birthday, is it?' I said, pondering. 'This opens up a social problem on which I should be glad to have your opinion. Ought I to weigh in with a present?'

'No, sir.'

'Not necessary, you think?'

'No, sir. Not after what has occurred.'

I was glad to hear him say so. I mean, while one wants on all occasions to do the *preux* thing, it is a tricky business, this bestowing of gifts, and apt to put ideas into a girl's head. Coming on top of 'Spindrift' and Spinoza, the merest bottle of scent at this juncture might well have set such a seal upon my glamour as to cause the beasel to decide to return Stilton to store and make other arrangements.

'Well, I defer to your judgement, Jeeves. No present for La Craye, then.'

'No, sir.'

'But, while on this subject, we shall shortly have to be nosing round for one for La Hopwood.'

'Sir?'

'A wedding gift. She's gone and got engaged to Boko Fittleworth.'

'Indeed, sir? I am sure I wish the young lady and gentleman every happiness.'

'Well spoken, Jeeves. Me, too. The projected union, I may say at once, is one that has my complete approval. Which is not always the case when a pal puts the banns up.'

'No, sir.'

'Too often on such occasions one feels, as I feel so strongly with regard to poor old Stilton, that the kindly thing to do would be to seize the prospective bridegroom's trousers in one's teeth and draw him back from danger, as faithful dogs do to their masters on the edge of precipices on dark nights.'

'Yes, sir.'

'But in the present case I have no such misgivings. Each of the contracting parties, in my opinion, has picked a winner, and it is with a light heart that I shall purchase the necessary fish slice. I am even prepared, if desired, to be best man and make a speech at the wedding breakfast, and one cannot say more than that.'

'No, sir.'

'Right ho, Jeeves,' I said, flinging back the bedclothes and rising from the couch. 'Unchain the eggs and bacon. I will be with you in a moment.'

After I had broken the fast and smoked a soothing cigarette, I sallied forth, for I had a busy morning before me. I popped in at Aspinall's and pocketed the brooch, and thence repaired to the establishment of the Cohen Bros. in Covent Garden, well known among the cognoscenti as the Mecca for the discriminating seeker after fancy dress costumes. They were fortunately able to supply me with the required Sindbad, the last they had in stock, and a visit to a near-by theatrical wiggery put me in possession of an admirable set of ginger whiskers, thus giving me a full hand.

The car was at the door on my return, a suitcase of feminine aspect in its rumble. This seemed to indicate that Nobby had arrived, and as I had expected I found her in the sitting-room, sipping a refresher.

It having been some considerable time since we had foregathered, there ensued, of course, a certain period of leaping about and fraternizing. Then, having put away a refresher myself, I escorted her to the car and bunged her in. Jeeves, following my instructions, had placed the small suitcase with the Sindbad in it beneath the front seat, so that it should be under my personal eye, and we were thus all set. I trod on the self-starter and we began the journey, Jeeves standing on the pavement, seeing us off like an archbishop blessing pilgrims, his air that of one who would shortly be following by train with the heavy luggage.

Though sorry to be deprived of this right-hand man's society, for his conversation always tends to elevate and instruct, I was glad to get Nobby alone. I wanted to hear all about this pending merger with Boko. Each being a valued member of my entourage, the news that they were affianced had interested me strangely.

I am never much of a lad for chatting in traffic, and until I had eased the vehicle out of the congested districts I remained strong and silent, the lips tense, the eyes keen. But when we were bowling along the Portsmouth Road, with nothing to distract the attention, I got down to it.

6

'So you and Boko are planning to leap in among the orange blossoms?' I said. 'I had the news from Stilton yesterday, and was much stirred.'

'I hope you approve?'

'Thoroughly. Nice work, in my opinion. I think you're both on to a good thing, and would be well advised to push it along with the utmost energy. I have always considered you an extremely sound young potato.'

She thanked me for these kind words, and I assured her that the tribute was well deserved.

'As for Boko,' I proceeded, 'one of the best, of course. I could tell you things about Boko which would drive it well into your nut that you have picked a winner.'

'You don't have to.'

Her voice was soft and tender, like that of a hen crooning over its egg, and it was easy to see that, as far as she was concerned, Cupid's dart had done its stuff. I gave the wheel a twiddle, to avoid a casual dog, and went into my questionnaire. I always like to know all the facts on these occasions.

'When did you arrange this match?'

'About a week ago.'

'But you felt it coming on before that, I take it?'

'Oh, yes. Directly we met.'

'When was that?'

'At the end of May.'

'It was love at first sight, was it?'

'It was.'

'On his side, also?'

'On his side, also.'

Well, I could readily understand Boko falling in love
at first sight with Nobby, of course, for she is a girl
liberally endowed with oomph. But how she could have
fallen in love at first sight with Boko beat me. The first
sight of Boko reveals to the beholder an object with a
face like an intellectual parrot. Furthermore, as is the
case with so many of the younger literati, he dresses like
a tramp cyclist, affecting turtleneck sweaters and grey
flannel bags with a patch on the knee and conveying a
sort of general suggestion of having been left out in the
rain overnight in an ash can. The only occasion on
which I have ever seen Jeeves really rattled was when he
met Boko for the first time. He winced visibly and
tottered off to the kitchen, no doubt to pull himself
together with cooking sherry.

I mentioned this to Nobby, and she said she knew
what I meant.

'You would think he was the sort of man who would
have to grow on a girl – gradually, as it were – wouldn't
you? But no. There was one startled moment when I
wondered if I was seeing things, and then – bang – like a
thunderbolt.'

'As quick as that, was it?'

'Yes.'

'And his reactions were similar?'

'Yes.'

'Well, here's something I don't understand. You say
you met in May, and we are now in July. Why did he
take such a dickens of a time wooing you?'

'He didn't exactly woo me.'

'How do you mean, not exactly? A man either woos or
he does not woo. There can be no middle course.'

'There were reasons why he couldn't let himself go.'

'You speak in riddles, young Nobby. Still, as long as
he got round to it eventually. And when are the bells
going to ring out in the little village church?'

'I don't know if they ever are.'

'Eh?'

'Uncle Percy doesn't seem to think so.'

'What do you mean?'

'He disapproves of the match.'

'What!'

I was astounded. It seemed to me for an instant that she must be pulling the Wooster leg. Then, scrutinizing her closely, I noted that the lips were tight and the brow clouded. This young Hopwood is a blue-eyed little half portion with, normally, an animated dial. The dial to which I refer was now contorted with anguish, as if she had just swallowed a bad oyster.

'You don't mean that?'

'I do.'

'Egad!' I said.

For this was serious. Nobby, you see, was peculiarly situated. As often occurs, I believe, when Girl A becomes the ward of Bloke B, a clause had been inserted in the contract to the effect that there must be no rot about her marrying without the big chief's consent till she was twenty-one or forty-one or something. So if Uncle Percy really had an anti-Boko complex, he was in a position to bung a spanner into the works with no uncertain hand.

I couldn't get it.

'But why? The man must be cuckoo. Boko is one of our most eligible young bachelors. He makes pots of money with his pen. You see his stuff everywhere. That play he had on last year was a substantial hit. And they were saying at the Drones the other day that he's had an offer to go to Hollywood. Has he?'

'Yes.'

'Well, then.'

'Oh, I know all that. But what you're overlooking is the fact that Uncle Percy is the sort of man who is suspicious of writers. He doesn't believe in their solvency. He's been in business all his life, and he can't

44

imagine anybody having any real money except a business man.'

'But he must know that Boko's dashed near being a celebrity. He's had his photograph in the *Tatler*.'

'Yes, but Uncle Percy has the idea that an author's success is here to-day and gone to-morrow. Boko may be doing all right now, but he feels that his earning capacity may go phut at any moment. I suppose he pictures himself having to draw him out of the bread line a year or two from now and support him and me and half a dozen little Boko's for the rest of our lives. And then, of course, he was prejudiced against the poor darling from the start.'

'Because of those trousers?'

'They may have helped perhaps.'

'The man's an ass. Boko's a writer. He must know that writers are allowed a wide latitude. Besides, though I wouldn't care to have Jeeves hear me say so, trousers aren't everything.'

'But the real reason was that he thought Boko was a butterfly.'

I couldn't follow her. She had me fogged. Anything less like a butterfly than good old Boko I've never set eyes on.

'A butterfly?'

'Yes. Flitting from flower to flower and sipping.'

'And he doesn't like butterflies?'

'Not when they flit and sip.'

'What on earth has put the extraordinary idea into his head that Boko's a flitting sipper?'

'Well, you see, when he arrived in Steeple Bumpleigh, he was engaged to Florence.'

'What!'

'It was she who made him settle there. That was what I meant when I said that he couldn't woo me, as you call it, with any real abandon at first. Being engaged to Florence sort of hampered him.'

45

I was amazed. I nearly ran over a hen in my emotion.

'Engaged to Florence? He never told me.'

'You haven't seen him for some time.'

'No, that's true. Well, I'll be dashed. Did you know that I was once engaged to Florence?'

'Of course.'

'And now Stilton is.'

'Yes.'

'How absolutely extraordinary. It's like one of those great race movements you read about.'

'I suppose it's her profile that does it. She has a lovely profile.'

'Seen from the left.'

'Seen from the right, too.'

'Well, yes, in a measure, seen from the right, too. But would that account for it? I mean, in these busy days you can't spend your whole time dodging round a girl, trying to see her sideways. I still maintain that this tendency on the part of the populace to get engaged to Florence is inexplicable. And that made Uncle Percy a bit frosty to Boko?'

'Glacial.'

'I see. One understands his point of view, of course. He frowns on this in and out running. Florence yesterday, you to-day. I suppose he thinks you are just another of the flowers that Boko is flitting in on for sipping purposes.'

'I suppose so.'

'And, in addition, he doubts his earning capacity.'

'Yes.'

I pondered. If Uncle Percy really thought that Boko was a butterfly that might go broke at any moment, Love's young dream had unquestionably stubbed its toe. I mean, an oofy butterfly is bad enough. But it can at least pay the rent. I could well imagine a man of conservative views recoiling from one which might come asking for handouts for the rest of its life.

A thought occurred to me. With that Wooster knack of looking on the bright side, I saw that all was not yet lost.

'How old do you have to be before you can marry without Uncle Percy's kayo?'

'Twenty-one.'

'How old are you now?'

'Twenty.'

'Well, there you are, then. I knew that if we looked close enough we should find that the sun was still shining. You've only got to wait another year, and there you are.'

'Yes. But Boko leaves for Hollywood next month. I don't know how you feel about this dream man of mine, but to me, and I have studied his character with loving care, he doesn't seem the sort of person to be allowed to go to Hollywood without a wife at his side to distract his attention from the local fauna.'

Her outlook shocked me, causing me to put a bit of austere top-spin on my next crack.

'There can be no love where there is not perfect trust.'

'Who told you that?'

'Jeeves, I think. It sounds like one of his things.'

'Well, Jeeves is wrong. There jolly well can be love without perfect trust, and don't you forget it. I love Boko distractedly, but at the thought of him going to Hollywood without me I come over all faint. He wouldn't mean to let me down. I don't suppose he would even know he was doing it. But one morning I should get an apologetic cable saying that he couldn't quite explain how it had happened, but that he had inadvertently got married last night, and had I anything to suggest. It's his sweet, impulsive nature. He can't say No. I believe that's how he came to get engaged to Florence.'

I frowned meditatively. Now that she had outlined the position of affairs, I could see that the situation was a tricky one.

'Then what's the procedure?'

'I don't know.'

I frowned another meditative one.

'Something must be done.'

'But what?'

I had an idea. It is often like that with the Woosters. They appear baffled, and then suddenly – *bingo!* – an inspiration.

'Leave this to me,' I said.

What had crossed my mind was the thought that by establishing myself at Wee Nooke on his behalf, I was doing Uncle Percy a dashed good turn – so dashed that if he had a spark of gratitude in his composition he ought to be all over me. I could picture him clasping my hand and saying that thanks to me that merger had come off and was there any reward I cared to ask, for he could deny me nothing.

'What you need here,' I said, 'is the suave intervention of a polished man of the world, a silver-tongued orator who will draw Uncle Percy aside and plead your cause, softening his heart and making him take the big broad view. I'll attend to it.'

'You?'

'In person. Within the next day or two.'

'Oh, Bertie!'

'It will be a pleasure to put in a word for you. I anticipate notable results. I shall probably play on the old crumb as on a stringed instrument.'

She registered girlish joy.

'Bertie, you're a lamb!'

'Maybe you're right. A touch of the lamb, perhaps.'

'It's a wonderful idea. You see, you've known Boko so long.'

'Virtually from the egg.'

'You'll be able to think of all sorts of things to say about him. Did he ever save your life, when you were a boy?'

'Not that I remember.'

'You could say he did.'

'I doubt if it would go well. Uncle Percy was none to keen on me at that epoch. It would be more likely to strike a chord if I told him that Boko had repeatedly tried to assassinate me, when I was a boy. However, leave it to me. I'll find words.'

All this while, of course, the old two-seater had been humming along towards Steeple Bumpleigh with the needle in the sixties, and at this point Nobby notified me that we were approaching our destination.

'Those chimneys through the trees are the Hall. You see that little lane to the left. You go down it, and you come to Boko's place. Yours is about half a mile beyond it, up another sort of side turning. You really will plead with Uncle Percy?'

'Like billy-o.'

'You won't weaken?'

'Not a chance.'

'Of course, it's just possible that you may not have to. You see, I thought that if Boko and Uncle Percy could really get together, Uncle Percy might learn to love him. So, though it wasn't easy, I arranged that Boko should give him lunch to-day. I hope everything has gone all right. A lot depends on how Boko behaved. I mean, up till now, whenever they have met, he has always been so stiff in his manner. I begged him with tears in my eyes to let himself go and be bright and genial, and he promised he would try. So I'm hoping for the best.'

'Me, too,' I said, and – if I remember correctly – patted her little hand. I then drove to the Hall and decanted her at its gates, assuring her that, even if Boko had failed to fascinate at the midday meal, I would see to it that everything came out all right. With a final cheery wave of the hand, I backed the car and headed for the lane of which she had spoken.

All this talking had, of course, left me with a well

defined thirst, and it seemed to me, despite a householder's natural desire to take possession as soon as possible, that my first move had better be to stop off at Boko's and touch him for the needful. I assumed that the whitewashed cottage standing on the river bank must be the Bokeries, for Nobby had indicated that I had to pass it on my way to Wee Nooke.

I hove to alongside, accordingly, and noting that one of the windows at the side was open I approached it and whistled.

A hoarse shout from within and a small china ornament whizzing past my head informed me that my old friend was at home.

7

The passing of the china ornament, which had come
within an ace of copping me on the napper, drew from
my lips a sharp 'Oi!' and as if in answer to the cry Boko
now appeared at the window. His hair was disordered
and his face flushed, presumably with literary
composition. In appearance, as I have indicated, this
man of letters is a cross between a comedy juggler and a
parrot that has been dragged through a hedge backwards,
and you never catch him at his nattiest in the workshop.
I took it that I had interrupted him at a difficult point in
a chapter.

He had been glaring at me through horn-rimmed
spectacles, but now, as he perceived who it was that
stood without, the flame faded behind the lenses, to be
replaced by a look of astonishment.

'Good Lord, Bertie! Is that you?'

I assured him that such was the case, and he
apologized for having bunged china ornaments at me.

'Why did you imitate the note of the lesser screech
owl?' he said, rebukingly. 'I thought you were young
Edwin. He comes sneaking round here, trying to do me
acts of kindness, and that is always how he announces
his presence. I am never without a certain amount of
ammunition handy on the desk. Where on earth did you
spring from?'

'The metropolis. I've just arrived.'

'Well, you might have had the sense to send a wire. I'd
have killed the fatted calf.'

I saw that he was under a misapprehension.

'I haven't come to stay with you. I'm hanging out at a

cottage which they tell me is a little farther down the road.'

'Wee Nooke?'

'That's right.'

'Have you taken Wee Nooke?'

'Yes.'

'What made you suddenly decide to do that?'

I had foreseen that some explanation of my presence might be required, and was ready with my story. My lips being sealed, of course, on the real reason which had brought me to Steeple Bumpleigh, it was necessary to dissemble.

'Jeeves thought he would like to do a bit of fishing. And,' I added, making the thing more plausible, 'they tell me a fancy dress dance is breaking out in these parts to-morrow night. Well, you know me when I hear rumours of these entertainments. The war horse and the bugle. And now,' I said, licking the lips, 'how about a cooling drink? The journey has left me a little parched.'

I climbed through the window, and sank into a chair, while he went off to fetch the ingredients. Presently he returned with the jingling tray, and after we had done a bit of stag-at-eve-ing and exchanged some desultory remarks about this and that, I did the civil thing by congratulating him on his engagement.

'I was saying to Nobby, whom I drove down here in my car, how extraordinary it was that any girl should have fallen in love with you at first sight. I wouldn't have thought it could be done.'

'It came as quite a surprise to me, too. You could have knocked me down with a feather.'

'I don't wonder. Still, all sorts of unlikely people do seem to excite the spark of passion. Look at my Aunt Agatha.'

'Ah.'

'And Stilton.'

'You know about Stilton?'

'I ran into him in a jeweller's, buying the ring, and he told me of his fearful predicament.'

'Sooner him than me.'

'Just how I feel. Nobby thinks it's Florence's profile that does it.'

'Quite possibly.'

There was a silence, broken only by the musical sound of us having another go at the elixir. Then he heaved a sigh and said that life was rummy, to which I assented that in many respects it was very rummy.

'Take my case,' he said. 'Did Nobby tell you what the position was?'

'About Uncle Percy gumming the works, you mean? Oh, rather.'

'A nice bit of box fruit, what?'

'So it struck me. Decidedly. The heart bled.'

'Fancy having to get anyone's consent to your getting married in this enlightened age! The thing's an anachronism. Why, you can't use it as a motive for a story even in a woman's magazine nowadays. Doesn't your Aunt Dahlia run some sort of women's rag?'

' "Milady's Boudoir". Sixpence weekly. I once contributed an article to it on What The Well-Dressed Man Is Wearing.'

'Well, I've never read "Milady's Boudoir", but I have no doubt it is the lowest dregs of the publishing world. Yet if I were to submit a story to your aunt about a girl who couldn't marry a fellow without some blasted head of the family's consent, she would hoot at it. That is to say, I am not allowed to turn an honest penny by using this complication in my work, but it is jolly well allowed to come barging in and ruining my life. A pretty state of things!'

'What happens if you go ahead regardless?'

'I believe I get jugged. Or is that only when you marry a ward in Chancery without the Lord Chancellor hoisting the All Right flag?'

'You have me there. We could ask Jeeves.'

'Yes, Jeeves would know. Have you brought him?'

'He's following with the heavy luggage.'

'How is he these days?'

'Fine.'

'Brain all right?'

'Colossal.'

'Then he may be able to think of some way out of this mess.'

'We shan't need Jeeves. I am handling the whole thing. I'm going to get hold of Uncle Percy and plead your cause.'

'You?'

'Oddly enough, that's what Nobby said. In the same surprised tone.'

'But I thought the man scared you stiff.'

'He does. But I've been able to do him a good turn, and my drag with him is now substantial.'

'Well, that's fine,' he said, brightening. 'Snap into it, Bertie. But,' he added, coming unbrightened again, 'you've got a tough job.'

'Oh, I don't know.'

'I do. After what happened at lunch to-day.'

I was conscious of a sudden, quick concern.

'Your lunch with Uncle Percy?'

'That's the one.'

'Didn't it go well?'

'Not too well.'

'Nobby was anticipating that it would bring home the bacon.'

'Ha! God bless her optimistic little soul.'

I gave him one of my keen looks. There was a sombre expression on his map. The nose was wiggling in an overwrought way. It was easy to perceive that pain and anguish racked the brow.

'Tell me all,' I said.

He unshipped a heavy sigh.

54

'You know, Bertie, the whole idea was a mistake from the start. She should never have brought us together. And, if she had to bring us together, she ought not to have told me to be bright and genial. You know about her wanting me to be bright and genial?'

'Yes. She said you were inclined to be a bit stiff in your manner with Uncle Percy.'

'I am always stiff in my manner with elderly gentlemen who snort like foghorns when I appear and glare at me as if I were somebody from Moscow distributing Red propaganda. It's the sensitive, highly strung artist in me. Old Hardened Arteries does not like me.'

'So Nobby said. She thinks it's because he regards you as a butterfly. My personal view is that it's those grey flannel bags of yours.'

'What's wrong with them?'

'The patch on the knee, principally. It creates a bad impression. Haven't you another pair?'

'Who do you think I am? Beau Brummel?'

I forbore to pursue the subject.

'Well, go on.'

'Where was I?'

'You were saying you made a bloomer in trying to be bright and genial.'

'Ah, yes. That's right. I did. And this is how it came about. You see, the first thing a man has to ask himself, when he is told to be bright and genial, is "How bright? How genial?" Shall he, that is to say, be just a medium ray of sunshine, or shall he go all out and shoot the works? I thought it over, and decided to bar nothing and be absolutely rollicking. And that, I see now, is where I went wrong.'

He paused, and remained for a space in thought. I could see that some painful memory was engaging his attention.

'I wonder, Bertie,' he said, coming to the surface at

length, 'if you were present one day at the Drones when
Freddie Widgeon sprang those Joke Goods on the
lunchers there?'

'Joke Goods?'

'The things you see advertised in toy-shop catalogues
as handy for breaking the ice and setting the table in a
roar. You know. The Plate Lifter. The Dribble Glass.
The Surprise Salt Shaker.'

'Oh, those?'

I laughed heartily. I remembered the occasion well.
Catsmeat Potter-Pirbright was suffering from a hangover
at the moment, and I shall not readily forget his emotion
when he picked up his roll and it squeaked and a rubber
mouse ran out of it. Strong men had to rally round with
brandy.

And then I stopped laughing heartily. The frightful
significance of his words hit me, and I started as if
somebody had jabbed a red-hot skewer through the
epidermis.

'You aren't telling me you worked those off on Uncle
Percy?'

'Yes, Bertie. That is what I did.'

'Golly!'

'That about covers it.'

I groaned a hollow one. The heart had sunk. One has,
of course, to make allowances for writers, all of them
being more or less loony. Look at Shakespeare, for
instance. Very unbalanced. Used to go about stealing
ducks. Nevertheless, I couldn't help feeling that in
springing Joke Goods on the guardian of the girl he loved
Boko had carried an author's natural goofiness too far.
Even Shakespeare might have hesitated to go to such
lengths.

'But why?'

'I suppose the idea at the back of my mind was that I
ought to show him my human side.'

'Did he take it big?'

'Pretty big.'

'He didn't like it?'

'No. I can answer that question without reservation. He did not like it.'

'Has he forbidden you the house?'

'You don't have to forbid people houses after looking at them as he looked at me over the Surprise Salt Shaker. The language of the eyes is enough. Do you know the Surprise Salt Shaker? You joggle it, and out comes a spider. The impression I received was that he was allergic to spiders.'

I rose. I had heard enough.

'I'll be pushing along,' I said, rather faintly.

'What's the hurry?'

'I ought to be going to Wee Nooke. Jeeves will be arriving at any moment with the luggage, and I shall have to get settled in.'

'I see. I would come with you, only I am in the act of composing a well-expressed letter of apology to my Lord Worplesdon. I had better finish it, though it may not be needed, if all you say about being in a position to plead with him is true. Plead well, Bertie. Pitch it strong. Let the golden phrases come rolling out like honey. For, as I say, I don't think you've got an easy job on your hands. Eloquence beyond the ordinary will be required. And, by the way. Not a word to Nobby about that lunch. The facts will have to be broken to her gently and by degrees, if at all.'

My mood, as I set a course for Wee Nooke, was, as you may well suppose, a good deal less effervescent than it had been. The idea of pleading with Uncle Percy had lost practically all its fascination.

There rose before me a vision of this relative by marriage, as he would probably appear directly I mentioned Boko's name – the eyes glaring, the moustache bristling and the *tout ensemble* presenting a strong resemblance to a short-tempered tiger of the jungle which has just seen its peasant shin up a tree. And while it would be going too far, perhaps, to say that Bertram Wooster shuddered, a certain coolness of the feet unquestionably existed.

I was trying to hold the thought that, once that merger had gone through, joy would most likely reign so supreme that the old bounder would look even on Boko with the eye of kindliness, when there came the ting of a bicycle bell, and a voice called my name, Woostering with such vehemence that I immediately braked the car and glanced round. The sight I saw smote me like a blow.

Heaving alongside was Stilton Cheesewright, and on his face, as he alighted from his bicycle and confronted me, there was about as unpleasant a look as ever caught me in the eyeball. It was a look pregnant with amazement and hostility. A Gorblimey-what's-this-blighter-doing-here look. The sort of look, in fine, which the heroine of a pantomime gives the Demon King when he comes popping up out of a trap at her elbow. And I could follow what was passing in his mind as clearly as if it had been broadcast on a nation-wide hook-up.

All along, I had been far from comfortable when speculating as to what this Othello's reactions would be on discovering me in the neighbourhood. The way in which he had received the information that I was an old acquaintance of Florence's had shown that his thoughts had been given a morbid turn, causing him to view Bertram with suspicion, and I had been afraid that he was going to place an unfortunate construction on my sudden arrival in her vicinity. It was almost inevitable, I mean, that the thing should smack, in his view, far too strongly of Young Lochinvar coming out of the West. And, of course, my lips being sealed, I couldn't explain.

A delicate and embarrassing situation.

And yet, amazing though you will find the statement, what was causing me to goggle at him with saucer eyes was not this look that told me that my fears had been well founded, but the fact that the face attached to it was topped by a policeman's helmet. The burly frame, moreover, was clad in a policeman's uniform, and on the feet one noted the regulation official boots or beetle crushers which go to complete the panoply of the awful majesty of the Law.

In a word, Stilton Cheesewright had suddenly turned into a country copper, and I could make nothing of it.

8

I stared at the man.

'Stap my vitals, Stilton,' I cried, in uncontrollable astonishment. 'Why the fancy dress?'

He, too, had a question to ask.

'What the hell are you doing here, you bloodstained Wooster?'

I held up a hand. This was no time for side issues.

'Why are you got up like a policeman?'

'I am a policeman.'

'A policeman?'

'Yes.'

'When you say "policeman",' I queried, groping, 'do you mean "policeman"?'

'Yes.'

'You're a policeman?'

'Yes, blast you. Are you deaf? I'm a policeman.'

I grasped it now. He was a policeman. And, my mind flashing back to yesterday's encounter in the jewellery bin, I realized what had made his manner furtive and evasive when I had asked him what he did at Steeple Bumpleigh. He had shrunk from revealing the truth, fearing lest I might be funny at his expense – as, indeed, I would have been, extraordinarily funny. Even now, though the gravity of the situation forbade their utterance, I was thinking of at least three priceless cracks I could make.

'What about it? Why shouldn't I be a policeman?'

'Oh, rather.'

'Half the men you know go into the police nowadays.'

I nodded. This was undoubtedly true. Since they

started that College at Hendon, the Force has become congested with one's old buddies. I remember Barmy Fotheringay-Phipps describing to me with gestures his emotions on being pinched in Leicester Square one Boat Race night by his younger brother George. And much the same thing happened to Freddie Widgeon at Hurst Park in connection with his cousin Cyril.

'Yes,' I said, spotting a flaw, 'but in London.'

'Not necessarily.'

'With the idea of getting into Scotland Yard and rising to great heights in their profession.'

'That's what I'm going to do.'

'Get into Scotland Yard?'

'Yes.'

'Rise to great heights?'

'Yes.'

'Well, I shall watch your future progress with considerable interest,' I said.

But I spoke dubiously. At Eton, Stilton had been Captain of the Boats, and he had also rowed assiduously for Oxford. His entire formative years, therefore, as you might say, had been spent in dipping an oar into the water, giving it a shove and hauling it out again. Only a pretty dumb brick would fritter away his golden youth doing that sort of thing – which, in addition to being silly, is also the deuce of a sweat – and Stilton Cheesewright was a pretty dumb brick. A fine figure of a young fellow as far northwards as the neck, but above that solid concrete. I could not see him as a member of the Big Four. Far more likely that he would end up as one of those Scotland Yard bunglers who used, if you remember, always to be getting into Sherlock Holmes's hair.

However, I didn't say so. As a matter of fact, I didn't say anything, for I was too busy pondering on this new and unforeseen development. I was profoundly thankful that Jeeves had voted against my giving Florence a birthday present. Such a gift, if Stilton heard of it, would have led to his tearing me limb from limb or, at the best, summoning me for failing to abate a smoky chimney. You can't be too careful how you stir up policemen.

I had succeeded in sidetracking his question for a space, but I knew that the respite would be merely temporary. They train these cops to stick to the point. I was not surprised, therefore, when he now repeated it. I'm not saying I didn't wish he hadn't. All I'm saying is that I wasn't surprised.

'Well, to blazes with all that. You haven't told me what you are doing in Steeple Bumpleigh.'

I temporized.

'Oh, just making a passing sojourn,' I said nonchalantly, the old, careless Bertram Wooster.

'You mean you've come to stay?'

'For a while. Somewhere over yonder is my little nest. I hope you will frequently drop in, when off duty.'

'And what made you suddenly decide to come taking little nests in these parts?'

I went into my routine.

'Jeeves wanted to do a bit of fishing.'

'Oh?'

'Yes. He tells me it is admirable here. You find the hook, and the fish do the rest.'

For quite a while he had been staring at me in an unpleasant, boiled sort of way, the brows drawn, the eyes bulging in their sockets. The austerity of his gaze now became intensified. Except for the fact that he hadn't taken out a notebook and a stub of pencil, he might have been questioning some rat of the underworld as to where he had been on the night of June the twenty-fifth.

'I see. That is your statement, is it? Jeeves wanted to do a bit of fishing?'

'That's right.'

'Oh? Well, I'll tell you what you wanted to do, young blasted Wooster. A bit of snake in the grassing.'

I affected not to have grabbed the gist, though in reality I had got it nicely.

'Snake in the whatting?'

'Grassing.'

'I don't follow you.'

'Then I'll make it clearer. You've come here to sneak round Florence.'

'My dear chap!'

He ground a tooth or two. It was plain that he was in dangerous mood.

'I may as well tell you,' he resumed, 'that I was not at all satisfied with your evidence – with what you said when I saw you yesterday. You stated that you had known Florence – '

'Just one moment, Stilton. Sorry to interrupt, but do we bandy a woman's name?'

'Yes, we do, and ruddy well keep on bandying it.'

'Oh, right ho. I just wanted to know.'

'You stated that you had known Florence only slightly. "Pretty well" was the exact expression you used, and it seemed to me that your manner was suspicious. So when I got back, I saw her and questioned her about you. She confessed that you and she had once been engaged.'

I moistened the lips with the tip of the tongue. I am never at my best *tête à tête* with the constabulary. They always seem somehow to quell my manly spirit. It may be the helmet that does it, or possibly the boots. And, of course, when one of the *gendarmerie* is accusing you of trying to pinch his girl, the embarrassment deepens. At moment of going to press, with Stilton's eyes boring holes through me, I had begun to feel like Eugene Aram just before they put the gyves on his wrists. I don't know if you remember the passage? 'Ti-tum-ti-tum ti-tumty

tum, ti-tumty tumty mist (I think it's mist), and Eugene
Aram walked between, with gyves upon his wrist.'

I cleared the throat, and endeavoured to speak with a
winning frankness.

'Why, yes. That's right. It all comes back to me. We
were. Long ago.'

'Not so long ago.'

'Well, it seems like long ago.'

'Oh?'

'Yes.'

'Is that so?'

'Positively.'

'The whole thing's over, eh?'

'Definitely.'

'Nothing between you now?'

'Not a thing.'

'Then how do you account for the fact that she gives
you a copy of her novel and writes "To Bertie, with love
from Florence" in it?'

I tottered. And at the same time, I'm bound to
confess, I found myself feeling a new respect for Stilton.
At first, if you recollect, when he had spoken of rising to
great heights at Scotland Yard, I had thought lightly of
his chances. It seemed to me now that he must have the
makings of a very hot detective indeed.

'You had the book with you when you came into that
jeweller's shop. You left it on the counter, and I looked
inside.'

I revised my views about his sleuthing powers. Not so
hot, after all. Sherlock Holmes, if you remember, always
said that it was a mistake for a detective to explain his
methods.

'Well?'

I laughed lightly. At least, I tried to. As a matter of
fact, the thing came out more like a death rattle.

'Oh, that was rather amusing.'

'All right. Go on. Make me laugh.'

'I was in the book shop, and she came in –'

'You had an assignation with her in a book shop?'

'No, no. Just an accidental meeting.'

'I see. And you've come down here to arrange another.'

'Good Lord, no.'

'Do you seriously expect me to believe that you aren't trying to steal her from me?'

'Nothing could be farther from my thoughts, old man.'

'Don't call me "old man".'

'Right ho, if you don't like it. The whole thing, officer, is one of those absurd misunderstandings. As I was starting to tell you, I was in this book shop –'

Here he interrupted me, damning the book shop with a good deal of heartiness.

'I'm not interested in the book shop. The point is that you have come down here to make a snake in the grass of yourself, and I'm not going to have it. I have just one thing to say to you, Wooster. Get out!'

'But –'

'Push off. Remove your beastly presence. Pop back to your London residence and stay there. And do it quick.'

'But I can't.'

'What do you mean?'

Well, as I said before, my lips were sealed. But the Woosters are swift thinkers.

'Old Boko,' I explained. 'I am acting for him in a rather delicate matter. As you possibly may know, my Uncle Percy is endeavouring to put the bee on his union with Nobby, and I have promised the young couple that I will plead for them. This will, of course, involve my remaining *in statu* – what is it?'

'Pah!'

'No, not pah. *Quo.* That's the word I'm trying to think of. You can't plead with an uncle by marriage unless you're *in statu quo.*'

It seemed to me a pretty good and reasonable

explanation, and I was distressed, accordingly, to observe that he was sneering unpleasantly.

'I don't believe a word of it. You plead? What's the good of you pleading? As if anything you could say would have any weight with anybody. I repeat – clear out. Otherwise – '

He didn't mention what would happen otherwise, but the menacing way in which he hopped on his bicycle and pedalled off spoke louder than words. I don't think I have ever seen anyone pedal with a more sinister touch to the ankle work.

I was still looking after him, feeling a little weak, when from the opposite or Wee Nooke direction there came the ting of another bicycle bell and, swivelling round, I perceived Florence approaching. As perfect an instance of one damn' thing after another as I have ever experienced.

In sharp contradistinction to those of Stilton, her eyes were shining with a welcoming light. She hopped off as she reached the car, and flashed a bright smile at me.

'Oh, here you are, Bertie. I have just been putting a few flowers in Wee Nooke for you.'

I thanked her, but with a sinking heart. I hadn't liked that smile, and I didn't like the idea of her sweating about strewing flowers in my path. The note struck seemed to me altogether too matey. Then I reminded myself that if she was betrothed to Stilton there could be no real cause for alarm. After all, her father had married my aunt, which made us sort of cousins, and there was nothing necessarily sinister in a bit of cousinly bustling about. Blood, I mean to say, when you come right down to it, being thicker than water.

'Frightfully decent of you,' I said. 'I've just been having a chat with Stilton.'

'Stilton?'

'Your affianced.'

'Oh, D'Arcy? Why do you call him Stilton?'

'Boyish nickname. We were at school together.'

'Oh? Then perhaps you can tell me if he was always such a perfect imbecile as he is to-day.'

I didn't like this. It didn't seem the language of love.

'In what sense do you use the word "imbecile"?'

'I use it as the only possible description of a man who, with a wealthy uncle willing and anxious to do everything for him, deliberately elects to become a common constable.'

'Why did he?' I asked. 'Become a common constable, I mean.'

'He says that every man ought to stand on his own feet and earn a living.'

'Conscientious.'

'Rubbish.'

'You don't think it does him credit?'

'No, I don't. I think he's a perfect idiot.'

There was a pause. It was plain that his behaviour rankled, and it seemed to me what was required here was a strong boost for the young copper. For I need scarcely say that, now that I was face to face again with this girl, all thought of carrying on with the promotion of that Save Stilton Cheesewright campaign was farther from my mind than ever.

'I should have thought you would have been rather bucked about it all. As giving evidence of Soul, I mean.'

'Soul?'

'It shows he's got a great soul.'

'I should be extremely surprised to find that he has any soul above those great, clodhopping boots he wears. He is just pig-headed. I have reasoned with him over and over again. His uncle wants him to stand for Parliament and is prepared to pay all his expenses and to finance him generously for the rest of his life, but no, he just looks mulish and talks about earning his living. I am sick and tired of the whole thing, and I really don't know what I shall do about it. Well, good-bye, Bertie, I must be getting along,' she concluded abruptly, as if she found the subject too painful to dwell on, and was off – just at the very moment when I had remembered that it was her birthday and that I had a brooch in my pocket to deliver to her from Aunt Agatha.

I could have called her back, I suppose, but somehow didn't feel in the mood. Her words had left me shaking in every limb. The revelation of the flimsiness of the foundations on which the Florence-Stilton romance appeared to be founded had appalled me, and I had to remain *in statu quo* and smoke a couple of cigarettes before I felt strong enough to resume my journey.

Then, feeling a little better and trying to tell myself that this was just a passing tiff and that matters would speedily adjust themselves, I pushed on and in another couple of minutes was coming to anchor abaft Wee Nooke.

9

Wee Nooke proved to be a decentish little shack, situated in agreeable surroundings. A bit Ye Olde, but otherwise all right. It had a thatched roof and a lot of those windows with small leaded panes, and there was a rockery in the front garden. It looked, in short, as I subsequently learned was the case, as if it had formerly been inhabited by an elderly female of good family who kept cats.

I had walked in and deposited the small suitcase in the hall, when, as I stood gazing about me and inhaling the fug which always seems to linger about these antique interiors, I became aware that there was more in this joint than met the eye. In a word, I suddenly found myself speculating on the possibility of it not only being fuggy, but haunted.

What started this train of thought was the fact that odd noises were in progress somewhere near at hand, here a bang and there a crash, suggesting the presence of a poltergeist or what not.

The sounds seemed to proceed from the other side of a door at the end of the hall, and I was hastening thither to investigate, for I was dashed if I was going to have poltergeists lounging about the place as if it belonged to them, when I took a toss over a pail which had been placed in the fairway. And I had just picked myself up, rubbing the spot, when the door opened and there entered a small boy with a face like a ferret. He was wearing the uniform of a Boy Scout, and I had no difficulty, in spite of the fact that his features were liberally encrusted with dirt, in identifying him as

Florence's little brother Edwin – the child at whom Boko Fittleworth was accustomed to throw china ornaments.

'Oh, hullo, Bertie,' he said, grinning all over his loathsome face.

'Hullo, you frightful young squirt,' I responded civilly. 'What are you doing here?'

'Tidying up.'

I touched on a point of absorbing interest.

'Was it you who left that bally pail there?'

'Where?'

'In the middle of the hall.'

'Coo! Yes, I remember now. I put it there to be out of the way.'

'I see. Well, you'll be amused to learn that I've nearly broken my leg.'

He started. A fanatic gleam came into his eyes. He looked like a boy confronted with an unexpected saucer of ice cream.

'I say! Have you really? This is a bit of bunce. I can give you first aid.'

'No, you jolly well can't.'

'But if you've bust your leg –'

'I haven't bust my leg.'

'You said you had.'

'A mere figure of speech.'

'Well, you may have sprained your ankle.'

'I haven't sprained my ankle.'

'I can do first aid for contusions.'

'I haven't any contusions. Stand back!' I cried, for I was prepared to defend myself with iron resolution.

There was a pause. His manner was that of one who finds the situation at a deadlock. My spirited attitude had plainly disconcerted him.

'Can't I bandage you?'

'You'll get a thick ear, if you try.'

'You may get gangrene.'

'I anticipate no such contingency.'

'You'll look silly if you get gangrene.'

'No, I shan't. I shall look fine.'

'I knew a chap who bumped his leg, and it turned black and had to be cut off at the knee.'

'You do seem to mix with the most extraordinary people.'

'I could turn the cold tap on it.'

'No, you couldn't.'

Again, that baffled air came into his demeanour. I had nonplussed him.

'Then I'll be getting back to the kitchen,' he said. 'I'm going to do the chimney. It needs a jolly good cleaning out. This place would have been in a fearful mess, if it hadn't been for me,' he added, with a smugness which jarred upon my sensibilities.

'How do you mean, if it hadn't been for you?' I riposted, in my keen way. 'I'll bet you've been spreading ruin and desolation on all sides.'

'I've been tidying up,' he said, with a touch of pique. 'Florence put some flowers for you in the sitting-room.'

'I know. She told me.'

'I fetched the water. Well, I'll go and do that chimney, shall I?'

'Do it, if it pleases you, till your eyes bubble,' I said, and dismissed him with a cold gesture.

Now, I don't know how you would have made a cold gesture – no doubt people's methods vary – but the way I did it was by raising the right arm in a sort of salute and allowing it to fall to my side. And, as it fell, I became aware of something missing. The coat pocket against which the wrist impinged should have contained a small, solid object – to wit, the package containing the brooch which Aunt Agatha had told me to convey to Florence for her birthday. And it didn't. The pocket was empty.

And at the same moment the kid Edwin said 'Coo!' and stooped, and came up holding the thing.

'Did you drop this?' he asked.

Any doubts that may have lingered in the child's mind as to my having broken my leg must have been dispelled by the spring I made. I flew through the air with the greatest of ease. A panther could not have moved more nippily. I wrenched the thing from his grasp, and once more pocketed it.

He seemed intrigued.

'What was it?'

'A brooch. Birthday present for Florence.'

'Shall I take it to her?'

'No, thanks.'

'I will, if you like.'

'No, thanks.'

'It would save you trouble.'

Had the circumstances been other than they were, I might have found this benevolence of his cloying – so much so, indeed, as to cause me to kick him in the pants. But he had rendered me so signal a service that I merely smiled warmly at the young blister, a thing I hadn't done for years.

'No, thanks,' I said. 'I don't let it out of my hands. I will run across and deliver it this evening. Well, well, young Edwin,' I continued affably, 'a smart piece of work, that. They train you sprouts to keep your eyes open. Tell me, how have you been all this while? All right? No colds, colics or other juvenile ailments? Splendid. I should hate to feel that you had been suffering in any way. It was decent of you to suggest putting my leg under the tap. Greatly appreciated. I wish I had a drink to offer you. You must come up and see me some time, when I am more settled.'

And on this cordial note our interview terminated. I tottered out into the garden, and for a space stood leaning on the front gate, for my spine was still feeling a bit jellified and I needed support.

I say my spine had become as jelly, and if you knew

my Aunt Agatha you would agree that so it jolly well
might.

This relative is a woman who, like Napoleon, if it
was Napoleon, listens to no excuses for failure, however
sound. If she gives you a brooch to take to a
stepdaughter, and you lose it, it is no sort of use trying
to tell her that the whole thing was an Act of God,
caused by your tripping over unforeseen pails and having
the object jerked out of your pocket. Pawn though you
may have been in the hands of Fate, you get put through
it just the same.

If I had not recovered this blighted trinket, I should
never have heard the last of it. The thing would have
marked an epoch. World-shaking events would have
been referred to as having happened 'about the time
Bertie lost that brooch' or 'just after Bertie made such an
idiot of himself over Florence's birthday present'. Aunt
Agatha is like an elephant – not so much to look at, for
in appearance she resembles more a well-bred vulture,
but because she never forgets.

Leaning on the gate, I found myself seething with
kindly feelings towards young Edwin. I wondered how I
could ever have gone so astray in my judgement as to
consider him a ferret-faced little son of a what not. And I
was just going to debate in my mind the idea of buying
him some sort of a gift as a reward for his admirable
behaviour, when there was a loud explosion and,
turning, I saw that Wee Nooke had gone up in flames.

It gave me quite a start.

IO

Well, everybody enjoys a good fire, of course, and for a while it was in a purely detached and appreciative spirit that I stood eyeing the holocaust. I felt that this was going to be value for money. Already the thatched roof was well ablaze, and it seemed probable that before long the whole edifice, being the museum piece it was, all dry rot and what not, would spit on its hands and really get down to it. And so, as I say, for about the space of two shakes of a duck's tail I stood watching it with quiet relish.

Then, putting a bit of a damper on the festivities, there came floating into my mind a rather disturbing thought – to wit, that the last I had seen of young Edwin, he had been seeping back into the kitchen. Presumably, therefore, he was still on the premises, and the conclusion to which one was forced was that, unless somebody took prompt steps through the proper channels, he was likely 'ere long to be rendered unfit for human consumption. This was followed by a second and still more disturbing thought that the only person in a position to do the necessary spot of fireman-save-my-child-ing was good old Wooster.

I mused. I suppose you would call me a fairly intrepid man, taken by and large, but I'm bound to admit I wasn't any too keen on the thing. Apart from anything else, my whole attitude towards the stripling who was faced with the prospect of being grilled on both sides had undergone another quick change.

When last heard from, if you remember, I had been thinking kindly thoughts of young Edwin and even going to the length of considering buying him some inexpensive present. But now I found myself once more viewing him with the eye of censure. I mean to say, it was perfectly obvious to the meanest intelligence that it was owing to some phonus-bolonus on his part that the conflagration had been unleashed, and I was conscious of a strong disposition to leave well alone.

It being, however, one of those situations where *noblesse* more or less *obliges*, I decided that I had better do the square thing, and I had torn off my coat and flung it from me and was preparing to plunge into the burning building, though still feeling that it was a bit thick having to get myself all charred up to gratify a kid who would be far better cooked to a cinder, when he emerged. His face was black, and he hadn't any eyebrows, but in other respects appeared reasonably bobbish. Indeed, he seemed entertained rather than alarmed by what had occurred.

'Coo!' he said, in a pleased sort of voice. 'Bit of a bust up, wasn't it?'

I eyed him sternly.

'What the dickens have you been playing at, you abysmal young louse?' I demanded. 'What was that explosion?'

'That was the kitchen chimney. It was full of soot, so I shoved some gunpowder up it. And I think I may have used too much. Because there was a terrific bang and everything sort of caught fire. Coo! It didn't half make me laugh.'

'Why didn't you pour water on the flames?'

'I did. Only it turned out to be paraffin.'

I clutched the brow. I was deeply moved. It had just come home to me that this blazing pyre was the joint which was supposed to be the Wooster G.H.Q., and the householder spirit had awoken in me. Every impulse urged me to give the little snurge six of the best with a bludgeon. But you can't very well slosh a child who has just lost his eyebrows. Besides, I hadn't a bludgeon.

'Well, you've properly messed things up,' I said.

'It didn't all work out quite the way I meant,' he admitted. 'But I wanted to do my last Friday's act of kindness.'

At these words, all was suddenly made plain to me. It was so long since I had seen the young poison sac that I had forgotten the kink in his psychology which made him such a menace to society.

This Edwin, I now recalled, was one of those thorough kids who spare no effort. He had the same serious outlook on life as his sister Florence. And when he joined the Boy Scouts, he did so, resolved not to shirk his responsibilities. The programme called for a daily act of kindness, and he went at it in a grave and earnest spirit. Unfortunately, what with one thing and another, he was always dropping behind schedule, and would then set such a clip to try and catch up with himself that any spot in which he happened to be functioning rapidly became a perfect hell for man and beast. It was so at the house in Shropshire where I had first met him, and it was evidently just the same now.

It was with a grave face and a thoughtful tooth chewing the lower lip that I picked up my coat and donned it. A weaker man, contemplating the fact that he was trapped in a locality containing not only Florence Craye, Police Constable Cheesewright and Uncle Percy, but also Edwin doing acts of kindness, would probably have given at the knees. And I am not so sure I might not have done so myself, had not my mind been diverted by a frightful discovery, so ghastly that I uttered a hoarse cry and all thoughts of Florence, Stilton, Uncle Percy and Edwin were wiped from my mind.

I had just remembered that my suitcase with the Sindbad the Sailor costume in it was in the Wee Nooke front hall and the flames leaping ever nearer.

There was no hesitation, no vacillating about my movements now. When it had been a matter of risking my life to save Boy Scouts, I may have stood scratching the chin a bit, but this was different. I needed that Sindbad. Only by retrieving it would I be able to attend the fancy dress ball at East Wibley to-morrow night, the one bright spot in a dark and sticky future. Well, I suppose I could have popped up to London and got something else, but probably a mere Pierrot, and my whole heart was set on the Sindbad and the ginger whiskers.

Edwin was saying something about fire brigades, and I righthoed absently. Then, snapping into it like a jack rabbit, I commended my soul to God, and plunged in.

Well, as it turned out, I needn't have worried. It is true that there was a certain amount of smoke in the hall, billowing hither and thither in murky clouds, but nothing to bother a man who had often sat to leeward of Catsmeat Potter-Pirbright when he was enjoying one of those cigars of his. In a few minutes, it was plain, the whole place would be a cheerful blaze, but for the nonce conditions were reasonably normal.

It is no story, in short, of a jolly-nearly-fried-to-a-crisp Bertram Wooster that I have to tell, but rather of a Bertram Wooster who just scooped up the old suitcase, whistled a gay air and breezed out without a mark on him. I may have coughed once or twice, but nothing more.

But though peril might have failed to get off the mark inside the house, it was very strong on the wing outside. The first thing I saw, as I emerged, was Uncle Percy standing at the gate. And as Edwin had now vanished, presumably in search of fire brigades, I was alone with him in the great open spaces – a thing I've always absolutely barred being from the days of childhood.

'Oh, hullo, Uncle Percy,' I said. 'Good afternoon, good afternoon.'

A casual passer-by, hearing the words and noting the hearty voice in which they had been spoken, might have been deceived into supposing that Bertram was at his ease. Such, however, was far from being the case. Whether anyone was ever at his ease in the society of this old Gawd-help-us, I cannot say, but I definitely was not. The spine, and I do not attempt to conceal the fact, had become soluble in the last degree.

You may wonder at this, arguing that as I was not responsible for the disaster which had come upon us, I had nothing to fear. But a longish experience has taught me that on these occasions innocence pays no dividends. Pure as the driven snow though he may be, or even purer, it is the man on the spot who gets the brickbats.

My civil greeting elicited no response. He was staring past me at the little home, now beyond any possible doubt destined to be a total loss. Edwin might return with all the fire brigades in Hampshire, but nothing was going to prevent Wee Nooke winding up as a heap of ashes.

'What?' he said, speaking thickly, as if the soul were bruised, as I imagine to have been the case. 'What? What? What? What . . . ?'

I saw that, unless checked, this was going to take some time.

'There's been a fire,' I said.

'What do you mean?'

Well, I didn't see how I could have put it much clearer.

'A fire,' I repeated, waving a hand in the direction of the burning edifice, as much as to tell him to take a glance for himself. 'How are you, Uncle Percy? You're looking fine.'

He wasn't, as a matter of fact, nor did this attempt to ease the strain by giving him the old oil have the desired effect. He directed at me a kind of frenzied glare, containing practically nil in the way of an uncle's love, and spoke in a sort of hollow, despairing voice.

'I might have known! My best friends would have warned me what would come of letting a lunatic like you loose in the place. I ought to have guessed that the first thing you would do – before so much as unpacking – would be to set the whole damned premises ablaze.'

'Not me,' I said, wishing to give credit where credit was due. 'Edwin.'

'Edwin? My son?'

'Yes, I know,' I said sympathetically. 'Too bad. Yes, he's your son, all right. He's been tidying up.'

'You can't start a fire by tidying up.'

'You can if you use gunpowder.'

'Gunpowder?'

'He appears to have touched off a keg or two in the kitchen chimney, to correct a disposition on its part to harbour soot.'

Well, I had naturally supposed, as anyone would have supposed, that this frank explanation would have set me right, causing him to dismiss me without a stain on my character, and that the rather personal note which had crept into his remarks would instantly have been switched off. What I had anticipated was that he would issue an apology for that crack of his about lunatics, which I would gracefully accept, and that we would then get together like two old buddies and shake our heads over the impulsiveness of the younger generation.

Not a bit of it, however. He continued to bend upon me the accusing gaze which I had disliked so much from the start.

'Why the devil did you give the boy gunpowder?'

I saw that he had still got the wrong angle.

'I didn't give the boy gunpowder.'

'Only a congenital idiot would give a boy gunpowder. There's not a man in England, except you, who wouldn't know what would happen if you gave a boy gunpowder.

Do you realize what you have done? The sole reason for your coming here was that I should have a place where I could meet an old friend and discuss certain matters of interest, and now look at it. I ask you. Look at it.'

'Not too good,' I was forced to concede, as the roof fell in, sending up a shower of sparks and causing a genial glow to play about our cheeks.

'I suppose it never occurred to you to throw water on the flames?'

'It did to Edwin. Only he used paraffin.'

He started, staring at me incredulously.

'You tried to put the fire out with paraffin? You ought to be certified, and as soon as I collect a couple of doctors, I'll have it seen to.'

What was making this conversation so difficult was, as you have probably spotted, the apparent impossibility of getting the old ass to sort out the principals in the affair and assign to each his respective role. He was one of those men you meet sometimes who only listen to about two words of any observation addressed to them. I suppose he had got that way through presiding at board meetings and constantly chipping in and squelching shareholders in the middle of sentences.

Once more, I tried to drive it home to him that it was Edwin who had done all the what you might call heavy work, Bertram having been throughout merely an innocent bystander, but it didn't penetrate. He was left with the settled conviction that I and the child had got together, forming a quorum, and after touching off the place with gunpowder had nursed the conflagration along with careful injections of paraffin, each encouraging each, as you might say, on the principle that it is team-work that tells.

When he finally pushed off, instructing me to send Jeeves along to him the moment he arrived, he was reiterating the opinion that I ought not to be at large, and wishing – though here I definitely could not see eye to eye with him – that I was ten years younger, so that he could have got after me with that hunting crop of his. He then withdrew, leaving me to my meditations.

These, as you may suppose, were not of the juiciest. However, they didn't last long, for I don't suppose I had been meditating more than about a couple of minutes when a wheezing, rattling sound made itself heard off-stage and there entered left upper centre a vehicle which could only have been a station taxi. There was luggage on it, and looking more closely I saw Jeeves protruding from the side window.

The weird old object – the cab, I mean, not Jeeves – came to a halt at the gate. Jeeves paid it off, the luggage was dumped by the roadside, and he was at liberty to get into conference with the young master, not an instant too soon for the latter. I had need of his sympathy, encouragement and advice. I also wanted to tick him off a bit for letting me in for all this.

11

'Jeeves,' I said, getting right down to it in the old Wooster way, 'here's a nice state of things!'

'Sir?'

'Hell's foundations have been quivering.'

'Indeed, sir?'

'The curse has come upon me. As I warned you it would, if I ever visited Steeple Bumpleigh. You have long been familiar with my views on this leper colony. Have I not repeatedly said that, what though the spicy breezes blow soft o'er Steeple Bumpleigh, the undersigned deemed it wisest to give it the complete miss in baulk?'

'Yes, sir.'

'Very well, Jeeves. Perhaps you will listen to me another time. However, let us flit lightly over the recriminations and confine ourselves to the facts. You notice our little home has been gutted?'

'Yes, sir. I was just observing it.'

'Edwin did that. There's a lad, Jeeves. There's a boy who makes you feel that what this country wants is somebody like King Herod. Started in with gunpowder and carried on with paraffin. Just cast your eye over those smouldering ruins. You would scarcely have thought it possible, would you, that one frail child in a sport shirt and khaki shorts could have accomplished such devastation. Yet he did it, Jeeves, and did it on his head. You understand what this means?'

'Yes, sir.'

'He has properly put the kybosh on the trysting-place

82

of Uncle Percy and his nautical pal. You'll have to think again.'

'Yes, sir. His lordship is fully alive to the fact that in the existing circumstances a meeting at Wee Nooke will not be feasible.'

'You've seen him, then?'

'He was emerging from the lane, as I entered it, sir.'

'Did he tell you he wants you to go and hobnob with him at your earliest convenience?'

'Yes, sir. Indeed, he insists on my taking up my residence at the Hall.'

'So as to be handy, in case you have a sudden inspiration?'

'No doubt that was in his lordship's mind, sir.'

'Was I invited?'

'No, sir.'

Well, I hadn't expected to be. Nevertheless, I was conscious of a pang.

'We part, then, for the nonce, do we?'

'I fear so, sir.'

'You taking the high road, and self taking the low road, as it were?'

'Yes, sir.'

'I shall miss you, Jeeves.'

'Thank you, sir.'

'Who was the chap who was always beefing about losing gazelles?'

'The poet Moore, sir. He complained that he had never nursed a dear gazelle, to glad him with its soft black eye, but when it came to know him well and love him, it was sure to die.'

'It's the same with me. I am a gazelle short. You don't mind me alluding to you as a gazelle, Jeeves?'

'Not at all, sir.'

'Well, that's that, then. I suppose I had better go and stay with Boko.'

'I was about to suggest it, sir. I am sure Mr Fittleworth will be most happy to accommodate you.'

'I think so. I hope so. Only recently, he was speaking about killing fatted calves. But to return to Uncle Percy and the old salt from America, have you any ideas on the subject of bringing them together?'

'Not at the moment, sir.'

'Well, bend the bean to it, because it's important. You remember me telling you that Boko and young Nobby were betrothed?'

'Yes, sir.'

'She can't marry without Uncle Percy's consent.'

'Indeed, sir?'

'Not till she's twenty-one. Legal stuff. And here's the nub, Jeeves. I haven't time to give you the full details now, but Boko, the silly ass, has been making a silly ass of himself, with the result that he has – what's the word that means making somebody froth at the mouth and chew pieces out of the carpet?'

' "Alienate", sir, is, I think, the verb for which you are groping.'

'That's it. Alienate. Well, as I say, I've no time to give you the inside story now, but Boko has played the goat and alienated Uncle Percy, and not a smell of a guardian's blessing is the latter prepared to give him. So you see what I mean about this meeting. It is vital that it takes place at the earliest possible date.'

'In order that his lordship may be brought to a more amiable frame of mind?'

'Exactly. If that merger comes off, the milk of human kindness will slosh about in him like the rising tide, swamping all animosity. Or don't you think so?'

'Undoubtedly, in my opinion, sir.'

'That's what I felt. And that is why you found me moody just now, Jeeves. I had just concluded an unpleasant interview with Uncle Percy, in the course of which he came out openly as not one of my admirers, thinking – incorrectly – that I had played an impressive part in the recent spot of arson.'

'He wronged you, sir?'

'Completely. I had nothing to do with it. I was a mere cipher in the affair. Edwin attended to the whole thing. But that was what he thought, and he blinded and stiffed with a will.'

'Unfortunate, sir.'

'Most. Of course, for the actual vote of censure that was passed I care little. A few poohs and a tush about cover that. Bertram Wooster is not a man who minds a few harsh words. He laughs lightly and snaps the fingers. It is wholly immaterial to me what the old bounder thinks of me, and in any case he didn't say a tithe of the things Aunt Agatha would have got off in similar circumstances. But the point is that I had promised Nobby that I would plead for her loved one, and what was saddening me when you came along was the thought that my potentialities in that direction had become greatly diminished. As far as Uncle Percy is concerned, I am not the force I was. So push that meeting along.'

'I will certainly use every endeavour, sir. I fully appreciate the situation.'

'Right. Now, what else have I to tell you? Oh, yes. Stilton.'

'Mr Cheesewright?'

'Police Constable Cheesewright, Jeeves. Stilton turns out to be the village bluebottle.'

He seemed surprised, and I didn't wonder. To him, of course, on the occasion when they had met at the flat, Stilton had been a mere, ordinary, tweed-suited popper-in. I mean, no uniform, no helmet and not a suggestion of any regulation boots.

'A policeman, sir?'

'Yes, and a nasty, vindictive policeman, too. With him, also, I have been having an unpleasant interview. He resents my presence here.'

'I suppose a great many young gentlemen enter the Force nowadays, sir.'

'I wish one fewer had. It is a tricky business falling foul of the constabulary, Jeeves.'

'Yes, sir.'

'I shall have to employ ceaseless vigilance, so as to give him no loophole for exercising his official powers. No drunken revels at the village pub.'

'No, sir.'

'One false step, and he'll swoop down on me like the – who was it who came down like a wolf on the fold?'

'The Assyrian, sir.'

'That's right. Well, that is what I have been through since I saw you last. First Stilton, then Edwin, then the fire, and finally Uncle Percy – all in about half an hour. It just shows what Steeple Bumpleigh can do, when it starts setting about you. And, oh my gosh, I was forgetting. You know the brooch?'

'Sir?'

'Aunt Agatha's brooch.'

'Oh, yes, sir.'

'I lost it. Oh, it's all right. I found it again. But what I mean is, picture my embarrassment. My heart stood still.'

'I can readily imagine it, sir. But you have it safely now?'

'Oh, rather,' I said, dipping a hand into the pocket. 'Or, rather,' I went on, bringing it out again with ashen face and bulging eyes. 'Oh, rather not. Jeeves,' I said, 'you will scarcely credit this, but the bally thing has gone again!'

It occasionally happens, and I have had to tell him off for doing so, that this man receives announcements that the young master's world is rocking about him with a mere 'Most disturbing, sir'. But now it was plain that he recognized that the thing was too big for that. I don't think he paled, and he certainly didn't say 'Golly!' or anything of that nature, but he came as near as he ever does to what they call in the movies 'the quick take 'um'. There was concern in his eyes, and if it hadn't been that his views are rigid in the matter of the correct etiquette between employee and employer, I have an idea that he would have patted me on the shoulder.

'This is a serious disaster, sir.'

'You are informing me, Jeeves!'

'Her ladyship will be vexed.'

'I can picture her screaming with annoyance.'

'Can you think where you could have dropped it, sir?'

'That's just what I'm trying to do. Wait, Jeeves,' I said, closing my eyes. 'Let me brood.'

I brooded.

'Oh, my gosh!'

'Sir?'

'I've got it.'

'The brooch, sir?'

'No, Jeeves, not the brooch. I mean I've reconstructed the scene and have now spotted where I must have parted company with it. Here's the sequence. The place caught fire, and I suddenly remembered I had left the small suitcase in the hall. I need scarcely remind you of its contents. My Sindbad the Sailor costume.'

'Ah, yes, sir.'

'Don't say "Ah, yes", Jeeves. Just keep on listening. I suddenly remembered, I repeat, that I had left the small suitcase in the hall. Well, you know me. To think is to act. I was inside, gathering it up, without a moment's delay. This involved stooping. This stooping must have caused the thing to fall out of my pocket.'

'Then it would still be in the hall, sir.'

'Yes. And take a look at the hall!'

We both took a look at it. I shook my head. He shook

his. Wee Nooke was burning lower now, but its interior was still something which only Shadrach, Meshach and Abednego could have entered with any genuine enjoyment.

'No hope of getting it, if it's there.'

'No, sir.'

'Then what's to be done?'

'May I brood, sir?'

'Certainly, Jeeves.'

'Thank you, sir.'

He passed into the silence, and I filled in the time by thinking of what Aunt Agatha was going to say. I did not look forward to getting in touch with her. In fact, it almost seemed as if another of my quick trips to America would be rendered necessary. About the only advantage of having an aunt like her is that it makes one travel, thus broadening the mind and enabling one to see new faces.

And I was just saying to myself 'Young man, go West', when, happening to glance at the thinker, I observed that his face was wearing the brainy expression which always signifies that there is a hot one coming along.

'Yes, Jeeves?'

'I think I have hit on quite a simple solution of your difficulty, sir.'

'Let me have it, Jeeves, and speedily.'

'What I would suggest, sir, is that I take the car, drive to London, call at the emporium where her ladyship made her purchase and procure another brooch in place of the one that is missing.'

I weighed this. It sounded promising. Hope began to burgeon.

'You mean, put on an understudy?'

'Yes, sir.'

'Delivering it to addressee as the original?'

'Precisely, sir.'

I went on weighing. And the more I did so, the fruitier the idea seemed.

'Yes, I see what you mean. The mechanism is much the same as that which you employed in the case of Aunt Agatha's dog McIntosh.'

'Not dissimilar, sir.'

'There we were in the position of being minus an Aberdeen terrier, when we should have been plus an Aberdeen terrier. You reasoned correctly that all members of this particular canine family look very much alike, and rang in a ringer with complete success.'

'Yes, sir.'

'Would the same system work with brooches?'

'I think so, sir.'

'Is one brooch just like another brooch?'

'Not invariably, sir. But a few words of inquiry will enable me to obtain a description of the lost trinket and to ascertain the price which her ladyship paid for it. I shall thus be enabled to return with something virtually indistinguishable from the original.'

I was convinced. It was as if a heavy weight had been removed from my soul. I have mentioned that a short while back he had seemed to be thinking of patting me on the shoulder. It was now all I could do to restrain myself from patting him on his.

'A winner, Jeeves!'

'Thank you, sir.'

'*Rem* – what is it again?'

'*Acu tetigisti*, sir.'

'I might have known that you would find the way.'

'I am gratified to feel that I enjoy your confidence, sir.'

'I have an account at Aspinall's, so you can tell them to chalk it up on the slate.'

'Very good, sir.'

'Buzz off instanter.'

'There is ample time, sir. I shall be able to reach

London long before the establishment closes for the day. Before proceeding thither, I think it would be best for me to stop at Mr Fittleworth's residence, apprise him of what has occurred, deposit the luggage and warn him of your coming.'

'Is "warn" the word?'

' "Inform" I should have said, sir.'

'Well, don't cut it too fine. The sands are running out, remember. That brooch must be in recipient's hands to-night. What one aims at is to have it lying alongside her plate at the dinner-table.'

'I shall undoubtedly be able to reach Steeple Bumpleigh on my return journey at about the dinner hour, sir.'

'Right ho, Jeeves. I know I can rely on you to run to time. First stop, Boko's, then. I, meanwhile, will be nosing round here. There is just a chance that I may have dropped the thing somewhere in the open. I can't remember exactly how the sight of that fire affected me, but I have no doubt that I sprang up and down a bit – quite nimbly enough to jerk packages out of pockets.'

Of course, I didn't think so, really. My original theory that I had become unbrooched while picking up the suitcase persisted. But on these occasions the instinct is to turn every stone and leave no avenue unexplored.

I nosed round, accordingly, scanning the turf and even going so far as to feel about in the rockery. As I had foreseen, no dice. It wasn't long before I gave it up and started to stroll along to Boko's. And I had just reached his gate, when there was a ting of a bicycle bell – I noted as a curious phenomenon that the denizens of Steeple Bumpleigh seemed to do practically nothing but ride about on bicycles, tinging bells – and I saw Nobby approaching.

I hastened to meet her, for she was just the girl

I wanted to get in touch with. I was anxious to thresh out with her the whole topic of Stilton and his love life.

Part 2

12

She dismounted with lissom grace, beaming welcomingly. Since I had last seen her, she had washed off the stains of travel and changed her frock and was looking spruce and dapper. Why she should have bothered to smarten herself up, when she was only going to meet a bird in patched grey flannel trousers and a turtle-neck sweater, I was at a loss to understand, but girls will, of course, be girls.

'Hullo, Bertie,' she said. 'Are you paying a neighbourly call on Boko?'

I replied that that was about what it amounted to, but added that first I required a few moments of her valuable time.

'Listen, Nobby,' I said.

She didn't, of course. I've never met a girl yet who did. Say 'Listen' to any member of the delicately nurtured sex, and she takes it as a cue to start talking herself. However, as the subject she introduced proved to be the very one I had been planning to ventilate, the desire to beat her brains out with a brick was not so pronounced as it would otherwise have been.

'What have you been doing to inflame Stilton, Bertie? I met him just now and asked if he had seen you, and he turned vermilion and gnashed every tooth in his head. I don't think I've ever seen a more incandescent copper.'

'He didn't explain?'

'No. He simply pedalled on furiously, as if he had been competing in a six-day bicycle race and had just realized he was dropping behind the leaders. What was the trouble?'

I tapped her on the arm with a grave forefinger.

'Nobby,' I said, 'there has been a bit of a mix-up. What's that word that begins with "con"?'

'Con?'

'I've heard Jeeves use it. There's a cat in it somewhere.'

'What on earth are you drivelling about?'

'Concatenation,' I said, getting it. 'Owing to an unfortunate concatenation of circumstances, Stilton is viewing me with concern. He has got the idea rooted in his bean that I've come down here to try to steal Florence from him.'

'Have you?'

'My dear young blister,' I said, with some impatience, 'would anybody want to steal Florence? Do use your intelligence. But, as I say, this unfortunate concatenation has led him to suspect the worst.'

And in a few simple words I gave her the run of the scenario, featuring the Young Lochinvar aspect of the matter. When I had finished, she made one of those foolish remarks which do so much to confirm a man in his conviction that women as a sex should be suppressed.

'You should have told him you were guiltless of the charge.'

I tut-tutted impatiently.

'I did tell him I was guiltless of the charge, and a fat lot he believed me. He continued to hot up, finally reaching a condition of so much Fahrenheit that I was surprised he didn't run me in on the spot. In which connection, you might have told me he was a cop.'

'I forgot to.'

'It would have spared me a very disconcerting shock. When I heard someone calling my name and looked round and saw him cycling towards me in the complete rig-out of a rural policeman, I nearly got the vapours.'

She laughed – a solo effort. Nothing in the prevailing

circumstances made me feel like turning it into a duet.

'Poor old Stilton!'

'Yes, that's all very well, but –'

'I think it's rather sporting of him, wanting to earn his living, instead of sitting on the knee of that uncle of his and helping himself out of his pockets.'

'I dare say, but –'

'Florence doesn't. And it's rather funny, because it was she who turned his thoughts in that direction. She talked Socialism to him, and made him read Karl Marx. He's very impressionable.'

I agreed with her there. I had never forgotten the time at Oxford when somebody temporarily converted him to Buddhism. It led to a lot of unpleasantness with the authorities, I recall, he immediately starting to cut chapels and go and meditate beneath the nearest thing the neighbourhood could provide to a bo tree.

'She's furious now, and says he was a fool to take her literally.'

She paused, in order to laugh again, and I seized the opportunity to get a word in edgeways.

'Exactly. As you state, she is furious. And that's just the aspect of the matter that I want to discuss. I could put up with a green-eyed Stilton, a Stilton who turns vermilion and gnashes the molars at the mention of my name. I don't say it could ever be pleasant, going about knowing that the Force was gnashing its teeth at you, but one learns to take the rough with the smooth. The real trouble is that I believe Florence is weakening on him.'

'What makes you think that?'

'She's just been talking to me about him. She used the expression "pigheaded", and said she was sick and tired of the whole thing and really didn't know what she was going to do about it. Her whole attitude seemed to me that of a girl on the very verge of giving her heart-throb the raspberry and returning the ring and presents. You spot the frightful menace?'

'You mean that if she breaks it off with Stilton, she may consider taking you on again?'

'That's what I mean. The peril is appalling. Owing to another unfortunate concatenation of circumstances, my stock has recently gone up with her to a fearful extent, and anything may happen at any moment.'

And I briefly outlined the Spindrift-Spinoza affair. When I had concluded, a meditative look came into her face.

'Do you know, Bertie,' she said, 'I've often thought that, of all the multitude Florence has been engaged to, you were the one she really wanted?'

'Oh, my gosh!'

'It's your fault for being so fascinating.'

'I dare say, but too late to do anything about that now.'

'Still, I don't see what you've got to worry about. If she proposes to you, just blush a little and smile tremulously and say "I'm sorry – so, so sorry. You have paid me the greatest compliment a woman can pay a man. But it cannot be. So shall we be pals – just real pals?" That'll fix her.'

'It won't do anything of the sort. You know what Florence is like. Propose, forsooth! She'll just notify me that the engagement is on again, like a governess telling a young charge to eat his spinach. And if you think I've got the force of character to come back with a *nolle prosequi* –'

'With a what?'

'One of Jeeves's gags. It means roughly "Nuts to you!" If, I say, you think I'm capable of asserting myself and giving her the bird, you greatly overestimate the Wooster fortitude. She must be reconciled to Stilton. It is the only way. Listen, Nobby. I wrote you a letter yesterday, giving my views on Florence and urging you to employ every means in your power to open Stilton's eyes to what he was in for. Have you read it?'

'Every syllable. It gripped me tremendously. I never knew you had such a vivid prose style. It reminded me of Ernest Hemingway. You don't by any chance write under the name of Ernest Hemingway, do you?'

I shook the head.

'No. The only thing I've ever written was an article for "Milady's Boudoir" on What The Well-Dressed Man Is Wearing. It appeared under my own name. But what I want to say is, pay no attention to that letter. I am now wholeheartedly in favour of the match. The wish to save Stilton has left me. The chap I have my eye on for saving purposes is B. Wooster. When chatting with Florence, therefore, boost Stilton in every possible way. Make her see what a prize she has got. And if you have any influence with him, endeavour to persuade him to chuck all this policeman nonsense and stand for Parliament, as she wants him to.'

'I'd love to see Stilton in Parliament.'

'So would I, if it means healing this rift.'

'Wouldn't he be a scream!'

'Not necessarily. There are bigger fatheads than Stilton among our legislators – dozens of them. They would probably shove him in the Cabinet. So push it along, young Nobby.'

'I'll do what I can. But Stilton isn't the easiest person to persuade, once the trend of his mind has set in any direction. You remember the deaf adder?'

'What deaf adder?'

'The one that stopped its ear, and would not listen to the voice of the charmers, charming never so wisely. That's Stilton. However, as I say, I'll do what I can. And now let's go and rout Boko out. I'm dying to hear what happened at that lunch of his.'

'You haven't seen Uncle Percy, then?'

'Not yet. He was out. Why?'

'Oh, nothing. I was only thinking that, if you had, you would have got an eye-witness's report from him,' I said, and was conscious of a pang of pity for my old friend and a hope that by this time he would have succeeded in thinking up a reasonably good story to cover the binge in question.

The sound of a typewriter greeted us as we crossed the threshold, indicating that Boko was still at work on that letter to Uncle Percy. It ceased abruptly as Nobby yoo-hooed, and when we passed on into the sitting-room, he was hastily dropping a sheet of paper into the basket.

'Oh, hullo darling,' he said brightly. Watching him bound from his chair and fold Nobby in a close embrace, the casual observer would have supposed him to have had nothing on his mind except the hair which he had apparently not brushed for days. 'I was just roughing out a *morceau*.'

'Oh, angel, have we interrupted the flow?'

'Not at all, not a-tall.'

'I was so anxious to hear how the lunch went off.'

'Of course, of course. I'll tell you all about it. By the way, Bertie, Jeeves delivered your effects. They are in the spare room. Delighted to put you up, of course. Too bad about that fire.'

'What fire?' asked Nobby.

'Jeeves tells me that Edwin has succeeded in burning Wee Nooke to the ground. Correct, Bertie?'

'Quite correct. It was his last Friday's act of kindness.'

'What a shame!' said Nobby, with a womanly sympathy that well became her.

Boko, however, looked on the bright side.

'Personally,' he said, 'I consider that Bertie has got off lightly. He appears not to have been even singed. A burned house is a mere bagatelle. Generally, when Edwin is trying to catch up with his acts of kindness, human life is imperilled. The mind flits back to the time when he mended my egg boiler. Occasionally, when I am much occupied with a job of work, sparing no effort to give my public of my best, I rise early, before my housekeeper turns up in the morning. On these occasions, it is my practice to boil myself a refreshing egg, using one of those patent machines for the purpose. You know the sort of thing I mean. It rings an alarm, hopes you've slept well, pours water on the coffee, lights a flame underneath and gets action on the egg. Well, the day after Edwin had fixed some trifling flaw in the apparatus, the egg was scarcely in position when it flew at me like a bullet, catching me on the tip of the nose and knocking me base over apex. I bled for hours. So I maintain that if you got off with a mere fire that destroyed your house, you are sitting pretty.'

Nobby speculated as to the chances of somebody some day murdering Edwin, and we agreed that the hour must eventually produce the man.

'And now,' said Boko, still with that strange brightness which, knowing the facts, I could not but admire, 'you will want to hear all about the lunch. Well, it was a great success.'

'Darling!'

'Yes, a notable success. I think I have made an excellent start.'

'Were you bright?'

'Very bright.'

'And genial?'

'The word understates it.'

'Angel!' said Nobby, and kissed him about fifteen times in rapid succession.

'Yes,' said Boko, 'I think I have got him on the run. It is difficult to tell with a man like that, who conceals his emotions behind a poker face, but I believe he's weakening. And we never expected him to fall on my neck right away, did we? It was agreed that the lunch was merely to prepare the soil.'

'What did you talk about?'

'Oh, this and that. The subject of spiders, I remember, was one that came up.'

'Spiders?'

'He seemed interested in spiders.'

'I never knew that.'

'Just a side of his character which he hasn't happened to reveal to you, I suppose. And then, of course, after talking of this and that, we talked of that and this.'

'There weren't any awkward pauses?'

'I didn't notice any. No, he rather prattled on, as it were, especially towards the end.'

'Did you tell him what a lot of money you were making?'

'Oh, yes, I touched on that.'

'I hope you explained that you were a steady young fellow and were bound to go on making it? That's what worries him. He thinks you may blow up at any moment.'

'Like Wee Nooke.'

'You see, when he was a young man, just starting in the shipping business, Uncle Percy used to go about with rather a rackety set in London, and he knew a lot of writers who made quite a bit from time to time and spent it all in a couple of days and then had to live on what they could borrow. My darling father was one of them.'

This was news to me. I had never pictured Uncle Percy as a bird who had gone about with rackety sets as a young man. In fact, I had never pictured him as ever having been a young man at all. It's always the way. If an old buster has a bristling moustache, a solid, lucrative business and the manners of a bear aroused while hibernating, you do not probe into his past and ask yourself whether he, too, in his day may not have been one of the boys.

'I covered that point,' said Boko. 'It was one of the

first I stressed. The modern author, I told him, is keen
and hard-headed. He is out for the stuff, and when he
gets it he salts it away.'

'That ought to have pleased him.'

'Oh, it did.'

'Then everything's fine.'

'Splendid.'

'All we need now is for Bertie to do his act.'

'Exactly. The future hinges on Bertie.'

'When he pleads –'

'Ah, I didn't mean quite that. I'm afraid you are not
abreast of the quick rush and swirl of recent events. I
doubt if it would be any good for Bertie to plead now.
His name has become mud.'

'Mud?'

' "Mud", I think, is the *mot juste*, Bertie?'

I was obliged to concede that this was more or less so.

'Uncle Percy,' I explained, 'has got it into his head
that I aided and encouraged Edwin in his fire-bug
activities. This has put me back in the betting a good
bit, considered as a pleader. I should find it difficult now
to sway him like a reed.'

'Then where are we?' said Nobby, registering anguish.

Boko patted her encouragingly on the shoulder.

'We're all right. Don't you worry.'

'But if Bertie can't plead –'

'Ah, but you're forgetting how versatile he is. What
you are overlooking is the scullery-window-breaking
side of his nature. That is what is going to see us
through. Brooding tensely over this business, I have had
an idea, and it is a pippin. Suppose, I said to myself, I
were to save the heavy's home from being looted by a
midnight marauder, that would make him feel I had the
right stuff in me, I fancy. He would say "Egad! A fine
young fellow, this Fittleworth!" would he not?'

'I suppose so.'

'You speak doubtfully.'

'I was only thinking that there isn't much chance of that happening. There hasn't been a burglary in Steeple Bumpleigh for centuries. Stilton was complaining about it only the other day. He said the place gave an ambitious young copper no scope.'

'These things can be arranged.'

'How do you mean?'

'It only needs a little organization. There is going to be a burglary in Steeple Bumpleigh this very night. Bertie will attend to it.'

There was only one comment to make on this, and I made it.

'Hey!' I cried.

'Don't interrupt, Bertie,' said Boko reprovingly. 'It prevents one marshalling one's thoughts. Here in a nutshell is the scheme I have evolved. Somewhere in the small hours, Bertie and I make our way to the Hall. We approach the scullery window. He busts it. I raise the alarm. He pops off –'

'Ah!' I said. It was the first point he had mentioned of which I found myself approving.

' – while I stay on, to accept the plaudits of all and be fawned on. I don't see how it can fail. The one thing a sturdy householder of the Worplesdon type dislikes is having the house he is holding broken into, and anyone who nips such a venture in the bud creeps straight into his heart. Before the night is out, I expect to have him promising to dance at our wedding.'

'Darling! It's wonderful!'

It was Nobby who said that, not me. I was still chewing the lower lip in open concern. I should have remembered, I was telling myself, that that play of Boko's, to which I alluded earlier, had been one of those mystery thrillers, and that it was only natural that some such set-up as this should have occurred to his diseased mind.

I mean to say, you get a chap whose thoughts run

persistently in the direction of screams in the night and
lights going out and mysterious hands appearing through
the wall and people rushing about shouting 'Here comes
The Shadow!' and it is inevitable that that will be the
sort of stuff he will dish out in an emergency. I resolved
there and then that I would put in a firm *nolle prosequi*.
Nobody is more anxious than Bertram Wooster to lend a
helping hand to Love's young dream, but there are limits
to what he is prepared to sign on for, and sharply defined
limits, at that.

Nobby's joyous animation had died away a bit. Like
me, she was chewing the lip.

'Yes, it's wonderful. But –'

'I don't like to hear that word "but".'

'I was only going to say, How do you explain?'

'Explain?'

'Your being there to raise alarms and be fawned on.'

'Perfectly simple. My love for you is the talk of
Steeple Bumpleigh. What more natural than that I
should have come to stand beneath your window, gazing
up at it?'

'I see! And then you heard a noise –'

'A curious noise that sounded like the splintering of
glass. And I popped round the house to investigate, and
there was a bounder smashing the scullery window.'

'Of course!'

'I knew you would see it.'

'Then everything depends on Bertie.'

'Everything.'

'You don't think he'll object?'

'I wish you wouldn't say things like that. You'll hurt
his feelings. You don't realize the sort of fellow Bertie is.
His nerve is like chilled steel, and when it is a question
of helping a pal, he sticks at nothing.'

Nobby drew a deep breath.

'He's wonderful, isn't he?'

'He stands alone.'

'I've always been devoted to Bertie. When I was a child, he once gave me threepennyworth of acid drops.'

'Generous to a fault. These splendid fellows always are.'

'How I admired him!'

'Me, too. I don't know a man I admire more.'

'Doesn't he remind you rather of Sir Galahad?'

'The name was on the tip of my tongue.'

'Of course, he wouldn't dream of not doing his bit.'

'Of course not. All settled, eh, Bertie?'

It's odd what a few kind words will do. Until now, I had, as I say, been all ready with the *nolle prosequi*, and had indeed opened my lips to shoot it across with all the emphasis at my disposal. But as I caught Nobby's eye, fixed on me in a devout sort of way, and at the same time was conscious of Boko shaking my hand and kneading my shoulder, something seemed to check me. I mean, there really didn't seem to be any way of *nolle-prosequi*-ing without spoiling the spirit of the party.

'Oh, rather,' I said. 'Absolutely.'

But not blithely. Not with any real chirpiness.

13

No, not with any real chirpiness. And this shortage of c.,
I must confess, continued to make its presence felt right
up to zero hour. All through the quiet evenfall, the
frugal dinner and the long, weary waiting for midnight
to strike on the village clock, I was conscious of a
growing concern. And when the moment arrived and
Boko and self passed through the silent gardens of
Bumpleigh Hall on our way to start the doings, it was
growing stronger than ever.

Boko was in gay and effervescent mood, speaking
from time to time in a low but enthusiastic voice of the
beauties of Nature and drawing my attention in a
cautious whisper to the agreeable niffiness of the flowers
past which we flitted, but it was far different with
Bertram. Bertram, and I do not attempt to conceal it, was
not at his fizziest. His spine crawled, and his heart was
bowed down with weight of woe. The word of a Wooster
was pledged; I had placed my services at the disposal of
the young couple and there was no question of my doing
a quick sneak and edging out of the enterprise, but
nothing was going to make me like it.

I think I have mentioned before my dislike for
creeping about strange gardens in the dark. Too many
painful episodes in my past have been connected with
other people's gardens, notably the time when
circumstances compelled me to slide out in the small
hours and ring the fire bell at Brinkley Court and that
other occasion when Roberta Wickham induced me
against my better judgement to climb a tree and drop a

flower-pot through the roof of a green-house, in order to create a diversion which would enable her cousin Clementina, who was A.W.O.L. from her school, to ooze back into it unobserved.

Of all these experiences, the last named had been, to date, the most soul searing, because it had culminated in the sudden appearance of a policeman saying 'What's all this?' And it was the thought that there might quite possibly be a repetition of this routine, and the realization that if a policeman did come muscling in now it would be Stilton, that curdled the blood and made me feel a dry, fluttering feeling in the pit of the stomach, as if I had swallowed a heaping tablespoonful of butterflies.

So pronounced was this sensation that I found myself clutching Boko's arm in ill-concealed panic and drawing him beneath a passing tree.

'Boko,' I gurgled, 'what about Stilton? Have you considered the Stilton angle?'

'Eh?'

'Suppose he's on duty at night? Suppose he's prowling? Suppose he suddenly pops out at us, complete with whistle and notebook?'

'Nonsense.'

'It would be an awful thing to be pinched by a chap you were boys together with. And he would spring to the task. He's got it in for me.'

'Nonsense, nonsense,' said Boko, continuing debonair to the gills. 'You mustn't allow your thoughts to take this morbid trend, Bertie. These tremors are unworthy of you. Don't you worry about Stilton. You have only to look at him – that clear eye, those rosy cheeks – to know that he is a man who makes a point of getting his regular eight hours. Early to bed and early to rise, is his slogan. Stilton is tucked up between the sheets, sleeping like a little child, and won't start functioning again till his alarm clock explodes at seven-thirty.'

Well, that was all right, as far as it went. His reasoning was specious, and did much to reassure me. Stilton's cheeks unquestionably were rosy. But it was only for a moment that I was strengthened. After all, I reflected, Stilton was merely a part of the menace. Even leaving him out of it, there was the Uncle Percy-Aunt Agatha side of the business. You couldn't get away from it that these gardens and messuages whose privacy we were violating belonged to the former, and that the latter had a joint interest in them. I might, that is to say, be safe from the dragon, but what about the hippogriffs? That was the question I asked myself. What price the hippogriffs?

If anything were to go wrong, if this frightful binge on which I had embarked were in the slightest detail to slip a cog, what would be the upshot? I'll tell you what would jolly well be the upshot. Not only should I be placed in the position of having to explain to a slavering uncle, justly incensed at being deprived of his beauty sleep, why I was going about the place breaking his scullery windows, but the whole story would be told to Aunt Agatha on her return with a wealth of detail, and then what?

Far less serious offences on my part in the past had brought the old relative leaping after me with her hatchet, like a Red Indian on the warpath, howling for my blood.

I mentioned this to Boko as we fetched up at journey's end, and he patted me on the shoulder. Well meant, no doubt, and a kindly gesture, but one that accomplished little or nothing in the way of stiffening my *morale*.

'If you're copped,' said Boko, 'just pass it off.'

'Pass it off?'

'That's right. Nonchalantly. Got the treacle?'

I said I had got the treacle.

'And the paper?'

'Yes.'

'Then I'll take a stroll for ten minutes. That will give you eight minutes to screw your courage to the sticking-point, one minute to break window and one to make getaway.'

This treacle idea was Boko's. He had insisted upon it as an indispensable adjunct to the proceedings, claiming that it would lend the professional touch at which we were aiming. According to him, and he is a chap who has studied these things, the knowledgeable burglar's first act is to equip himself with treacle and brown paper. He glues the latter to the window by means of the former, and then hauls off and busts the glass with a sharp buffet of the fist.

What a way to earn a living! I suppose I must have used up quite three minutes of my ten in meditating on these hardy fellows and wondering what made them go in for such an exacting life work. Large profits, no doubt, and virtually no overhead, but think what they must have to spend on nerve specialists and rest cures. Some sort of tonic alone must form a heavy item of a burglar's expenses.

I could have gone on for quite a while musing along these lines, but was obliged to dismiss the subject from my mind, for time was passing and I might expect Boko's return at any minute. And I shrank from the prospect of having to explain to him that I had been frittering away in daydreaming the moments which should have been earmarked for action.

Feeling, therefore, that if the thing was to be smacked into, 'twere well 'twere smacked into quickly, as Shakespeare says, I treacled the paper and attached it to the window. All that now remained to be done was to deliver the sharp buffet. And it was at this point that I suddenly came over all cat-in-the-adage-y. The chilliness of the feet became intensified, and I began to hover, as Stilton had done outside that jeweller's shop.

I had thought, while watching him on that occasion,

that he had accomplished what you might call the last
word in backing and filling, but I now realized that he
had merely scratched the surface. Compared with mine
at this juncture, Stilton's hovering could scarcely be
termed at all. I moved towards my objective and away
from my objective, and some of the time I moved
sideways. To an observer, had one been present, it might
have seemed that I was trying out the intricate steps of
some rhythmic dance.

Finally, however, stiffening the sinews and
summoning up all the splendid Wooster courage, I made
a quick forward movement and was in the act of raising
my fist, when it was as if a stick of dynamite had been
touched off beneath me. The hair rose in a solid mass,
and every nerve in the body stood straight up, curling at
the ends. There have been moments in his career, many
of them, when Bertram Wooster has not felt at his ease,
but this one was the top.

From somewhere above, a voice had spoken.

'Coo!' it said. 'Who's there?'

If it hadn't been for that 'Coo!' I might have supposed
it the voice of Conscience. As it was, I was enabled to
ticket it correctly as that of young blasted Edwin. Glued
against the wall, as if I had been a bit of treacled paper, I
could just see him leaning out of an adjacent window.
And when I reflected that, after all I had gone through, I
was now being set upon by Boy Scouts, I don't mind
admitting that the iron entered into my soul. Very
bitter, the whole thing.

After he had said 'Who's there?' he was silent for a
space, as if pausing for a reply, though you would have
thought even a cloth-headed kid like that would have
known that it's hopeless to expect burglars to keep the
conversation going.

'Who's that?' he said, at length.

I maintained a prudent reserve. He then said 'I can see
you all right,' but in an uncertain voice which told me

he was lying in his teeth. The one thing that was serving to buoy me up and still the fluttering heart-strings at this most unpleasant moment was the fact that it was a dark night, without a moon or any rot of that sort. Stars, yes. Moon, no. A lynx might have seen me, but only a lynx, and it would have had to be a pretty sharpsighted lynx, at that.

My silence seemed to discourage him. These one-sided conversations always flag fairly quickly. He brooded over the scene a bit longer – Jeeves would have spotted a resemblance to the Blessed Damozel gazing out from the gold bar of heaven – then drew his head in, and I was alone at last.

Not, however, for long. A moment later, Boko hove alongside.

'All set?' he asked, in a hearty voice that seemed to boom through the garden like a costermonger calling attention to his brussels sprouts, and I grabbed him feverishly, begging him to pipe down a bit.

'Not so loud!'

'What's the matter?'

'Edwin.'

'Edwin?'

'He just poked his foul head out of a window and wanted to know who was there.'

'Did you tell him?'

'No.'

'Excellent. Very wise move. He's probably gone to sleep again.'

'Boy Scouts never sleep.'

'Of course they do. In droves. Have you smashed the window?'

'No.'

'Why not?'

'Because of Edwin.'

He clicked his tongue, causing me to quiver from stem to stern. To me, a little nervous at the moment, as

I have shown, it sounded like a mass meeting of Spanish dancers playing the castanets.

'You mustn't let yourself be diverted from the task in hand by trifles, Bertie. I can't help wondering if you're taking this thing with the proper seriousness. I may be wrong, but there seems to me something frivolous in your attitude. Do pull yourself together and try to remember what this means to Nobby and me.'

'But I can't smash windows, with Edwin lurking above.'

'Of course you can. I can't see your difficulty. Pay no attention whatever to Edwin. If he is on the alert, so much the better. It will all help when the moment comes for me to put on my act. His story will support mine. I'll give you another ten minutes, and then I really must insist on a little action. Got a cigarette?'

'No.'

'Then I shall simply have to go on smoking mine. That's what it amounts to,' said Boko, and breezed off.

Now, reading the above splash of dialogue, you will have noticed something. I don't know if you happen to know the meaning of the French expression *sang-froid*, but, if you do, you can scarcely have failed to observe to what an extraordinary extent the recent Fittleworth had been exhibiting this quality. While I trembled and twittered, he remained as cool and calm as a turbot on ice, and it now occurred to me that the reason for this might very possibly be that he was keeping on the move.

It helps on these occasions to be able to circulate freely instead of standing on point duty outside the scullery windows, and it was quite on the cards, I felt, that a short stroll might do something towards keying up my sagging nervous system. With this end in view, I wandered off round the house.

Any hope I may have entertained, however, that the vibrating ganglions would cease to quiver and the fluttering feeling in the pit of the stomach simmer down was shattered before I had gone a dozen yards. A dim figure suddenly loomed up before me in the darkness, causing me to leap perhaps five feet in the air and utter a sharp yip.

My composure was somewhat restored – not altogether, but somewhat – when the dim f. spoke, and I recognized Jeeves's voice.

14

'Good evening, sir,' he said.

'Good evening, Jeeves,' I responded.

'You gave me quite a start, sir.'

'Nothing to the one you gave me. I thought the top of my head had come off.'

'I am sorry to have been the cause of you experiencing any discomfort, sir. I was unable to herald my approach, the encounter being quite unforeseen. You are up late, sir.'

'Yes.'

'One could scarcely desire more delightful conditions for a nocturnal ramble.'

'That is your view, is it?'

'It is indeed, sir. I always feel that nothing is so soothing as a walk in a garden at night.'

'Ha!'

'The cool air. The scent of growing things. That is tobacco plant which you can smell, sir.'

'Is it?'

'The stars, sir.'

'Stars?'

'Yes, sir.'

'What about them?'

'I was merely directing your attention to them, sir. Look how the floor of heaven is thick inlaid with patines of bright gold.'

'Jeeves –'

'There's not the smallest orb which thou beholdest, sir, but in his motion like an angel sings, still quiring to the young-eyed cherubims.'

'Jeeves –'

'Such harmony is in immortal souls. But whilst this muddy vesture of decay doth grossly close it in, we cannot hear it.'

'Jeeves –'

'Sir?'

'You couldn't possibly switch it off, could you?'

'Certainly, sir, if you wish it.'

'I'm not in the mood.'

'Very good, sir.'

'You know how one isn't, sometimes.'

'Yes, sir. I quite understand. I procured the brooch, sir.'

'Brooch?'

'The one which you wished me to purchase in place of the trinket lost in the fire, sir. Lady Florence's birthday present.'

'Oh, ah.' It will give you some rough indication of how what he had called this nocturnal ramble of mine had affected me, when I say that I had completely forgotten about the damn' thing. 'You got it, eh?'

'Yes, sir.'

'And handed it in?'

'Yes, sir.'

'Good. That's off my mind, then. And, believe me, Jeeves, the more I can get off my mind at this juncture, the better I shall like it, because it's already loaded down well above the Plimsoll mark.'

'I am sorry to hear that, sir.'

'Do you know why I'm prowling about this garden?'

'I was hoping that you might enlighten me, sir.'

'I will. This is no careless saunter on which you find me engaged, Jeeves, but an enterprise whose consequences may well stagger humanity.'

He listened attentively while I sketched out the events which had led up to the tragedy, interrupting only with a respectful intake of the breath as I spoke of

Uncle Percy, Boko and the Joke Goods. It was plain that my story had gripped him.

'An eccentric young gentleman, Mr Fittleworth, sir,' was his comment, as I concluded.

'Loony to the eyebrows,' I agreed.

'The scheme which he had formulated is not, however, without its ingenuity. His lordship would undoubtedly be most grateful to anyone whom he supposed to have foiled a raid on the premises on this particular night. I happen to be aware that, despite her ladyship's repeated instructions to him to attend to the matter, he forgot to post the letter renewing his burglary insurance.'

'How do you know that?'

'I had the facts from his lordship in person, sir. Ascertaining that I was about to drive to London this afternoon, he gave me the communication to dispatch in the metropolitan area, so that it should reach its destination to-morrow morning by the first delivery. His emotion, as he urged me not to fail him and alluded to what her ladyship would say if she ever discovered his negligence, was very noticeable. He shook visibly.'

I was amazed.

'You don't mean he's scared of Aunt Agatha?'

'Intensely, sir.'

'A tough bird like him? Practically a bucko mate of a tramp steamer?'

'Even bucko mates stand in awe of the captains of their vessels, sir.'

'Well, you absolutely astound me. I should have thought that if ever there was a bimbo who was master in his own home, that bimbo was Percival, Lord Worplesdon.'

'I am inclined to doubt whether the gentleman exists who could be master in a home that contained her ladyship, sir.'

'Perhaps you're right.'

'Yes, sir.'

I breathed deeply. For the first time since Boko had outlined the night's programme, I was conscious of a relaxation of the strain. It would be paltering with the truth to say that even now Bertram Wooster looked forward with any actual relish to busting that scullery window, but it was stimulating to feel that the action was likely to produce solid results.

'Then you think this scheme of Boko's will drag home the gravy?'

'Quite conceivably, sir.'

'That's a comfort.'

'On the other hand –'

'Oh, golly, Jeeves. What's wrong now?'

'I was merely about to say that Mr Fittleworth has selected a somewhat unfortunate moment for his enterprise, sir. It tends to clash with his lordship's arrangements.'

'How do you mean?'

'By an unfortunate coincidence, his lordship will in a few moments from now be proceeding to the potting shed to confer with Mr Chichester Clam.'

'Chichester Clam?'

'Yes, sir.'

I shook the head.

'I think the strain to which I have been subject must have affected my hearing. You sound to me just as if you were saying Chichester Clam.'

'Yes, sir. Mr J. Chichester Clam, managing director of the Clam Line.'

'What on earth's a clam line?'

'The shipping line, sir, which, if you remember, is on the eve of being merged with his lordship's Pink Funnel.'

I got it at last.

'You mean the chap Uncle Percy is trying to get together with? The ancient mariner from America?'

'Precisely, sir. Owing to the conflagration at Wee

Nooke, it became necessary to think of some other spot where the two gentlemen could meet and discuss their business without fear of interruption.'

'And you chose the potting shed?'

'Yes, sir.'

'God bless you, Jeeves.'

'Thank you, sir.'

'Is this bird in the potting shed now?'

'I should be disposed to imagine so, sir. When I motored to London this afternoon, it was with instructions from his lordship to establish telephonic communication with Mr Clam at his hotel and urge him to hasten to Steeple Bumpleigh and be in the potting shed half an hour after midnight. The gentleman expressed complete understanding and agreement, and assured me that he would drive down in good time to keep the appointment.'

I could not repress a pang of gentle pity for this hand across the sea. Born and brought up in America, he would, of course, not have the slightest idea of the sort of place Steeple Bumpleigh was and what he was letting himself in for in going there. I couldn't, offhand, say what Steeple Bumpleigh was saving up for Chichester Clam, but obviously he was headed for a sticky evening.

I saw, too, what Jeeves meant about Boko having selected an unfortunate moment for his enterprise.

'Half an hour after midnight? It must be nearly that now.'

'Exactly that, sir.'

'Then Uncle Percy will be manifesting himself at any moment.'

'If I am not mistaken, sir, this would be his lordship whom you can hear approaching.'

And, sure enough, from somewhere to the nor'-nor'-east there came the sound of some solid object shuffling through the night.

I inhaled in quick concern.

'Egad, Jeeves!'

'Sir?'

''Tis he!'

'Yes, sir.'

I mused a moment.

'Well,' I said, though not liking the prospect and wishing that the civility could have been avoided, 'I suppose I'd better pass the time of day. What ho,' I continued, as he came abreast. 'What ho, what ho!'

I must say the results were not unpleasing – to a man, I mean, who, like myself, had twice to-night been forced to skip like the hills on finding himself unexpectedly addressed from the shadows. Watching the relative soar skywards with a wordless squeak, obviously startled out of a year's growth, I was conscious of a distinct sensation of getting a bit of my own back. I felt that, whatever might befall, I was at least that much to the good.

In introducing this uncle by marriage, I showed him to be a man who, in moments of keen emotion, had a tendency to say 'What?' and keep on saying it. He did so now.

'What? What? What? What? What?' he ejaculated, making five in all. 'What?' he added, bringing it up to the round half dozen.

'Lovely evening, Uncle Percy,' I said, hoping by the exercise of suavity to keep the conversation on an amicable plane. 'Jeeves and I were just talking about the stars. What was it you said about the stars, Jeeves?'

'I alluded to the fact that there was not the smallest orb which did not sing in its motion like an angel, still quiring to the young-eyed cherubims, sir.'

'That's right. Worth knowing, that, eh, Uncle Percy?'

During these exchanges, the relative had been going on saying 'What?' in a sort of strangled voice, as if still finding it a bit hard to cope with the pressure of events. He now came forward and peered at me, feasting the eyes as far as was possible in the uncertain light.

'You!' he said, with a kind of gasp, like some strong swimmer in his agony. 'What the devil are you doing here?'

'Just sauntering.'

'Then go and saunter somewhere else, damn it.'

The Woosters are quick to take a hint, and are generally able to spot when our presence is not desired. Reading between the lines, I could see that he was wishing me elsewhere.

'Right ho, Uncle Percy,' I said, still maintaining the old suavity, and was about to withdraw, when another of those voices which seemed to be so common in these parts spoke in my immediate rear, causing me to equal, if not to improve upon, the old relative's recent standing high jump.

'What's all this?' it said, and with what is sometimes called a sickening qualm I perceived that it was Stilton who had joined our little group. Boko had been completely wrong about the man. Rosy though his cheeks may have been, here was no eight-hour slumberer, who had to be brought to life by alarm clocks, but a vigilant guardian of the peace who was always up and doing, working while others slept.

Stilton was looking gruesomely official. His helmet gleamed in the starlight. His regulation boots had settled themselves solidly into the turf. I rather think he had got his notebook out.

'What's all this?' he repeated.

I suppose Uncle Percy was still feeling a bit edgy. Nothing else could have explained the crisp, mouth-filling expletive which now proceeded from him like a shot out of a gun. It sounded to me like something he must have picked up from one of the sea captains in his employment. These rugged mariners always have excellent vocabularies, and no doubt they frequently drop in at the office on their return from a voyage and teach them something new.

'What the devil do you mean, what's all this? And who the devil are you to come trespassing in my grounds, asking what's all this? What's all this yourself? What,' proceeded Uncle Percy, warming to his work, 'are you doing here, you great oaf? I suppose you're just sauntering, too? Good God! I try to enjoy a quiet stroll in my garden, and before I can so much as inhale a breath of air I find it crawling with nephews and policemen. I come out to be alone with Nature, and the first thing I know I can't move for the crowd. What is this place? Piccadilly Circus? Hampstead Heath on Bank Holiday? The spot chosen for the annual outing of the police force?'

I saw his point. Nothing is more annoying to a man who is seeking privacy than to discover that, without knowing it, he had thrown his grounds open to the public. In addition to which, of course, Chichester Clam was waiting for him in the potting shed.

The acerbity of his tone had not been lost on Stilton. Well, I mean to say, it couldn't very well have been. That expletive alone would have been enough to tell him that he was not a welcome visitor. I could see that he was piqued. His was in many ways a haughty spirit, and it was plain that he resented this brusqueness. From the fact that the top of his helmet moved sharply in the direction of the stars, I knew that he had drawn himself to his full height.

He found himself, however, in a somewhat embarrassing position. He could not come back with anything really snappy, Uncle Percy being a Justice of the Peace and, as such, able to put it across him like the dickens if he talked out of his turn. Besides being his future father-in-law. He was compelled, accordingly, to temper his resentment with a modicum of reserve and to take it out in stiffness of manner.

'I am sorry –'

'No use being sorry. Thing is not to do it, blast it.'

' – to intrude – '

'Then stop intruding.'

' – but I am here in the performance of my duty.'

'What do you mean? Never heard such nonsense.'

'I received a telephone call just now, desiring me to proceed to the Hall immediately.'

'Telephone call? Telephone call? What rot! At this time of night? Who telephoned you?'

I suppose that stiff, official manner is difficult to keep up. Quite a bit of a strain, probably. At any rate, Stilton now lapsed from it.

'Young ruddy Edwin,' he replied sullenly.

'My son Edwin?'

'Yes. He said he had seen a burglar in the grounds.'

A spasm seemed to pass through Uncle Percy. The word 'burglar' had plainly touched a chord. He spun round with passionate gesture.

'Jeeves!'

'M'lord?'

'Did you post that letter?'

'Yes, m'lord.'

'Phew!' said Uncle Percy, and mopped his brow.

He was still mopping it, when there came the sound of galloping feet and somebody started giving tongue in the darkness.

'Hi! Hi! Hi! Wake up, everybody. Turn out the guard. I've caught a burglar in the potting shed.'

The voice was Boko's, and with another pang of pity I realized that J. Chichester Clam's troubles had begun. He knew now what happened to people who came to Steeple Bumpleigh.

15

In the brief interval which elapsed before Boko sighted us and came to join our little circle, I fell to musing on this Clam and thinking how different he must be feeling all this from what he had been accustomed to.

Here, I mean to say, was one of those solid businessmen who are America's pride, whose lives are as regular and placid as that of a bug in a rug. On my visits to New York I had met dozens of them, so I could envisage without difficulty a typical Clam day.

Up in the morning bright and early in his Long Island home. The bath. The shave. The eggs. The cereal. The coffee. The drive to the station. The 8.15. The cigar. The *New York Times*. The arrival at the Pennsylvania terminus. The morning's work. The lunch. The afternoon's work. The cocktail. The 5.50. The drive from the station. The return home. The kiss for the wife and tots, the pat for the welcoming dog. The shower. The change into something loose. The well-earned dinner. The quiet evening. Bed.

That was the year in, year out routine of a man like Chichester Clam, Sundays and holidays excepted, and it was one ill calculated to fit him for the raw excitements and jungle conditions of Steeple Bumpleigh. Steeple Bumpleigh must have come upon him as a totally new experience, causing him to wonder what had hit him – like a man who, stooping to pluck a nosegay of wild flowers on a railway line, is unexpectedly struck in the small of the back by the Cornish Express. As he now sat in the potting shed, listening to Boko's view halloos, he was probably convinced that all this must be that

Collapse of Civilization, of which he had no doubt so often spoken at the Union League Club.

In spite of the floor of heaven being thick inlaid with patines of bright gold, it was, as I have said, a darkish night, not easy to see things in. The visibility was, however, quite good enough to enable one to perceive that Boko was pretty pleased with himself. Indeed, it would not be overstating it to say that he had got it right up his nose. That this was so was borne in upon me by the fact that he started right away calling Uncle Percy 'my dear Worplesdon' – a thing which in his calmer moments he wouldn't have done on a bet.

'Ah, my dear Worplesdon,' he said, having peered into the relative's face and identified him, 'so you're up and about, are you? Capital, capital. Stilton, too? And Jeeves? And Bertie? Fine. Between the five of us, we ought to be well able to overpower the miscreant. I don't know if you were listening to what I was saying just now, but I've locked a burglar up in the potting shed.'

He spoke these words with the air of a man getting ready to receive the thanks of the nation, tapping Uncle Percy's chest the while as if to suggest that the latter was a lucky chap to have Boko Fittleworths working day and night in his interests. It did not surprise me to observe the relative's growing restiveness under the treatment.

'Will you stop prodding me, sir!' he cried, plainly stirred. 'What's all this nonsense about burglars?'

Boko seemed taken aback. One could see that he was feeling that this was not quite the tone.

'Nonsense, Worplesdon?'

'How do you know the fellow's a burglar?'

'My dear Worplesdon! Would anybody but a burglar be lurking in potting sheds at this time of night? But, if you still need convincing, let me tell you that I was passing the scullery window just now, and I noticed that it was covered with a piece of brown paper.'

'Brown paper?'

'Brown paper. Pretty sinister, eh?'

'Why?'

'My dear Worplesdon, it proves to the hilt the man's criminal intentions. You were possibly not aware of it, but when these fellows plan to enter a house and snaffle contents, they always stick a bit of brown paper on a window with treacle and then smash it with a blow of the fist. It's the regular procedure. The fragments of glass adhere to the paper, and they are thus enabled to climb in without mincing themselves to hash. Oh, no, my dear Worplesdon, there can be no doubt concerning the scoundrel's guilty purpose. I bottled him up in the nick of time. I heard something moving in the potting shed, peeped in, saw a dark form, and slammed the door and fastened it, thus laying him a dead stymie and foiling all his plans.'

This statement drew a word of professional approbation from the sleepless guardian of the law.

'Good work, Boko.'

'Thanks, Stilton.'

'You showed great presence of mind.'

'Nice of you to say so.'

'I'll go and pinch him.'

'Just what I was about to suggest.'

'Has he a gun?'

'I don't know. You'll soon find out.'

'I don't care if he has.'

'The right spirit.'

'I shall just make a quick spring –'

'That's the idea.'

' – and disarm him.'

'We will hope so. We will certainly hope so. Yes, let us hope for the best. Still, whatever happens, you will have the satisfaction of knowing that you have done your duty.'

Throughout these exchanges, starting at the words

'Good work' and continuing right through to the tab line 'done your duty', Uncle Percy had been exhibiting much of the frank perturbation of a cat on hot bricks. Nor could one blame him. He had invited J. Chichester Clam for a quiet talk in the potting shed, and the thought of constables making quick springs at him must have been a very bitter one. You can't conduct delicate business negotiations with that sort of thing going on. In his agony of spirit, he now began saying "What?" again, leading Boko to apply that patronizing finger to his brisket once more.

'It's quite all right, my dear Worplesdon,' said Boko, tapping like a woodpecker. 'Have no concern about Stilton. He won't get hurt. At least, I don't thing so. One may be wrong, of course. Anyway, he is paid to take these risks. Ah, Florence,' he added, addressing the daughter of the house, who had just come alongside in a dressing-gown, with her hair in curling pins.

It was plain that Florence was not her usual calm and equable self. When she spoke, one noted a testiness.

'Never mind the "Ah, Florence". What is going on out here? What is all this noise and disturbance? I was woken up by someone shouting.'

'Me,' said Boko, and even in the uncertain light I could see that he was smirking. I doubt if in all Hampshire that night you could have found a fellow more thoroughly satisfied with himself. He had got it firmly rooted in his mind that he was the popular hero, beloved of all – little knowing that Uncle Percy's favourite reading would have been his name on a tombstone. Rather saddening, the whole thing.

'Well, I wish you wouldn't. It is perfectly impossible to sleep, with people romping all over the garden.'

'Romping? I was catching a burglar.'

'Catching a burglar?'

'You never spoke a truer word. A great desperate brute of a midnight marauder, who may or may not be armed

to the teeth. That question we shall be able to answer
better after Stilton has got together with him.'

'But how did you catch a burglar?'

'Oh, it's just a knack.'

'I mean, what were you doing here at this time of night?'

It was as if Uncle Percy had been waiting for someone
to come along and throw him just that cue.

'Exactly,' he cried, having snorted the snort of a
lifetime. 'The very thing I want to know. The precise
question I was about to ask myself. What the devil are
you doing here? I am not aware that I invited you to
infest my private grounds and go charging about them
like a buffalo, making an appalling din and rendering
peace and quiet impossible. You have a garden of your
own, I believe? If you must behave like a buffalo, kindly
go and do so there. And the idea of locking people in my
potting shed! I never heard of anything so officious in
my life.'

'Officious?'

'Yes, damned officious.'

Boko was patently stunned. One sensed that thoughts
about birds biting the hand that fed them were racing
through his mind. He stuttered a while before speaking.

'Well!' he said, at length, having ceased to imitate a
motor bicycle. 'Well, I'm dashed! Well, I must say! Well,
I'm blowed! Officious, eh? That is the attitude you take,
is it? Ha! One desires no thanks, of course, for these
little good turns one does people – at some slight
inconvenience to oneself, one might perhaps mention –
but I should have thought that in the circumstances one
was entitled to expect at least decent civility. Jeeves!'

'Sir?'

'What did Shakespeare say about ingratitude?'

' "Blow, blow, thou winter wind", sir, "thou art not so
unkind as man's ingratitude". He also alludes to the
quality as "thou marble-hearted fiend".'

'And he wasn't so dashed far wrong! I brood over his

house like a guardian angel, sacrificing my sleep and leisure to its interests. I sweat myself to the bone, catching burglars –'

Uncle Percy turned in again.

'Burglars, indeed! All silly nonsense. The man is probably some harmless wayfarer, who had taken refuge in my potting shed from the storm –'

'What storm?'

'Never mind what storm.'

'There isn't a storm.'

'All right, all right!'

'It's a lovely night. No suggestion of a storm.'

'All right, all *right*! We aren't talking about the weather. We're talking about this poor waif in my potting shed. I say he is probably just some harmless wayfarer, and I refuse to persecute the unfortunate fellow. What harm has he done? All the riff-raff for miles around have been using my garden as if it were their own, so why shouldn't he? This is Liberty Hall, damn it – or seems to be.'

'So you don't think he's a burglar?'

'No, I do not.'

'Worplesdon, you're a silly ass. How about the brown paper? What price the treacle?'

'Damn the treacle. Curse the brown paper. And how dare you call me a silly ass? Jeeves!'

'M'lord?'

'Here's ten shillings. Go and give it to the poor chap and let him go. Tell him to buy himself a warm bed and supper.'

'Very good, m'lord.'

Boko uttered a sharp, yapping sound, like a displeased hyena.

'And, Jeeves!' he said.

'Sir?'

'When he's got the warm bed, better tuck him up and see that he has a hot water bottle.'

'Very good, sir.'

'Ten shillings, eh? Supper, egad? Warm bed, forsooth?
Well, this lets me out,' said Boko. 'I wash my hands
of the whole affair. This is the last occasion on which
you may expect my help when you have burglars in
this loony bin. Next time they come flocking round,
I shall pat them on the back and hold the ladder for
them.'

He strode off into the darkness, full to the brim of
dudgeon, and I can't say I was much surprised. The way
things had panned out had been enough to induce
dudgeon in the mildest of men, let alone a
temperamental young author, accustomed to calling on
his publishers and raising hell at the smallest
provocation.

But though seeing his viewpoint, I mourned. In fact, I
would go further, I groaned in spirit. The tender Wooster
heart had been deeply touched by the non-smooth
running of the course of the Boko-Nobby true love, and I
had hoped that to-night's rannygazoo would have
culminated in a thorough sweetening of Uncle Percy and
a consequent straightening out of the tangle.

Instead of which, this impulsive scrivener had gone
and deposited himself lower down among the wines and
spirits than ever. If the betting against his scooping in a
guardian's consent had been about four to one up to this
point, it could scarcely be estimated now at anything
shorter than a hundred to eight – and even at that
generous price I doubt if the punters would have
invested.

I was just wondering whether it would be any use my
putting in a soothing word, and feeling on the whole
perhaps not, when there came to my ears a low whistle,
which may or may not have been the note of the lesser
screech owl, and I observed something indistinct but
apparently feminine bobbing about behind a distant tree.
Everything seeming to point to this being Nobby, I

detached myself from the main body and oiled off in her direction.

My surmise was correct. It was Nobby, in a dressing-gown but not curling pins. Apparently, with her style of hair you don't use them. She was fizzing with excitement and the desire to learn the latest hot news.

'I didn't like to join the party,' she said, after the preliminary what-hoes had been exchanged. 'Uncle Percy would have sent me to bed. How's it coming along, Bertie?'

It wrenched the heart-strings to have to ladle out bad tidings to the eager young prune, but the painful task could not be avoided.

'Not too well,' I replied sombrely.

As I had foreseen, the statement got right in amongst her. She uttered a stricken yowl.

'Not too well?'

'No.'

'What went wrong?'

'It would be better to ask what went right. The enterprise was a flop from start to finish.'

She sharp-exclamationed, and I saw that she was giving me one of those unpleasant, suspicious looks.

'I suppose you fell down on your end of the thing?'

'Nothing of the kind. I did all that man could have done. But there was one of those unfortunate concatenations of circumstances, which led to what we had anticipated would be a nice little night's work for the two of us becoming a mob scene. We were just getting on with it most satisfactorily, when the gardens and messuages became a seething mass of Uncle Percies, Jeeveses, Stiltons, Florences and what not. It dished our aims completely. And I am sorry to say that Boko did not show himself at his best.'

'What do you mean?'

'He would keep calling Uncle Percy "my dear Worplesdon". You can't address a man like that as "my

dear Worplesdon" for long without something cracking
under the strain. Heated words ensued, quite a few being
contributed by Boko. The scene, a most painful one,
concluded with him calling Uncle Percy a silly ass, and
turning on his heel and stalking off. I fear his standing
with the above has hit a new low.'

She moaned softly, and I considered for a moment the
idea of patting her head. Not much use, though, I felt on
consideration, and gave it a miss.

'I did think I could have trusted Boko not to make an
ass of himself just for once,' she murmured with a wild
regret.

'I doubt if you can ever trust an author not to make an
ass of himself,' I responded gravely.

'Golly, I'll tick him off for this! Which way did he go,
when he turned on his heel?'

'Somewhere in that direction.'

'Wait till I find him!' she cried, baying like an
under-sized bloodhound, and was gone with the wind.

It was perhaps a couple of ticks later, or three, that
Jeeves came shimmering up.

'A disturbing evening, sir,' he said. 'I released Mr
Clam.'

'Never mind about Clam. Clam leaves me cold. The
chap I'm worrying about is Boko.'

'Ah, yes, sir.'

'Silly idiot, alienating Uncle Percy like that.'

'Yes, sir. It was a pity that the young gentleman's
manner should not have been more conciliatory.'

'He's sunk, unless you can think of some way of
healing the breach.'

'Yes, sir.'

'Get hold of him, Jeeves.'

'Yes, sir.'

'Confer with him.'

'Yes, sir.'

'Strain the bean to the utmost in order to hit upon some solution.'

'Very good, sir.'

'You will find him somewhere out there in the silent night. At least, it won't be so dashed silent, because Nobby will be telling him what she thinks of him. Circle around till you hear a raised soprano voice, and that will be the spot to head for.'

He popped off, as desired, and I started to do a bit of pacing to and fro, knitting the brows. I had been knitting them for about five minutes, when something loomed up in the offing and I saw that it was Boko, come to play a return date.

16

Boko was looking subdued and chastened, as if his soul had been passed through the wringer. He wore the unmistakable air of a man who has just been properly told where he gets off by the girl of his dreams and has not yet reassembled the stunned faculties.

'Hullo, Bertie,' he said, in a sort of hushed, saintlike voice.

'Pip-pip, Boko.'

'Some night!'

'Considerable.'

'You haven't a flask on you, have you?'

'No.'

'A pity. One should always carry a flask about in case of emergencies. Saint Bernard dogs do it in the Alps. Fifty million Saint Bernard dogs can't be wrong. I have just passed through a great emotional experience, Bertie.'

'Did Nobby find you?'

He gave a little shiver.

'I've just been chatting with her.'

'I had a sort of idea you had.'

'It shows in my appearance, does it? Yes, I suppose it would. It wasn't you who told her about those Joke Goods, was it?'

'Of course not.'

'Somebody did.'

'Uncle Percy, probably.'

'That's true. She would have asked him how the lunch came out. Yes, I imagine that was the authoritative source from which she had her information.'

'So she touched on the Joke Goods?'

'Oh, yes. Yes, she touched on them. Her conversation dealt partly with them and partly with what happened to-night. She was at no loss for words on either theme. You're absolutely sure you haven't a flask?'

'Quite, I'm afraid.'

'Ah, well,' said Boko, and relapsed into silence for a while, emerging from it to ask me in a wondering sort of voice where girls picked up these expressions.

'What expressions?'

'I couldn't repeat them, with gentlemen present. I suppose they learn them at their finishing schools.'

'She gave you beans, did she?'

'With no niggardly hand. It was an extraordinary feeling, standing there while she put me through it. One had a dazed sensation of something small and shrill whirling about one, seething with fury. Like being attacked by a Pekinese.'

'I've never been attacked by a Pekinese.'

'Well, ask the man who has. He'll tell you. Every moment, I was expecting to get a nasty nip in the ankle.'

'How did it all end?'

'Oh, I got away with my life. Still, what's life?'

'Life's all right.'

'Not if you've lost the girl you love.'

'Have you lost the girl you love?'

'That's what I'm trying to figure out. I can't make up my mind. It all depends what construction you place on the words "I never want to see or speak to you again in this world or the next, you miserable fathead".'

'Did she say that?'

'Among other things.'

I saw that the time had come to soothe and encourage.

'I wouldn't let that worry me, Boko.'

He seemed surprised.

'You wouldn't?'

'No. She didn't mean it.'

'Didn't mean it?'

135

'Of course not.'

'Just said it for something to say? Making conversation, as it were?'

'Well, I'll tell you, Boko, I've made a pretty deep study of the sex, observing them in all their moods, and the conclusion I've come to is that when they shoot their heads off in the manner described, little attention need be paid to the subject matter.'

'You would advise ignoring it?'

'Absolutely. Dismiss it from the mind.'

He was silent for a moment. When he spoke, it was on a note of hope.

'There's one thing, of course. She used to love me. As recently as this afternoon. Dearly. She said so. One's got to remember that.'

'She still does.'

'You really feel that, do you?'

'Of course.'

'In spite of calling me a miserable fathead?'

'Certainly. You are a miserable fathead.'

'That's true.'

'You can't go by what a girl says, when she's giving you the devil for making a chump of yourself. It's like Shakespeare. Sounds well, but doesn't mean anything.'

'Your view, then, is that the old affection still lingers?'

'Definitely. Dash it, man, if she could love you in spite of those grey flannel trousers of yours, it isn't likely that any mere acting of the goat on your part will have choked her off. Love is indestructible. Its holy flame burneth forever.'

'Who told you that?'

'Jeeves.'

'He ought to know.'

'He does. You can bank on Jeeves.'

'That's right. You can, can't you? You're a great comfort, Bertie.'

'I try to be, Boko.'

'You give me hope. You raise me from the depths.'

He had perked up considerably. He wasn't actually squaring his shoulders and sticking his chin out, but the morale had plainly stiffened. And I have an idea that in another minute or two he might have become almost jaunty, had there not cut through the night air at this juncture a feminine voice, calling his name.

'Boko!'

He shook like an aspen.

'Yes, darling?'

'Come here. I want you.'

'Coming, darling. Oh, my God!' I heard him whisper. 'An encore!'

He tottered off, and I was left to ponder over the trend of affairs.

I may say at once that I viewed the situation without concern. To Boko, who had actually been in the ring with the young geezer while she was exploding in all directions, it had naturally seemed that the end of the world had come and Judgement Day set in with unusual severity. But to me, the cool and level-headed bystander, the whole thing had been pure routine. One shrugged the shoulders and recognized it for what it was – viz. pure apple sauce.

Love's silken bonds are not broken just because the female half of the sketch takes umbrage at the loony behaviour of the male partner and slips it across him in a series of impassioned speeches. However devoutly a girl may worship the man of her choice, there always comes a time when she feels an irresistible urge to haul off and let him have it in the neck. I suppose if the young lovers I've known in my time were placed end to end – difficult to manage, of course, but what I mean is just suppose they were – they would reach half-way down Piccadilly. And I couldn't think of a single dashed one who hadn't been through what Boko had been through to-night.

Already, I felt, the second phase had probably set in, where the female lovebird weeps on the male lovebird's chest and says she's sorry she was cross. And that my surmise was correct was proved by Boko's demeanour, as he rejoined me some minutes later. Even in the dim light, you could see that he was feeling like a million dollars. He walked as if on air, and the whole soul had obviously expanded, like a bath sponge placed in water.

'Bertie.'

'Hullo?'

'Still there?'

'On the spot.'

'It's all right, Bertie.'

'She loves you still?'

'Yes.'

'Good.'

'She wept on my chest.'

'Fine.'

'And said she was sorry she had been cross. I said "There, there!" and everything is once more gas and gaiters.'

'Splendid.'

'I felt terrific.'

'I bet you did.'

'She withdrew the words "miserable fathead".'

'Good.'

'She said I was the tree on which the fruit of her life hung.'

'Fine.'

'And apparently it was all a mistake when she told me she never wanted to see or speak to me again in this world or the next. She does. Frequently.'

'Splendid.'

'I clasped her to me, and kissed her madly.'

'I bet you did.'

'Jeeves, who was present, was much affected.'

'Oh, Jeeves was there?'

'Yes. He and Nobby had been discussing plans and schemes.'

'For sweetening Uncle Percy?'

'Yes. For, of course, that still has to be done.'

I looked grave. Not much use, of course, in that light.

'It's going to be difficult –'

'Not a bit.'

' – after your not only addressing him as "my dear Worplesdon" but also calling him a silly ass.'

'Not a bit, Bertie, not a bit. Jeeves has come across with one of his ripest suggestions.'

'He has?'

'What a man!'

'Ah!'

'I often say there's nobody like Jeeves.'

'And well you may.'

'Have you ever noticed how his head sticks out at the back?'

'Often.'

'That's where the brain is. Packed away behind the ears.'

'Yes. What's his idea?'

'Briefly this. He thinks it would make an excellent impression and enable me to recover the lost ground, if I stuck up for old Worplesdon.'

'Stuck him up? I don't get that. With a gun, do you mean?'

'I didn't say "stuck him up". Stuck up for.'

'Oh, stuck up for?'

'That's right. Stuck up for. In other words, he advises me to take the old boy's part – protect him, as it were.'

'Protect Uncle Percy?'

'Oh, I know it sounds bizarre. But Jeeves thinks it will work.'

'I still don't get it.'

'It's perfectly simple, really. Look here. Suppose some great blustering brute of a chap barges into old

Worplesdon's study at ten sharp to-morrow morning and starts ballyragging him like the dickens, calling him every name under the sun and generally making himself thoroughly offensive. I'm waiting outside the study window, and at the psychological moment I stick my head in and in a quiet, reproving voice, say "Stop Bertie! –"'

'Bertie?'

'The chap's name is Bertie. But don't interrupt. I'll lose the thread. I stick my head in and say "Stop, Bertie! You are strangely forgetting yourself. I cannot stand by and listen to you abusing a man I admire and respect as highly as Lord Worplesdon. Lord Worplesdon and I may have had our differences – the fault was mine and I am heartily sorry for it – but I never deviated from the opinion that it is an honour to know him. And when I hear you calling him a –"'

I am pretty quick. Already, I had spotted the nature of the frightful scheme.

'You want me to go into Uncle Percy's lair and call him names?'

'At ten sharp. Most important, that. We shall have to synchronize to the second. Nobby tells me he always spends the morning in his study, no doubt writing stinkers to the captains of his ships.'

'And you bob up and tick me off for ticking him off?'

'That's the idea. It can hardly fail to show me in a sympathetic light, causing him to warm to me and feel that I'm a pretty good chap, after all. There he will be, I mean to say, cowering in his chair, while you stand over him, shaking your finger in his face –'

The vision conjured up by these words was so ghastly that I staggered and would have fallen, had I not clutched at a tree.

'You say Jeeves suggested that?'

'As I told you, just like a flash.'

'He might be tight.'

A stiffness crept into Boko's manner.

'I don't understand you, Bertie. I rank the scheme among his very subtlest efforts. It seems to me one of those simple stratagems, all the more effective for their simplicity, which can hardly drop a stitch. Coming in at the moment when you are intimidating old Worplesdon, and throwing the whole weight of my sympathy and support on his side, I shall –'

There are moments when we Woosters can be very firm – adamant is perhaps the word – and one of these is when we are asked to intimidate men like Uncle Percy.

'I'm sorry, Boko.'

'Sorry? Why?'

'Include me out.'

'What!'

'Nothing doing.'

He leaned forward, the better to stare incredulously into my face. The man seemed stunned.

'Bertie!'

'Yes, I know. But I repeat – nothing doing.'

'Nothing doing?'

'Nothing doing.'

A pleading note came into his voice, the same sort of note I've sometimes heard in Bingo Little's, when asking a bookie to take the broad, spacious view and wait for his money till Wednesday week.

'But, Bertie, you're fond of Nobby?'

'Of course.'

'Of course you are, or you would never have given her that threepennyworth of acid drops. And you don't, I take it, dispute the fact that you and I were at school together? Of course, you don't. When I thought I heard you say you wouldn't sit in, I must have misunderstood you.'

'You didn't.'

'I didn't?'

'No.'

'You refuse to do your bit?'

'I do.'

'You – I want to get this straight – you really decline to play your part – your simple, easy part – in this enterprise?'

'That's right.'

'This *is* Bertie Wooster speaking?'

'It is.'

'The Bertie Wooster I was at school with?'

'That's right.'

He drew in his breath with a sort of whistle.

'Well, if anybody had told me this would happen, I wouldn't have believed it. I would have laughed mockingly. Bertie Wooster let me down? No, no, I would have said – not Bertie, who was not only at school with me but is at this very moment bursting with my meat.'

This was a nasty one. I wasn't actually bursting with his meat, of course, because there hadn't been such a frightful lot of it, but I saw what it meant. For an instant, when he put it like that, I nearly weakened. Then I thought of Uncle Percy 'cowering in his chair' – cowering in his chair, my foot! – and was strong again.

'I'm sorry, Boko.'

'So am I, Bertie. Sorry and disappointed. Sick at heart is the expression that leaps to the lips. Well, I suppose I shall have to go and break the news to Nobby. Golly, how she'll cry!'

I could not repress a pang.

'I don't want to make Nobby cry.'

'You will, though. Gallons.'

He faded away into the darkness, sighing reproachfully, leaving me alone with the stars.

And I was just examining them and wondering what had given Jeeves the idea that they were quiring to the young-eyed cherubims – I couldn't see the slightest indication of such a thing myself – when they suddenly merged, as if they had been Uncle Percy and J.

Chichester Clam, and became a jagged sheet of flame.

This was because a hidden hand, creeping up behind me unperceived, had given me the dickens of a slosh with what I assumed to be some blunt instrument. It caught me squarely on the back hair, bringing me to earth with a sharp 'Ouch!'

17

I sat up rubbing the occiput, and a squeaky voice spoke in my earhole. Eyeing me solicitously, or else gloating over his handiwork, I couldn't tell which, was young blighted Edwin.

'Coo!' he said. 'Is that you, Bertie?'

'Yes, it jolly well is,' I replied with a touch of not unnatural asperity. I mean, life's difficult enough without having Boy Scouts beaning one every other minute, and I was incensed. 'What's the idea? What do you mean, you repellent young boll weevil, by socking me with a dashed great club?'

'It wasn't a club. It was my Scout's stick. Sort of like a hockey stick. Very useful.'

'Comes in handy, does it?'

'Rather! Did it hurt?'

'You may take it as definitely official that it hurt like blazes.'

'Coo! I'm sorry. I mistook you for the burglar. There's one lurking in the grounds. I heard him underneath my window. I said "Who's there?" and he slunk off with horrid imprecations. I say, I'm not having much luck to-night. The last chap I mistook for the burglar turned out to be father.'

'Father?'

'Yes. How was I to know it was him? I never thought he would be wandering about the garden in the middle of the night. I saw a shadowy form crouching down, as if about to spring, and I crept up behind it and –'

'You didn't biff him?'

'Yes. Rather a juicy one.'

I must say my heart leaped up, as Jeeves tells me his does when he beholds a rainbow in the sky. The thought of Uncle Percy stopping a hot one with the trouser seat was pretty stimulating. It had been coming to him for years. I had that sort of awed feeling one gets sometimes, when one has a close-up of the workings of Providence and realizes that nothing is put into this world without a purpose, not even Edwin, and that the meanest creatures have their uses.

'He was a bit shirty about it.'

'It annoyed him, eh?'

'He wanted to give me beans, but Florence wouldn't let him. She said, "Father, you are not to touch him. It was a pure misunderstanding". Florence is very fond of me.'

I raised my eyebrows. A girl, I felt, of strange, even morbid tastes.

'So all he did was to tell me to go to bed.'

'Then why aren't you in bed?'

'Bed? Coo! Not likely. How's your head?'

'Rotten.'

'Does it ache?'

'Of course it aches.'

'Have you got a contusion?'

'Yes, I have.'

'This is where I could give you first aid.'

'No, it isn't.'

'Don't you want first aid?'

'No, I don't. We have threshed all this out before, young Edwin. You know my views.'

'I don't ever seem able to get anyone to let me give them first aid,' he said wistfully. 'And what one needs is lots of practice. What are you doing here, Bertie?'

'Everybody asks me what I'm doing here,' I replied, with a touch of pique. 'Why shouldn't I be here? This place is related to me by ties of blood. If you really want to know, I came here for an after dinner saunter with Boko Fittleworth.'

'I haven't seen Boko.'

'A bit of luck for him.'

'D'Arcy Cheesewright's here.'

'I know.'

'I phoned him after I saw the burglar.'

'I know.'

'Did you know he was engaged to Florence?'

'Yes.'

'I'm not sure it's not off. They were having an awful row just now.'

He spoke lightly, throwing the statement out as if it had been some news item of merely negligible interest, and was probably surprised at the concern which I exhibited.

'What!'

'Yes.'

'An awful row?'

'Yes.'

'What about?'

'I don't know.'

'When you say an awful row, how awful a row do you mean?'

'Well, fairly awful.'

'High words?'

'Pretty high.'

My heart, which had leaped up as described at the bulletin about Uncle Percy's trouser seat, was now down in the basement again. The whole trend of my foreign policy, as I have made abundantly clear, being to promote cordial relations between these two, the information that they had been having even fairly high words was calculated to freeze the blood.

You see, what I was saying apropos to Nobby hauling up her slacks and coming the Pekinese on Boko – all that stuff, if you remember, about girls giving their loved one the devil just for the fun of the thing and to keep the pores open – didn't apply to serious minded females like

Florence and the sort of chap Stilton was. It's all a question of what Jeeves calls the psychology of the individual. If Florence and Stilton had gone to the mat and started chewing pieces out of each other, the outlook was unsettled.

'How much of it did you hear?'

'Not much. Because that was when I saw something moving in the darkness and went and biffed it with my Scout's stick, and it turned out to be you.'

This, of course, put a slightly better complexion on things. My first impression had been that he had had a ringside seat all through the conflict. If he had only heard the opening exchanges, it might be that matters had not proceeded too far. Cooler thoughts might have prevailed after his departure, causing the contestants to cheese it before the breach became irreparable. It often happens like that with girls and men of high spirit. They start off with a whoop and a holler, and then, their better selves prevailing, pipe down.

I mentioned this to Edwin, and he seemed to think that there might be something in it. But I noticed that he appeared distrait and not really interested, and after a pause of a few moments, during which I hoped for the best and he twiddled his Scout's stick, he revealed why this was so. He was worrying about a point of procedure.

'I say, Bertie,' he said, 'you know that slosh I gave you.'

I assured him that I had not forgotten it.

'I meant well, you know.'

'That's a comfort.'

'Still, of course, I did sock you, didn't I?'

'You did.'

'You can't get away from that.'

'No.'

'Then here's what I'm wondering. Have I wiped out the act of kindness I did you this afternoon?'

'When you tidied up Wee Nooke?'

'No, I'm afraid that doesn't count, because it didn't
work out right. I meant finding that brooch.'

I had to watch my step rather sedulously here. I mean
to say, the brooch he had found and the brooch Jeeves
had delivered to Florence were supposed to be one and
the same brooch, and he must never learn from my lips
that I had lost the dashed thing again after he had found
it that time in the hall.

'Oh, that?' I said. 'Yes, that was a Grade A act of
kindness.'

'I know. But do you think it still counts?'

'Oh, rather.'

'In spite of my socking you?'

'Unquestionably.'

'Coo! Then I'm all square up to last Thursday.'

'You mean last Friday.'

'Thursday.'

'Friday.'

'Thursday.'

'Friday, you fatheaded young faulty reasoner,' I said,
with some heat, for his inability to keep the score
correctly was annoying me as much as that 'We are
seven' stuff must have annoyed the poet – I forget his
name – who got talking figures with another child.
'Listen. Your last Friday's act of kindness would have
been the tidying up of Wee Nooke. Right. But owing to
the unfortunate sequel that has to be scratched off the
list. You admit that, don't you? Well, that makes the
finding of the brooch your last Friday's act of kindness.
Perfectly simple, if you'll only use the little grey cells a
bit.'

'Yes, but you haven't got it right.'

'I have got it right. Listen –'

'I mean, you're talking about the first time I found the
brooch. What I'm talking about is the second time. That
counts as well.'

I couldn't follow him.

'How do you mean, the second time? You didn't find it twice.'

'Yes, I did. The first time was when you dropped it in the hall, you remember. Then I went off to clean the kitchen chimney. Then there was that explosion, and I came out, and you were standing on the lawn in your shirt sleeves. You had taken off your coat and chucked it away.'

'Oh my gosh!'

What with the stress of this and that, I had completely forgotten that coat sequence. It all came back to me now, and a cold hand seemed to clutch my heart. I could see where he was heading.

'I suppose the brooch must have fallen out of your pocket, because when you had gone into the house I saw it lying there. And I thought it would be an act of kindness if I saved you the trouble by taking it to Florence.'

I gazed at him dully. With a lack-lustre eye is, I believe, the expression.

'So you took it to Florence?'

'Yes.'

'Saying it was a present from me?'

'Yes.'

'Did she seem pleased?'

'Frightfully. Coo!'

He vanished abruptly, like an eel going into mud, and I was aware of the approach of someone breathing heavily.

It did not need the child's impulsive dash into the shadows to tell me that this stertorous newcomer was Florence.

18

Florence was obviously in the grip of some powerful emotion. She quivered gently, as if in the early stages of palsy, and her face, as far as I could gather from the sketchy view I was able to obtain of it, was pale and set, like the white of a hard-boiled egg.

'D'Arcy Cheesewright,' she said, getting right off the mark without so much as a preliminary 'What ho, there', 'is an obstinate, mulish, pigheaded, overbearing, unimaginative, tyrannical jack in office!'

Her words froze me to the core. I was conscious of a sense of frightful peril. Owing to young Edwin's infernal officiousness, this pancake had been in receipt only a few hours earlier of a handsome diamond brooch, ostensibly a present from Bertram W., and now, right on top of it, she had had a falling out with Stilton, so substantial that it took her six distinct adjectives to describe him. When a girl uses six derogatory adjectives in her attempt to paint the portrait of the loved one, it means something. One may indicate a merely temporary tiff. Six is big stuff.

I didn't like the way things were shaping. I didn't like it at all. It seemed to me that what she must be saying to herself was 'Look here upon this picture and this one', as it were. I mean to say, on the one hand, a suave, knightly donor of expensive brooches; on the other, an obstinate, mulish, pigheaded, overbearing, unimaginative, tyrannical jack in office. If you were a girl, which would you prefer to link your lot with? Exactly.

I felt that I must spare no effort to plead Stilton's

cause, to induce her to overlook whatever it was he had
done to make her go about breathing like an asthma
patient and scattering adjectives all over the place. The
time had come for me to be eloquent and persuasive as
never before, pouring oil on the troubled waters with a
liberal hand, emptying the jug if necessary.

'Oh, dash it!' I cried.

'What do you mean by "Oh, dash it"?'

'Just "Oh, dash it!" Sort of protest, if you follow
me.'

'You do not agree with me?'

'I think you've misjudged him.'

'I have not.'

'Splendid fellow, Stilton.'

'He is nothing of the kind.'

'Wouldn't you say he was the sort of chap who has
made England what it is?'

'No.'

'No?'

'I said no.'

'Yes, that's right. So you did.'

'He is a mere uncouth Cossack.'

A cossack, I knew, was one of those things clergymen
wear, and I wondered why she thought Stilton was like
one. An inquiry into this would have been fraught with
interest, but before I could institute it she had
continued.

'He has been abominably rude, not only to me but to
father. Just because father would not allow him to arrest
the man in the potting shed.'

A bright light shone upon me. Her words had made
clear the root of the trouble. I had, if you remember,
edged away from the Stilton-Florence-Uncle Percy group
just after the last named had put the presidential veto on
the able young officer's scheme of pinching J. Chichester
Clam, and had, accordingly, not been there to hear
Stilton's comments. These, it was now evident, must

have been on the fruity side. Stilton, as I have indicated, is a man of strong passions – one who, when annoyed, does not mince his words.

My mind went back to that time at Oxford, when I had gone in for rowing and had drawn him as a coach. If what he had said to Uncle Percy had been even remotely in the same class as his remarks on that occasion with reference to my stomach, I could see that relations must inevitably have got pretty strained, and my heart sank as I visualized the scene.

'He said father was shackling the police and that it was men like him, grossly lacking in any sense of civic duty, who were the cause of the ever-growing crime wave. He said that father was a menace to the community and would be directly responsible if half the population of Steeple Bumpleigh were murdered in their beds.'

'You don't think he spoke laughingly?'

'No, I do not think he spoke laughingly.'

'With a twinkle in his eye, I mean.'

'There was not the slightest suggestion of any twinkle in his eye.'

'You might have missed it. It's a dark night.'

'Please do not be utterly absurd, Bertie. I have sufficient intelligence, I hope, to be able to recognize a vile exhibition of bad temper when I see it. His tone was most offensive. "And you", he said, looking at father as if he were some sort of insect, "call yourself a Justice of the Peace. Faugh!"'

'Fore? Like at golf?'

'F-a-u-g-h.'

'Oh, ah.'

I was beginning to be almost sorry for Uncle Percy, as far as it is possible to be sorry for a man like that. I mean, there was no getting away from it that it hadn't been a big evening for the poor old bloke. First, Boko with his 'My dear Worplesdon'; then Edwin with his hockey stick; and now Stilton with his 'Faughs'. One of those nights you look back to with a shudder.

'His behaviour was a revelation to me. It laid bare a brutal, inhuman side of his character, of the existence of which I had never till then had a suspicion. There was something positively horrible in the fury he exhibited, when he realized that he was not to be allowed to arrest the man. He was like some malignant wild beast deprived of its prey.'

It was plain that Stilton's stock was in or approaching the cellar, and I did what I could to stop the slump.

'Still, it showed zeal, what?'

'Tchah!'

'And zeal, after all, when you come right down to it, is what he draws his weekly envelope for.'

'Don't talk to me about zeal. It was revolting. And when I said that father was quite right, he turned on me like a tiger.'

Although by this time, as you may well imagine, I was rocking on my base and becoming more and more a prey to alarm and despondency, I couldn't help admiring Stilton for his intrepid courage. Circumstances had so arranged themselves as to extract most of the stuffing from what had been a closish boyhood friendship, but I had to respect a man capable of turning on Florence like a tiger. I would hardly have thought Attila the Hun could have done it, even if at the peak of his form.

All the time, I wished he hadn't. Oh, I was saying to myself, that the voice of Prudence had whispered in his ear. It was so vital to my interests that the mutual love of these two should continue unimpaired, and already much of the gilt, I feared, must have been rubbed off the gingerbread of their romance. Love is a sensitive plant, which needs cherishing and fostering. This cannot be done by turning on girls like tigers.

'I told him that modern enlightened thought held that imprisonment merely brutalizes the criminal.'

'And what did he say to that?'

'"Oh, yes?"'

'Ah, he agreed with you.'

'He did nothing of the kind. He spoke in a most unpleasant, sneering voice. "It does, does it?" he said. And I said "Yes, it does". He then said something about modern enlightened thought which I cannot repeat.'

I wondered what this had been. Evidently something red hot, for it was clear that it still rankled like a boil on the back of the neck. Her fists, I saw, were clenched, and she had started to tap her foot on the ground – sure indications that the soul is fed to the eye teeth. Florence is one of those girls who look on modern enlightened thought as a sort of personal buddy, and receive with an ill grace cracks at its expense.

I groaned in spirit. The way things were shaping, I was expecting her to say next that she had broken off the engagement.

And that was just what she did say.

'Of course, I broke off the engagement instantly.'

In spite of the fact that, as I say, I had practically known it was coming, I skipped like the high hills.

'You broke off the engagement?'

'Yes.'

'Oh, I say, you shouldn't have done that.'

'Why not?'

'Sterling chap like Stilton.'

'He is nothing of the kind.'

'You ought to forget those cruel words he spoke. You should make allowances.'

'I don't understand you.'

'Well, look at it from the poor old buster's point of view. Stilton, you must bear in mind, entered the police force hoping for rapid advancement.'

'Well?'

'Well, of course, the men up top don't advance a young rozzer rapidly unless he comes through with something so spectacular as to make them draw in their breath with an awed "Lord love a duck!" For weeks, months perhaps, he had been chafing like a caged eagle at the frightful law-abidingness of this place, hoping vainly for even a collarless dog or a decent drunk and disorderly that he could get his teeth into, and the sudden arrival of a burglar must have seemed to him manna from heaven. Here, he must have said to himself, was where at last he made his presence felt. And just as he was hitching up his sleeves and preparing to take his big opportunity, Uncle Percy goes and puts him on the leash. It was enough to upset any cop. Naturally he forgot himself and spoke with a generous strength. But he never means what he says in moments of heat. You should have heard him once at Oxford, talking to me about sticking out my stomach while toiling at the oar. You would have thought he loathed my stomach and its contents. Yet only a few hours later we were dining *vis-à-vis* at the Clarendon – clear soup, turbot and a saddle of mutton, I remember – and he was amiability itself. You'll find it's just the same now. I'll bet remorse is already gnawing him, and nobody is sorrier than he for having said nasty things about modern enlightened thought. He loves you devotedly. This is official. I happen to know. So what I would suggest is that you go to him and tell him that all is forgotten and forgiven. Only thus can you avoid making a bloomer, the memory of which will haunt you through the years. If you give Stilton the bum's rush, you'll kick yourself practically incessantly for the rest of your life. The whitest man I know.'

I paused, partly for breath and partly because I felt I had said enough. I stood there, waiting for her reply, wishing I had a throat lozenge to suck.

Well, I don't know what reaction I had expected on her part – possibly the drooping of the head and the silent tear, as the truth of my words filtered through her

system; possibly some verbal statement to the effect
that I had spoken a mouthful. What I had definitely not
expected was that she would kiss me, and with a
heartiness that nearly dropped me in my tracks.

'Bertie, you are extraordinary!' She laughed, a thing I
couldn't have done, if handsomely paid. 'So quixotic. It
is what I love in you. Nobody hearing you would dream
that it is your dearest wish to marry me yourself.'

I tried to utter, but could not. The tongue had got all
tangled up with the uvula, and the brain seemed
paralysed. I was feeling the same stunned feeling which,
I imagine, Chichester Clam must have felt as the door of
the potting shed slammed and he heard Boko starting to
yodel without – a nightmare sensation of being but a
helpless pawn in the hands of Fate.

She passed an arm through mine, and began to
explain, like a governess instructing a backward pupil in
the rudiments of simple arithmetic.

'Do you think I have not understood? My dear Bertie, I
am not blind. When I broke off our engagement, I
naturally supposed that you would forget – or perhaps
that you would be angry and resentful and think hard,
bitter thoughts of me. Tonight, I realized how wrong I
had been. It was that brooch you gave me that opened
my eyes to your real feelings. There was no need for you
to have given me a birthday present at all, unless you
wanted me to know that you still cared. And to give me
one so absurdly expensive . . . Of course, I knew at once
what you were trying to tell me. It all fitted in so clearly
with the other things you had said. About your reading
Spinoza, for instance. You had lost me, as you thought,
but you still went on studying good literature for my
sake. And I found you in the bookshop buying my novel.
I can't tell you how it touched me. And as the result of
that chance meeting you could not keep yourself from
coming to Steeple Bumpleigh, so that you might be near
me once more. And to-night, you crept out, to stand

beneath my window in the starlight . . . No, let us have
no more misunderstandings. I am thankful that I should
have seen the meaning of your shy overtures in time,
and that I should have had the real D'Arcy Cheesewright
revealed to me before it was too late. I will be your wife,
Bertie.'

There didn't seem much to say to this except 'Oh,
thanks'. I said it, and the interview terminated. She
kissed me again, expressed her preference for a quiet
wedding, with just a few relations and intimate friends,
and beetled off.

19

It was not immediately that I, too, departed. The hour was late, and my bed awaited me *chez* Boko, but for a considerable time I remained rooted to the spot, staring dazedly into the darkness. Winged creatures of the night came bumping into the old face and bumping off again, while others used the back stretches of my neck as a skating rink, but I did not even raise a hand to interfere with their revels. This awful thing that had come upon me had practically turned me into a pillar of salt. I doubt if the moth, or whatever it was that was doing Swedish exercises in and around my left ear, had the remotest notion that it had parked itself on the person of a once vivacious young clubman. A tree, it probably thought, or possibly even the living rock.

Presently, however, life returned to the rigid limbs, and I started to plod my weary way down the drive and out of the gate, eventually reaching Boko's door. It was open, and I heaved myself through. There was a light along the passage, and heading for it I won through to the sitting-room.

Boko was in an armchair, with his feet on the mantel-piece and his hand clasping a glass. The sight of another glass and a syphon and decanter drew me to the table like a magnet. The sloshing of the liquid seemed to rouse mine host from a reverie, causing him for the first time to become aware of my presence.

'Help yourself,' he said.

'Thanks, old man.'

'Though I'm surprised you have the heart to drink, after what has occurred to-night.'

He spoke coldly, and there was a distinct aloofness in his manner as he reached out and refilled his glass. He eyed me for a moment as if I had been a caterpillar in some salad of which he was about to partake, and resumed.

'I saw Nobby.'

'Oh, yes?'

'As I anticipated, she cried buckets.'

'I'm sorry.'

'So you should be. Yours was the hand that wrenched those pearly drops from her eyes.'

'Oh, dash it!'

'It's no good saying "Oh, dash it!" You have a conscience, I presume? Then it must have informed you that you were directly responsible for the downpour. Well, well, if anybody had told me that Bertie Wooster would let me down –'

'You said that before.'

'And I shall go on saying it. Even unto seventy times seven. One doesn't dismiss a thing like that with a single careless comment. When your whole faith in human nature has been shattered, you are entitled to repeat yourself a bit.'

He laughed a short, mirthless laugh, very rasping and hard on the ears. Then, as if dismissing an unpleasant subject for the time being, he drained his snootful and turned to the matter of my belated return, saying that he had expected me back hours ago.

'When I took you for an after dinner stroll, I didn't think you were going to stay out practically till the arrival of the morning milk. You will have to change these dissolute city ways, if you wish to fit in with the life of a decent English village.'

'I am a bit later than I had anticipated.'

'What kept you?'

'Well, for one thing, I was being biffed over the nut by Edwin with a hockey stick. That took time.'

'What?'

'Yes.'

'He socked you with a hockey stick?'

'Right on the bean.'

'Ah!' said Boko, and seemed to brighten quite a good deal. 'Fine little chap, Edwin. Good stuff in that boy. Got nice ideas.'

The circs being what they were, this absence of the sympathetic note distressed me, filling me with what I have heard Jeeves describe as thoughts that lie too deep for tears. A man in my position wants his friends to rally round him.

'Don't gibe and scoff,' I begged. 'I want sympathy, Boko – sympathy and advice. Do you know what?'

'What?'

'I'm engaged to Florence.'

'What, again? What's become of Stilton?'

'I will tell you the whole ghastly story.'

I suppose the poignant note in my voice stirred his better nature, for he listened gravely and with evidences of human feeling as I related my tragedy. When I had concluded, he shivered and reached out for the decanter, his whole aspect that of a man who needed one quick.

'There but for the grace of God,' he said, in a low voice, 'goes George Webster Fittleworth!'

I pointed out that he was missing the nub.

'Yes, that's all very well, Boko, and I am sure you have my heartiest congratulations, but the basic fact with which we have to deal is that there actually does go Bertram Wooster. Have you nothing to suggest?'

'Is any man safe?' he continued, still musing. 'I did think that the black spot had finally passed into Stilton's possession.'

'So did I.'

'It's a shame it hasn't, because he really loves that girl, Bertie. No doubt you have been feeling a decent pity for Stilton, but I assure you it was wasted. He loves her.

And when a man with a head as fat as that loves, it is for ever. You and I would say that it was impossible that anyone should really want to marry this frightful girl, but it is a fact. Did she make you read "Types of Ethical Theory"?'

'Yes.'

'Me, too. It was that that first awoke me to a sense of my peril. But when she slipped it to Stilton, he ate it alive. I don't suppose he understood a word of it, but I repeat, he ate it alive. Theirs would have been an ideal match. Too bad it has blown a fuse. Of course, if Stilton would resign from the Force, a way could readily be paved to an understanding. It's that that is at the root of the trouble.'

Once more, I saw that the nub had eluded him.

'It's not Stilton I'm worrying about, Boko, old man, it's me. I view Stilton with a benevolent eye, and would be glad to see him happily mated, but the really vital question is Where does Bertram get off? How do we extricate poor old Wooster?'

'You really want to be extricated?'

'My dear chap!'

'She would be a good influence in your life, remember. Steadying. Educative.'

'Would you torture me, Boko?'

'Well, how did you extricate yourself, when you were engaged to her last time?'

'It's a long story.'

'Then for goodness sake don't start it now. All I meant was, could the same technique be employed in the present crisis?'

'I'm afraid not. There was something she wanted me to do for her, and I failed to do it and she gave me the air. These circs could not arise again.'

'I see. Well, it's a pity you can't use the method I did. The Fittleworth System. Simple but efficacious. That would solve all your difficulties.'

'Why can't I use it?'

'Because you don't know what it is.'

'You could tell me.'

He shook his head.

'No, Bertie, not after the extraordinary attitude you have seen fit to take up with regard to my proposals for sweetening your Uncle Percy. The Fittleworth Method – tried and tested, I may say, and proved infallible – can be imparted only to the deserving. It is not a secret I would care to share with any except real friends who are as true as steel.'

'I'm as true as steel, Boko.'

'No, Bertie, you are not as true as steel, or anything like it. You may have shown that by your behaviour to-night. A real eye-opener it has been, causing me to revise my estimate of your friendship from the bottom up. Of course, if you were to reconsider your refusal to chip in on this scheme of Jeeves's and consent, after all, to play your allotted part, I should be delighted to . . . But what's the use of talking about it? You have declined, and that's that. I know your iron will. When you come to a decision, it stays come to.'

I didn't know so much about that. It is true, of course, that I have a will of iron, but it can be switched off if the circumstances seem to demand it. The strong man always knows when to yield and make concessions. I have frequently found myself doing so in my relation with Jeeves.

'You absolutely guarantee this secret method?' I asked earnestly.

'I can only tell you that it produced immediate and gratifying results in my own case. One moment, I was engaged to Florence; the next, I wasn't. As quick as that. It was more like magic than anything I can think of.'

'And you'll tell it me, if I promise to tick Uncle Percy off?'

'I'll tell it you *after* you've ticked him off.'

'Why not now?'

'Just a whim. It's not that I don't trust you, Bertie. It's not that I think that, having learned the Fittleworth secret, you would change your mind about carrying out your end of the contract. But it would be a temptation, and I don't want your pure soul to be sullied by it.'

'But you'll tell me without fail after I've done the deed?'

'Without fail.'

I pondered. It was a fearful choice to have to make. But I did not hesitate long.

'All right, Boko. I'll do it.'

He tapped me affectionately on the chest. It was odd how to-night's events had brought out the chest-tapper in him.

'Splendid fellow!' he said. 'I thought you would. Now, you pop off to bed, so as to get a good night's rest and rise alert and refreshed. I will sit up and rough out a few things for you to say to the old boy. It's no good your trusting to the inspiration of the moment. You must have your material all written out and studied. I doubt, too, if, left to yourself, you would be able to think of anything really adequate. This is one of the occasions when you need the literary touch.'

20

It was but a troubled slumber that I enjoyed that night, much disturbed by dreams of Uncle Percy chasing me with his hunting crop. Waking next morning, I found that though the heart was leaden, the weather conditions were of the best and brightest. The sun shone, the sky was blue, and in the trees outside my window the ear detected the twittering of a covey or platoon of the local fowls of the air.

But though all Nature smiled, there was, as I have indicated, no disposition on the part of Bertram to follow its example. I got no kick from the shining sun, no uplift from the azure firmament, as it is sometimes called: while as for the twittering birds their heartiness in the circumstances seemed overdone and in dubious taste. When you're faced with the sort of ordeal I was faced with, there is but little satisfaction to be derived from the thought that you've got a nice day for it.

My watch showed me that the hour was considerably less advanced than my customary one for springing from between the sheets, and it is possible that, had the burden on the soul been lighter, I might have turned over and got another forty minutes. But the realization of what dark deeds must be done 'ere this day's sun should have set – or, for the matter of that, 'ere this day's lunch should have been eaten – forbade sleep. I rose, accordingly, and assembling sponge and towel was about to proceed to the bathroom for a bit of torso sluicing, when my eye was caught by a piece of paper protruding from beneath the door. I picked it up, and found it to be the material which Boko had sat up on the

previous night composing for my benefit – the few
things, if you remember, which he wanted me to say to
Uncle Percy. And as my eye flitted over it, the persp.
started out on my brow and I sank back on the bed,
appalled. It was as if I had scooped in a snake.

I think that in an earlier chronicle I related how,
when a growing boy at my private school, I once sneaked
down at dead of night to the study of the headmaster,
the Rev. Aubrey Upjohn, in order to pinch a few mixed
biscuits from the store which I had been informed that
he maintained in the cupboard there; and how, having
got well ahead with the work in hand, I discovered that
their proprietor was also among those present, seated at
his desk regarding my activities with a frosty eye.

The reason I bring this up again is that on the occasion
to which I allude, after a brief pause – on my side, of
embarrassment, on his of working up steam – the Rev.
Aubrey had started to give a sort of character sketch of
the young Wooster, which until now I had always
looked upon as the last word in scholarly invective. It
was the kind of thing a minor prophet of the Old
Testament might have thrown together on one of his
bilious mornings, and, as I say, I considered it to have set
up a mark at which other orators would shoot in vain. I
had been wrong. This screed of Boko's left it nowhere.
Boko began where the Rev. Aubrey Upjohn left off.

Typewritten, with single spaces, I suppose the stuff
ran to about six hundred words, and of all those six
hundred words I don't think there were more than half a
dozen which I could have brought myself to say to a
man of Uncle Percy's calibre, unless primed to the back
teeth with the raw spirit. And Boko, you will recall, was
expecting me to deliver my harangue at ten o'clock in
the morning.

To shoot out of my room into his, bubbling over with
expostulations and what not, was with me the work of
an instant. But the eloquent outburst which I had been

planning was rendered null and void by the fact that he was not there, and an inquiry of an aged female whom I found messing about in the kitchen elicited the information that he had gone for a swim in the river. Repairing thither, I perceived him splashing about in mid-stream with many a merry cry.

But once more I was obliged to choke back the burning words. A second glance, revealing a pink, porpoise-like object at his side, told me that he was accompanied by Stilton. It was to Steeple Bumpleigh's zealous police constable that the merry cries were addressed, and I deemed it wisest to leave my presence unrevealed. It seemed to me that a chat with Stilton at this particular juncture could be fraught with neither pleasure nor profit.

I pushed along the bank, therefore, pondering deeply, and I hadn't gone far when there came to my ears the swish of a fishing line, and there was Jeeves, harrying the finny denizens like nobody's business. I might have known that his first act on finding himself established in Steeple Bumpleigh would have been to head for the fluid and cast a fly or two.

As it was to this fly-caster that I owed my present hideous predicament, you will not be surprised to learn that my manner, as I came abreast, was on the distant side.

'Ah, Jeeves,' I said.

'Good morning, sir,' he responded. 'A lovely day.'

'Lovely for some of us, perhaps, Jeeves,' I said coolly, 'but not for the Last of the Woosters, who, thanks to you, is faced by a binge beside which all former binges fade into insignificance.'

'Sir?'

'It's no good saying "Sir?" You know perfectly well what I mean. Entirely through your instrumentality, I shall shortly be telling Uncle Percy things about himself which will do something to his knotted and combined locks which at the moment has slipped my memory.'

'Make his knotted and combined locks to part and each particular hair to stand on end like quills upon the fretful porpentine, sir.'

'Porpentine?'

'Yes, sir.'

'That can't be right. There isn't such a thing. However, let that pass. The point is that you have let me in for the ghastly task of ticking Uncle Percy off, and I want to know what you did it for. Was it kind, Jeeves? Was it feudal?'

He registered surprise. Mild surprise, of course. He never goes as far as the other sort. One eyebrow flickered a little, and the tip of the nose moved slightly.

'You are alluding to the suggestion I offered Mr Fittleworth, sir?'

'That is the suggestion I am alluding to, Jeeves.'

'But surely, sir, if you have decided to fall in with the scheme, it was entirely your kind heart that led you to do so? It would have been optional for you to have declined to lend your assistance.'

'Ha!'

'Sir?'

'I said "Ha!" Jeeves. And I meant "Ha!" Do you know what happened last night?'

'So much happened last night, sir.'

'True. Among other things, I got properly biffed over the coconut by young Edwin with his Scout's stick, he thinking I was a burglar.'

'Indeed, sir?'

'We then fell into conversation, and he informed me that he had found the brooch which we assumed to have perished in the flames and had delivered it to Lady Florence, telling her it was a birthday present from me.'

'Indeed, sir?'

'It just turned the scale. She had a frightful row with

Stilton, gave him the air for saying derogatory things about modern enlightened thought, and is now betrothed once more to the toad beneath the harrow whom you see before you.'

I thought he was going to say 'Indeed, sir?' again, in which case I might easily have forgotten all the decencies of civilized life and dotted him one. At the last moment, however, he checked the utterance and merely pursed his lips in a grave and sympathetic manner. A vast improvement.

'And the reason I consented to sit in on this scheme of yours was that Boko confided to me last night that he had a simple infallible remedy for getting out of being engaged to this specific girl, and he won't tell me what it is till I have interviewed Uncle Percy.'

'I see, sir.'

'I must learn it at all costs. It's no use my trying the Stilton method and saying nasty things about modern enlightened thought, because I couldn't think of any. It is the Boko way or nothing. You don't happen to know what it was that made Lady Florence sever her relations with him, do you?'

'No, sir. Indeed, it is news to me that Mr Fittleworth was affianced to her ladyship.'

'Oh, yes. He was affianced to her, all right. Post-Wooster, but pre-Stilton. And something occurred, an imbroglio of some description took place, and the thing was instantly broken off. Just like magic, he said. I gathered that it was something he did. But what could it have been?'

'I fear I am unable to hazard a conjecture, sir. Would you wish me to institute inquiries among the domestic staff at the Hall?'

'An excellent idea, Jeeves.'

'It is possible that some member of that unit may have become cognizant of the facts.'

'The thing was probably the talk of the Housekeeper's

Room for days. Sound the butler. Question the cook.'

'Very good, sir.'

'Or try Lady Florence's personal maid. Somebody is sure to know. There's not much that domestic staffs don't become cognizant of.'

'No, sir. One has usually found them well informed.'

'And bear in mind that speed is essential. If you can hand me the data before I see Uncle Percy – that is to say, any time up to ten o'clock, for which hour the kick-off is slated – I shall be in a position to edge out of giving him that straight talk, at the thought of which I don't mind telling you that the flesh creeps. As for the happiness of Boko and soulmate, I am all for giving that a boost, of course, but I feel that it can be done by other and less drastic methods. So lose no time, Jeeves, in instituting those inquiries.'

'Very good, sir.'

'Be at the main gate of the Hall from half-past nine onwards. I shall be arriving about then, and shall expect your report. Try not to fail me, Jeeves. Now is the time for all good men to come to the aid of the party. If I could show you that list Boko drafted out of the things he wants me to say – I unfortunately left it in my room, where it fell from my nerveless fingers – your knotted and combined locks would part all right, believe me. You're sure it's porpentine?'

'Yes, sir.'

'Very odd. But I suppose half the time Shakespeare just shoved down anything that came into his head.'

Having been *en route* for the bathroom at the moment when I buzzed off to seek audience of Boko, I was still, of course, in the ordinary slumberwear of the English gentleman, plus a dressing-gown, and it was some little time, accordingly, after I had returned to the house, before I showed up in the dining-salon. I found Boko there, getting outside a breakfast egg. I asked him if he knew what a porpentine was, and he said to hell

with all porpentines and had I got that sheet of
instructions all right and, if so, what did I think of it.

To this, my reply was that I certainly had jolly well
got it and that it had frozen me to the marrow. No
human power, I added, would induce me to pass on to
Uncle Percy even a skeleton outline of the document's
frightful contents.

'Frightful contents.'

'That was what I said.'

He seemed wounded, and murmured something
about the artist and destructive criticism.

'I thought it was particularly good stuff. Crisp, terse
and telling. The subject inspired me, and I was under the
impression that I had given of my best. Still, if you feel
that I stressed the personal note a bit too much, you can
modify it here and there, if you like – preserving the
substance, of course.'

'As a matter of fact,' I said, thinking it best to prepare
him, 'you mustn't be surprised, Boko, if at the last
moment I change my plans and decide to give the whole
thing a miss.'

'What!'

'I am toying with the idea.'

'Well, I'm blowed! Is this – ?'

'Yes, it is.'

'You don't know what I was going to say.'

'Yes, I do. You were going to say "Is this Bertie
Wooster speaking?"'

'Quite right. I was. Well, is it?'

'Yes.'

His table talk then took on a rather acid tone,
touching disparagingly on so-called friends who,
supposed by him hitherto to be staunch and true, turned
out to his disappointment to be lily-livered poltroons
lacking even the meagre courage of a rabbit.

'Where are the boys of the bulldog breed? That's what
I want to know,' he concluded, plainly chagrined. 'Well,

you understand clearly what this means. Fail me, and not an inkling of the Fittleworth secret do you get.'

I smiled subtly, and helped myself to a slice of ham. He little knew, I felt.

'I shall watch you walking up the aisle with Florence Craye, and not stir a finger to save you. In fact, you will hear a voice singing "Oh, perfect love" rather louder than the rest of the congregation, and it will be mine. Reconsider, Bertie. That is what I advise.'

'Well, of course,' I said, 'I don't say I will back out of the assignment. I only say I may.'

This calmed him somewhat, and he softened – saying that he was sure that when the hour struck, my better self would prevail. And a bit later, we parted with mutual good wishes.

For it had been arranged that we should proceed to the Hall separately. In his case, Boko felt, not without some reason, that there was need for stealth, lest he be fallen upon and slung out. He proposed, therefore, to circle round the outskirts till he found a gap in the hedge and then approach the study by a circuitous route, keeping well in the shelter of the bushes and not letting a twig snap beneath his feet.

I set out by myself, accordingly, and arriving at the main entrance found Jeeves waiting for me in the drive. It needed but a glance to inform me that the man had good tidings. I can always tell. He doesn't exactly smile on these occasions, because he never does, but the lips twitch slightly at the corners and the eye is benevolent.

I gave tongue eagerly.

'Well, Jeeves?'

'I have the data you require, sir.'

'Splendid fellow! You saw the butler! You probed the cook?'

'Actually, it was from the boy who cleans the knives and boots that I secured the information, sir. A young fellow of the name of Erbut.'

'How did he come to be our special correspondent?'

'It appears that he was actually an eyewitness of the scene, sir, sheltered in the obscurity of a neighbouring bush, where he had been enjoying a surreptitious cigarette. From this point of vantage he was enabled to view the entire proceedings.'

'And what were they? Tell me all, Jeeves, omitting no detail, however slight.'

'Well, sir, the first thing that attracted the lad's attention was the approach of Master Edwin.'

'He comes into it, does he?'

'Yes, sir. His role, as you will see, is an important one. Master Edwin, Erbut reports, was advancing through the undergrowth, his gaze fixed upon the ground. He seemed to be tracking something.'

'Spooring, no doubt. It is a practice to which these Scouts are much addicted.'

'So I understand, sir. His movements, Erbut noted, were being observed with a sisterly indulgence by Lady Florence, who was cutting flowers in an adjacent border.'

'She was watching him, eh?'

'Yes, sir. Simultaneously, Mr Fittleworth appeared, following the young gentleman.'

'Spooring the spoorer?'

'Yes, sir. Erbut describes his manner as keen and purposeful. That, at least, was his meaning, though the actual phrasing of his statement was different. These knives and boots boys seldom express themselves well.'

'I've often noticed it. Rotten vocabularies. Go on, Jeeves. I'm all agog. Boko, you say, was trailing Edwin. Why?'

'That was what Erbut appears to have asked himself, sir.'

'He was mystified?'

'Yes, sir.'

'I don't blame him. I'm mystified myself. I gather, of

course, that the plot thickens, but I'm dashed if I can see where it's heading.'

'It was not long before Mr Fittleworth's motives were abundantly clear, sir. As Master Edwin approached the flower bed, he suddenly accelerated his movements –'

'Edwin did?'

'No, sir. Mr Fittleworth. He bounded forward at the young gentleman, and taking advantage of the fact that the latter, in the course of his spooring, had just adopted a stooping posture, proceeded to deliver a forceful kick upon his person –'

'Golly, Jeeves!'

'– causing him to fly through the air and fall at Lady Florence's feet. Her ladyship, horrified and incensed, rebuked Mr Fittleworth sharply, demanding an immediate explanation of this wanton assault. The latter endeavoured to justify his action by accusing Master Edwin of having tampered with his patent egg boiler, so disorganizing the mechanism that a new-laid egg had flown from its base and struck him on the tip of the nose. Her ladyship, however, was unable to see her way to accepting this as a palliation of what had occurred, and shortly afterwards announced that the betrothal was at an end.'

I drew in the breath. The scales had fallen from my eyes. I saw all. So that was the Fittleworth remedy – booting young Edwin! No wonder Boko had spoken of it as simple and efficacious. All you needed was a good stout shoe and a sister's love.

I heard Jeeves cough.

'If you will glance to your left, sir,' he said, 'you will observe that Master Edwin has just entered the drive and is stooping over some object on the ground that appears to have engaged his attention.'

21

I got the gist. The significance of his words was not lost
upon me. The grave, encouraging look with which he
had accompanied the news bulletin would alone have
been enough to enable me to sense the underlying
message he was trying to convey. It was the sort of look
a Roman father might have given his son, when handing
him shield and spear and pushing him off to battle, and
it ought, I suppose, to have stirred me like a bugle.

Nevertheless, I found myself hesitating. After that
sock on the head he had given me on the previous night,
the thought of kicking young Edwin was one that
presented many attractions, of course, and there was no
question but that the child had been asking for some
such little personal attention for years. But there's
something rather embarrassing about doing that sort of
thing in cold blood. Difficult, I felt, to lead up to it
neatly in the course of conversation. ('Hello, Edwin.
How are you? Lovely day. *Biff*'. You see what I mean.
Not easy.)

In Boko's case, of course, the whole set-up had been
entirely different, for he had been in the grip of the
berserk fury which comes upon a man when he is hit on
the tip of the nose with new-laid eggs. This had enabled
him, so to speak, to get a running start.

And so I fingered the chin dubiously.

'Yes,' I said. 'Yes, there he is, Jeeves – and, as you say,
stooping. But do you really advise –'

'I do, sir.'

'What, now?'

'Yes, sir. There is a tide in the affairs of men which,

taken at the flood, leads on to fortune. Omitted, all the
voyage of their life is bound in shallows and in miseries.'

'Oh, rather. Quite. No argument about that. But – '

'If what you are trying to say, sir, is that it is of the
essence that Lady Florence be present, to observe the
proceedings as she did in the case of Mr Fittleworth, I
fully concur. I would suggest that I go and inform her
ladyship that you are waiting on the drive and would be
glad of a word with her.'

I still hesitated. It was one of those cases where you
approve the broad, general principle of an idea, but can't
help being in a bit of a twitter at the prospect of putting
it into practical effect. I explained this to Jeeves, and he
said that much the same thing had bothered Hamlet.

'Your irresolution is quite understandable, sir.
Between the acting of a dreadful thing and the first
motion, all the interim is like a phantasma or a hideous
dream. The genius and the mortal instruments are then
in council; and that state of man, like to a little
kingdom, suffers then the nature of an insurrection.'

'Absolutely,' I said. He puts these things well.

'If it would assist you to stiffen the sinews and
summon up the blood, sir, may I remind you that it is
very nearly ten o'clock, and that only the promptest
action along the lines I have indicated can enable you to
avoid appearing in his lordship's study at that hour.'

He had found the talking-point. I hesitated no longer.

'You're right, Jeeves. How long do you think it will be
necessary to detail young Edwin in conversation before
you can bring Lady Florence on stage?'

'Not more than a few minutes, sir. I happen to know
that her ladyship is at the moment in her private
apartment, engaged upon literary work. There will be
but a brief interval before she appears.'

'Then tally ho!'

'Very good, sir.'

He flickered off upon his mission, while I, having

summoned up the blood a bit and stiffened the sinews as far as was possible at such short notice, squared the shoulders and headed for where Edwin was squatting. The weather continued uniformly fine. The sun shone, and a blackbird, I remember, was singing in an adjoining thicket. No reason why it shouldn't have been, of course. I mention the fact merely to stress the general peace and tranquillity of everything. And I must say it did strike me as a passing thought that the sort of setting a job like this really needed was a blasted heath at midnight, with a cold wind whistling in the bushes and three witches doing their stuff at the cauldron.

However, one can't have everything, and I doubt if an observer would have noted any diffidence in Bertram's bearing as he advanced upon his prey. Bertram, I rather fancy he would have thought, was in pretty good form.

I hove to at the stripling's side.

'Hullo, young Edwin,' I said.

His gaze had been riveted on the ground, but at the sound of the familiar voice a couple of pink-rimmed eyes came swivelling round in my direction. He looked up at me like a ferret about to pass the time of day with another ferret.

'Hullo, Bertie. I say, Bertie, I did another act of kindness this morning.'

'Oh, yes?'

'I finished pasting the notices of Florence's novel in her album. That puts me all right up to last Wednesday.'

'Good work. You're catching up. And what do you think you're doing now?'

'I'm studying ants. Do you know anything about ants, Bertie?'

'Only from meeting them at picnics.'

'I've been reading up about them. Very interesting.'

'Vastly, I shouldn't wonder.'

I was glad the topic had been introduced, for it promised to be one that would carry us along nicely until Florence's arrival on the scene. It was obvious that the young squirt was bulging with information about these industrious little creatures and asked nothing better than to be allowed to impart it.

'Did you know ants can talk?'

'Talk?'

'In a sort of way. To other ants, of course. They do it by tapping their heads on a leaf. How's your head this morning, Bertie? I nearly forgot to ask.'

'Still on the tender side.'

'I thought it would be. Coo! That was funny last night, wasn't it? I laughed for hours, when I got to bed.'

He emitted a ringing guffaw, and at the raucous sound any spark of compunction that might have been lingering in my bosom was quenched. A boy to whom the raising of a lump the size of a golf ball on the Wooster bean was a subject for heartless mirth deserved all that boot toe could do to him. For the first time, I found myself contemplating the task before me with real fire and enthusiasm – almost, as you might say, in a missionary spirit. I mean, I felt what a world of good a swift kick in the pants would do to this child. It might prove to be the turning-point in his life.

'You laughed, did you?'

'Rather!'

'Ha!' I said, and ground a few teeth.

The maddening thing was, of course, that though I was now keyed up to give of my best, and though the position he had assumed for this ant-studying session of his was the exact position demanded by the run of the scenario, I was debarred from getting action. You might have compared me to a greyhound on the leash. Until Florence came along, I could not fulfil myself. As Jeeves had said, her presence was of the essence. I scanned the horizon for a sight of her, like a shipwrecked mariner hoping for a sail, but she did not appear, and in the meantime we went on talking about ants, Edwin saying that they were members of the Hymenoptera family and self replying, 'Well, well. Quite the nibs, eh?'

'They are characterized by unusual distinctness of the three regions of the body – head, thorax and abdomen – and by the stalk or petiole of the abdomen having one or two scales or nodes, so that the abdomen moves very freely on the trunk or thorax.'

'You wouldn't fool me?'

'The female, after laying her eggs, feeds the larvae with food regurgitated from her stomach.'

'Try to keep it clean, my lad.'

'Both males and females are winged.'

'And why not?'

'But the female pulls off its wings and runs about without them.'

'I question that. I doubt if even an ant would be such an ass.'

'It's quite true. It says so in the book. Have you ever seen ants fight?'

'Not that I remember.'

'They rise on their hind legs and curve the abdomen.'

And, to my consternation and chagrin, whether because it was his intention to illustrate or because he found his squatting position cramping to the limbs, this was just what he did himself. He rose on his hind legs, and stood facing me, curving the abdomen – at the exact moment when I perceived Florence emerging from the house and walking briskly in our direction.

It was a crisis at which a less resourceful man might have supposed that all was lost. But the Woosters are quick thinkers.

'Hullo!' I said.

'What's the matter?'

'Have you dropped sixpence?'

'No.'

'Somebody has. Look.'

'Where?'

'Under that bush,' I said, and pointed to a shrub of sorts on the edge of the drive.

As you probably conjecture, in saying this I was descending to subterfuge, and anybody knowing Bertram Wooster and his rigid principles might have supposed that such wilful tampering with the truth would have caused the blush of shame to mantle his cheek. Not so, however. If there was a flush to be noted, it was the flush of excitement and triumph.

For my subtle appeal to the young blister's cupidity had not failed to achieve its end. Already, he was down on all fours, and if I had posed him with my own hands I could not have obtained better results. His bulging shorts seemed to smile up at me in a sort of inviting, welcoming way.

As Jeeves had rightly said, there is a tide in the affairs of men which, taken at the flood, leads on to fortune. I drew back the leg, and let him have it just where the pants were tightest.

It was a superb effort. Considering that I hadn't kicked anyone since the distant days of school, you might have thought that the machinery would have got rusty. But no. All the old skill still lingered. My timing was perfect, and so was my follow through. He disappeared into the bush, travelling as if out of a gun, and as he did so Florence's voice spoke.

'Ah!' she said.

There was no mistaking the emotion that animated the ejaculation. It was stiff with it. But with a dazed sensation of something having gone wrong I realized that it was not the emotion I had anticipated. Horror was completely absent, nor had there come through anything in the nature of indignation and sisterly resentment. Astounding as it may seem, joy was the predominating note. One might go further and say ecstasy. Her 'Ah!' in short, had been practically equivalent to 'Whoopee!' and I could make nothing of it.

'Thank you, Bertie!' she said. 'It was just what I was going to do myself. Edwin, come here!'

Down in the forest something stirred. It was the prudent child wriggling his way through the bush in a diametrically opposite direction. There came the sound of a faint and distant 'Coo!' and he was gone, leaving not a wrack behind.

Florence was gazing at me, a cordial and congratulatory light in her eyes, a happy smile playing about her lips.

'Thank you, Bertie!' she said again, once more with that wealth of emotion in her voice. 'I would like to skin him! I have just been looking at my album of press clippings, and he has gone and pasted in half the reviews of "Spindrift" wrong side up. I believe he did it on purpose. It's a pity I couldn't catch him, but there it is. I can't tell you how grateful I am, Bertie, for what you did. What gave you the idea?'

'Oh, it just came to me.'

'I understand. A sort of sudden inspiration. The central theme of "Spindrift" came like that. Jeeves says you want to speak to me. Is it something very important?'

'Oh, no. Not important.'

'Then we will keep it till later. I must go back now and see if there isn't some way of floating those clippings off with hot water.'

She hurried away, turning as she entered the house to wave a loving hand, and I was left alone to submit the situation to the analysis it demanded.

I don't know anything that seems to jar the back teeth like having a sure thing come unstuck, and it was with a dull sensation of having been hit in the stomach by a medicine ball, as once happened to me during a voyage to America, that I stood contemplating the future. Not even the fact that in the recent scene this girl had shown a warm, human side to her nature, which

I had not suspected that she possessed, could reconcile me to what I was now so unavoidably in for. A Florence capable of wanting to skin Edwin was better, of course, than a Florence susceptible of no such emotion, but no, I couldn't bring myself to like the shape of things to come.

How long I stood brooding there before I became aware of the squeaking that was going on at my side, I cannot say. Quite a time it must have been. For when at length I came out of my reverie, to find that Nobby was endeavouring to attract my attention, I saw that her manner was impatient, like that of one who has been trying to hobnob with a deaf mute and is finding the one-sided conversation weighing upon the spirits.

'Bertie!'

'Oh, sorry. I was musing.'

'Well, stop musing. You'll be late.'

'Late?'

'For Uncle Percy. In the study.'

I have mentioned earlier in this narrative that I am a pretty good silver-lining spotter, and that if there is a bright side to any cataclysm or disaster I seldom fail to put my finger on it sooner or later. Her words reminded me that there was one attached to the present catastrophe. Murky the future might be, what with all those wedding bells and what not which now seemed so inescapable, but at least I was in a position to save something out of the wreck. I could at any rate give Uncle Percy the go-by.

'Oh, that?' I said. 'That's off.'

'Off?'

'My reward for sitting in on the scheme,' I explained, 'was to have been the learning of the Fittleworth secret process for getting out of being engaged to Florence. I have learned it, and it is a wash-out. I, therefore, hand in my portfolio.'

'You mean you won't help us?'

'In some other way, to be decided on later, certainly. But not by inflaming Uncle Percy.'

'Oh, Bertie!'

'And it's no good saying, "Oh, Bertie!"'

She looked at me with bulging eyes, and it seemed for an instant as if those pearly drops, of which Boko had spoken so eloquently, were about to start functioning once more. But there was good stuff in the Hopwoods. The dam did not burst.

'But I don't understand.'

I explained in some detail what had occurred.

'Boko,' I concluded, 'claimed that this secret remedy of his was infallible. It is not. So unless he has something else to suggest –'

'But he has. I mean, I have.'

'You?'

'You want Florence to break off the engagement?'

'I do.'

'Well, go and talk to Uncle Percy, and I'll show her that letter you wrote me, saying what you thought of her. That'll work it.'

I started. In fact, I leaped about a foot.

'Golly!'

'Don't you agree?'

'Well, I'm dashed!'

I don't know when I've been so affected. I had forgotten all about that letter, but now, as its burning phrases came back to me, hope, which I had thought dead, threw off the winding sheet and resumed business at the old stand. The Fittleworth method might have failed, but there was no question that the Hopwood remedy would bring home the bacon.

'Nobby!'

'Think on your feet!'

'You promise you'll show Florence that letter?'

'Faithfully. If you will give Uncle Percy the treatment.'

'Is Boko at his post?'

'Sure to be by now.'

'Then out of my way! Here we go!'

And, moving as if on wings, I flitted to the house, plunged across the threshold, shot down the passage that led to the relative's sanctum and dived in.

Part 3

22

Uncle Percy's study, to which this was of course my first
visit, proved to be what they call on the stage a 'rich
interior', liberally equipped with desks, chairs, tables,
carpets and all the usual fixings. Books covered one side
of it, and on the opposite wall there hung a large picture
showing nymphs, or something similar, sporting with
what, from the look of them and the way they were
behaving, I took to be fauns. One also noted a terrestrial
globe, some bowls of flowers, a stuffed trout, a cigar
humidor, and a bust which might have been that of the
late Mr Gladstone.

In short, practically the only thing you could think of
that could have been in the room, but wasn't, was Uncle
Percy. He was not seated in the chair behind the desk,
nor was he pacing the carpet, twiddling the globe,
sniffing the flowers, reading the books, admiring the
stuffed trout or taking a gander at the nymphs and fauns.
Not a glimpse of him met the eye, and this total absence
of uncles, so different from what I had been led to
expect, brought me up with a bit of a turn.

It's a rummy feeling, when you've got yourself all
braced for the fray and suddenly discover that the fray
hasn't turned up. Rather like treading on the last stair
when it isn't there. I stood chewing the lip in some
perplexity, wondering what to do for the best.

The scent of a robust cigar, still lingering in the air,
showed that he must have been on the spot quite
recently, and the open French windows suggested that
he had popped out into the garden, there possibly to
wrestle with the problems which were weighing on his

mind – notably, no doubt, that of how the dickens life at
Steeple Bumpleigh being what it was, he was to obtain
an uninterrupted five minutes with Chichester Clam.
And what I was debating within myself was whether to
follow him or to remain in *status-quo* till he came back.

Much depended, of course, on how long he was going
to be. I mean, it wasn't as if the mood of fiery resolution
in which I had hurled myself across the threshold was a
thing which would last indefinitely. Already, the
temperature of the feet had become sensibly lowered,
and I was conscious of an emptiness behind the
diaphragm and a disposition to gulp. Postpone the
fixture for even another minute or two, and the evil
would spread to such an extent that the relative, when
he eventually showed up, would find a Bertram out of
whom all the sawdust had trickled – a Wooster capable
of nothing better than a mild 'Yes, Uncle Percy', and
'No, Uncle Percy'.

Looking at it from every angle, therefore, it seemed
that it would be best to go and tackle him in the great
open spaces, where Boko by this time was presumably
lurking. And I had reached the French windows, and was
about to pass through, though with little or no relish for
what lay before me, when my attention was arrested by
the sound of raised voices. They came from a certain
distance, and the actual wording of the dialogue escaped
the eardrum, but from the fact that they were addressing
each other as 'My dear Worplesdon' and 'You blot', I
divined that they belonged – respectively – to Boko and
the seigneur of Bumpleigh Hall.

A moment later, my conjecture was proved correct. A
little procession came into view, crossing the strip of
lawn outside the study. Heading it was Boko, looking
less debonair than I have sometimes seen him.
Following him came a man of gardeneresque appearance,
armed with a pitchfork and accompanied by a dog of
uncertain breed. The rear was brought up by Uncle

Percy, waving a cigar menacingly like the angel expelling Adam from the Garden of Eden.

It was he who seemed to be doing most of the talking. From time to time, Boko would look around, as if about to say something, but whatever eloquence he may have been intending was checked by the expression on the face of the dog, which was that of one fit for treasons, stratagems and spoils, and the fact that the pitchfork to which I have alluded was almost touching the seat of his trousers.

Half-way across the lawn, Uncle Percy detached himself from the convoy and came stumping rapidly towards me, puffing emotionally at his cigar. Boko and his new friends continued in the direction of the drive.

After the painful shock, inevitable on seeing an old friend given the push from enclosed premises, my first thought, as you may have surmised, had been that there was nothing to keep me. The whole essence of the scheme to which I had consented to lend my services had been that Boko should be within earshot while I was making my observations to Uncle Percy, and nothing was clearer than that by the time the latter reached his sanctum he would have drifted away like thistledown.

I shot off, accordingly, not standing upon the order of my going but going at once, as the fellow said, and was making good progress when, as I approached the door, I suddenly observed that there hung over it a striking portrait of Aunt Agatha, from the waist upwards. In making my entrance, I had, of course, missed this, but there it had been all the time, and now it caught my eye and halted me in my tracks as if I had run into a lamp-post.

It was the work of one of those artists who reveal the soul of the sitter, and it had revealed so much of Aunt Agatha's soul that for all practical purposes it might have been that danger to traffic in person. Indeed, I came within an ace of saying 'Oh, hullo!' at the same moment when I could have sworn it said 'Bertie!' in that compelling voice which had so often rung in my ears and caused me to curl up in a ball in the hope that a meek subservience would enable me to get off lightly.

The weakness was, of course, merely a temporary one. A moment later, Bertram was himself again. But the pause had been long enough to allow Uncle Percy to come clumping into the room, and escape was now impossible. I remained, therefore, and stood shooting my cuffs, trusting that the action would induce fortitude. It does sometimes.

Uncle Percy appeared to be soliloquizing.

'I trod on him! *Trod* on him! There he was, nestling in the grass, and I trod on him! It's not enough that the fellow comes roaming my grounds uninvited at all hours of the night. He comes also by day, and reclines in my personal grass. No keeping him out, apparently. He oozes into the place like oil.'

Here, for the first time, he seemed to become aware of a nephew's presence.

'Bertie!'

'Oh, hullo, Uncle Percy.'

'My dear fellow! Just the chap I wanted to see.'

To say that I was surprised at this remark would be to portray my emotions but feebly. It absolutely knocked me endways.

I mean, consider the facts. Man and boy, I had known this old buzzard a matter of fifteen years, and not once during that period had he even hinted that my society held any attraction for him. In fact, on most of the occasions when we had foregathered, he had rather gone out of his way to indicate that the reverse was the case. I have already alluded to the episode of the hunting crop, and there had been other similar passages through the course of the years.

I have, I think, made it sufficiently clear that few harder eggs ever stepped out of the saucepan than this

Percival, Lord Worplesdon. Rugged sea captains, accustomed to facing gales in the Western Ocean without a tremor, quivered like blancmanges when hauled up before him in his office and asked why the devil they had – or had not – ported the helm or spliced the mainbrace during their latest voyage in his service. In disposition akin to a more than ordinarily short-tempered snapping turtle, he resembled in appearance a malevolent Aubrey Smith, and usually, when one encountered him, gave the impression of being just about to foam at the mouth.

Yet now he was gazing at me in a manner which, when you came to look closely and got past the bristling moustache, revealed itself as not only part human, but actually kindly. From the pain in the neck generally induced by the sight of Bertram Wooster he appeared to be absolutely free.

'Who, me?' I said, weakly, my amazement, such that I was compelled to support myself against the terrestrial globe.

'Yes, you. The very fellow. Have a drink, Bertie.'

I said something about it being a bit early, but he pooh-poohed the suggestion.

'It's never too early to have a drink, if you've been wading ankle deep in blasted Fittleworths. I was taking a stroll with my cigar, my mind deeply occupied with vital personal problems, and my foot came down on something squashy, and there the frightful chap was, reclining in the lush grass by the lake as if he had been a dashed field-mouse or something. If I had had a weak heart, it might have been the end of me.'

I couldn't help mourning for Boko. I could picture what must have occurred. Making his way snakily towards the study window, he had heard Uncle Percy's approach and had taken cover, little knowing that a moment later the latter's number eleven foot was about to descend upon what – from the fact that the other

had described it as squashy – must have been some
tender portion of his anatomy. A nasty jar for the poor
chap. A nasty jar for Uncle Percy, too, of course. In fact,
one of those situations where the heart bleeds for both
the party of the first part and the party of the second
part.

'Fittleworth!' He shot an accusing glance at me.
'Friend of yours, isn't he?'

'Oh, bosom.'

'You would do well to choose your friends more
carefully,' he said, with the first lapse from that strange
benevolence of his which he had yet shown.

I suppose this was really the moment for embarking
upon an impassioned defence of Boko, stressing his
admirable qualities. Not being able to think of any,
however, I remained silent, and he carried on.

'But never mind him. My gardening staff is seeing him
off the premises, with strict orders to jab him in the seat
of his pants with a pitchfork if he dares to offer the
slightest resistance. I venture to think that these
grounds will see less of him in the future. And, by
George, that is what Bumpleigh Hall wants, to make it
an earthly Paradise – fewer and better Fittleworths. Have
a cigar, Bertie.'

'I don't think so, thanks.'

'Nonsense. I can't understand this in and out policy of
yours with regard to my cigars. When I don't want you
to smoke them, you do – remember that hunting crop,
eh, ha, ha? – and when I do want you to smoke them,
you don't. All silly nonsense. Put this in your face, you
young rascal,' he said, producing from the humidor
something that looked like a torpedo, 'and let's have no
more of this "I don't think so, thanks". I want you to be
all relaxed and comfortable, because I have something
very important to consult you about. Ah, bring it here,
Maple.'

On the cue 'It's never too early to have a drink', I

should have mentioned, he had pressed the bell, causing the butler to appear and book instruction. The latter had now re-entered with a half-bot from the oldest bin, and it was while genially uncorking this that the relative resumed his remarks.

'Yes, never mind Fittleworth,' he repeated, handing me a foaming goblet. 'Let us dismiss him from our thoughts. I have other things to talk about. First and foremost . . . Cheerio, Bertie.'

'Cheerio,' I said, faintly.

'Success to crime.'

'Skin off your nose,' I responded, still on the dazed side.

'Mud in your eye,' said this extraordinary changeling. 'First and foremost,' he proceeded, passing a rapid glassful down the hatch, 'I wish to express my appreciation of your spectacularly admirable conduct on the drive just now. I met Edwin out there, and he told me you had kicked him. A thing I've been wanting to do for years, but never had the nerve.'

Here he rose from his chair with outstretched hand, shook mine warmly and reseated himself.

'Thinking over some of our recent meetings, Bertie,' he said – I don't say softly, because he couldn't speak softly, but as softly as a chap who found it so difficult to speak softly could speak, 'I fancy you may have run away with the idea that I was a bad-tempered, cross-grained old fellow. I believe I spoke harshly to you last night. You must overlook it. You must make allowances. You can't judge a man with a son like Edwin by the same standards as men who haven't got a son like Edwin. Did you happen to hear that he got me squarely with that infernal Scout's stick of his last night?'

'Me, too.'

'Right on the –'

'He got me on the head.'

'Thinking I was a burglar, or some such nonsense.

And when I wanted to take steps, Florence wouldn't let me. You can imagine how I felt when I learned that you had kicked him. I wish I had seen it. Still, I gathered enough from his story to tell me that you behaved with notable gallantry and resource, and I don't mind admitting, my boy, that the thing has completely revolutionized my opinion of you. For years I have been looking on you as a mere lackadaisical, spiritless young man about town. I see now how wrong I was. You have shown yourself to be possessed of the highest executive qualities, and I have decided that you are the chap to advise me in the crisis which has arisen in my affairs. I am in a painful dilemma, Bertie. It is absolutely essential that . . . But perhaps you have heard about it from Jeeves?'

'He did give me a sort of outline.'

'Chichester Clam?'

'Yes.'

'My vital need for meeting him in secret session?'

'Yes.'

'That clears the ground then. Never mind why it is so urgent for me to meet Chichester Clam in secret session. So long as you understand that it is, that is all that matters. He was the man in the potting shed last night.'

'Yes.'

'You know that, do you? It was Jeeves's suggestion, and a very good one, too. In fact, if it hadn't been for that revolting Fittleworth . . . But don't let me get on to the subject of Fittleworth. I want to keep calm. Yes, Clam was in the potting shed. Curious fellow.'

'Oh, yes?'

'Most curious. I wonder how I can describe him to you. Ever seen a fawn?'

'Like the chaps in that picture?'

'No, not that sort of faun. I mean the animal. The timid fawn that shivers and shakes and at the slightest suspicion of danger starts like a . . . like a fawn. That's

Clam. Not to look at, I don't mean. He's stouter than
the average fawn, and he wears horn-rimmed spectacles,
which, of course, fawns don't. I'm referring to his
character and disposition. You agree with me?'

I reminded him that, owing to the fact that I had
never had the pleasure of making his acquaintance,
Clam's psychology was a sealed book to me.

'That's true. I was forgetting. Well, that's what he's
like. A fawn. Nervous. Quivering. Gets the wind up at
the slightest provocation. Came out of that potting shed,
I understand, shaking like a leaf and saying "Never
again!" Yes, every drop of his manly courage had
evaporated, and any scheme which we may devise for a
future meeting will have to be a good one, a foolproof
one, a scheme which even he can see involves him in no
peril. Odd, this neurotic tendency in the American
businessman. Can you account for it? No? I can. Too
much coffee.'

'Coffee?'

'That and the New Deal. Over in America, it appears,
life for the businessman is one long series of large cups
of coffee, punctuated with shocks from the New Deal.
He drinks a quart of coffee, and gets a nasty surprise
from the New Deal. To pull himself together, he drinks
another quart of coffee, and along comes another nasty
surprise from the New Deal. He staggers off, calling
feebly for more coffee, and . . . Well, you see what I
mean. Vicious circle. No nervous system could stand it.
Chichester Clam's nerves are in ruins. He wants to take
the next boat to New York. Knows he will be wrecking
the business deal of a lifetime by doing so, but says he
doesn't care, just so long as he gets God's broad, deep
Atlantic Ocean in between him and the English potting
shed. A most extraordinary prejudice he seems to have
taken against potting sheds, so keep steadily in your
mind the fact that whatever you may have to suggest
must be totally free from anything in the nature of a

potting-shed angle. What have you to suggest, Bertie?'

To this, of course, there was but one reply.

'I think we'd better consult Jeeves.'

'I have consulted Jeeves, and he says he's baffled.'

I shot out an aghastish puff of smoke. The thing seemed incredible.

'Jeeves says he's baffled?'

'Told me so himself. That's why I've come to you. Fresh mind.'

'When did he say that?'

'Last night.'

I saw that all was not lost.

'Ah, but he's had a refreshing sleep since then, and you know how a spot of sleep picks you up. And, by Jove, Uncle Percy, I'll tell you something I've just remembered. Early this morning I came upon him fishing in the river.'

'What of it?'

'The fact is tremendously significant. I didn't actually question him on the subject, but a man of his calibre would be bound to have caught a few. No doubt, he had them for breakfast. In which case, his faculties will have been greatly stimulated. Probably by now he's at the top of his form again, with his brain humming like a dynamo.'

It was plain that the relative found himself infected by my enthusiasm. In obvious excitement, he put the wrong end of his cigar in his mouth, singeing his moustache at the corner.

'I never thought of that,' he said, having cursed a bit.

'That often happens with Jeeves.'

'Is that so?'

'Most of his major triumphs have been accomplished on fish.'

'You don't say?'

'Absolutely. The phosphorus, you know.'

'Of course.'

'Even a single sardine will sometimes do the trick. Can you lay your hand on him?'

'I'll ring for Maple. Oh, Maple,' he said, as the butler fetched up at journey's end, 'send Jeeves to me.'

'Very good, m'lord.'

'And another half-bottle, I think, don't you Bertie?'

'Just as you say, Uncle Percy.'

'It would be rash not to have it. You have no conception how it shakes a man, bringing his foot down on what he thinks is solid ground and finding it's Fittleworth. Another of the same, Maple.'

'Very good, m'lord.'

During the stage wait, which was not of long duration, the old relative filled in with some *ad lib* stuff about Boko, mostly about how much he disliked his face. Then the door opened again to admit a procession headed by the half-bottle on a salver. This was followed by Maple, who in his turn was followed by Jeeves. Maple withdrew, and Uncle Percy got down to it.

'Jeeves.'

'M'lord?'

'Did you catch any fish this morning?'

'Two, m'lord.'

'Have 'em for breakfast?'

'Yes, m'lord.'

'Splendid. Capital. Excellent. Then come along. Hark for'rard.'

'M'lord?'

'I was telling his lordship how fish always gingered up your thought processes,' I explained. 'He is rather expecting that you may now have something constructive to suggest *in re* another meeting with Chichester Clam.'

'I am sorry, sir. I have used every endeavour to hit upon a solution of the problem confronting his lordship, but I regret to say that my efforts have not been crowned with success.'

'A wash-out, he says,' I construed, for Uncle Percy's benefit.

Uncle Percy said he had hoped for better things. Jeeves said he had, too.

'Any good offering you a glass of bubbly? Might buck you up.'

'I fear not, m'lord. Alcohol has a sedative rather than a stimulating effect on me.'

'In that case, nothing to be done, I suppose. All right, Jeeves. Thanks.'

A fairly sombre silence fell upon the room for some moments, after the man's departure. I gave the terrestrial globe a twirl. Uncle Percy stared at the stuffed trout.

'Well, that's that, what?' I said, at length.

'Eh?'

'I mean, if Jeeves is baffled, hope would appear to be more or less dead.'

To my surprise, he did not agree with me. His eye flashed fire. I had underestimated the fighting spirit of these blokes who have made large fortunes in the shipping business. You may depress them for a while, but you can't keep them down.

'Nonsense, nonsense. Nothing of the kind. Jeeves isn't the only man in this house with a head on his shoulders. Anyone who could conceive the idea of kicking Edwin and carry it out as brilliantly as you did is not to be beaten by a simple problem like this. I am relying on you, Bertie. Chichester Clam – how to meet him? Don't give it up. Think again.'

'Shall I go and brood a bit on the drive?'

'Brood wherever you like, all over the grounds.'

'Right ho,' I said, and took a meditative departure.

I had scarcely closed the door and started to push along the passage, when Nobby appeared, as if out of a trap.

23

She came leaping towards me, like Lady Macbeth coming to get first-hand news from the guest-room.

'Well?' she said, getting her hooks on my arm with girlish animation. 'I'm nearly expiring with excitement and suspense, Bertie. Did everything go off all right? I listened at the door for a bit, but it was so difficult to hear what was going on. All that came through was Uncle Percy's voice rumbling like thunder, and occasionally a bleat from you.'

I would have denied, and with some warmth, this charge that I had bleated, but she gave me no opportunity to speak.

'And what puzzled me was that, according to the programme, it should have been your voice rumbling like thunder and an occasional bleat from Uncle Percy. And I couldn't hear Boko at all. He might just as well not have been there.'

I winced. It seemed to be my constant task to have to dash the cup of joy from this young geezer's lips, and I didn't like it any more than I had the first time. However, I forced myself to give her the works.

'Boko wasn't there.'

'Not there?'

'No.'

'But the whole point –'

'I know. But he was unavoidably detained by a gardener with a pitchfork and a dog which seemed to me to have a dash of the wolf-hound in him.'

And in a few sympathetic words I related how the light of her life had become less than the dust beneath

Uncle Percy's gent's Oxfords and had been slung off the premises with all his music still within him.

A hard, set look came into her face.

'So Boko's made an ass of himself *again*?'

'I wouldn't call it actually making an ass of himself this time. More accurate, don't you think, to chalk him up as the helpless prey of destiny?'

'He could have rolled out of the way.'

'Not very easily. Uncle Percy's foot covers a wide area.'

She seemed to see the justice of this. Her map softened, and she asked if the poor darling had been hurt.

I weighed this.

'His physical injuries, I imagine, were slight. He seemed to be navigating under his own steam. Spiritually, he did not appear to be doing so well.'

'Poor lamb! He's so sensitive. What would you say his standing was now with Uncle Percy?'

'Lowish.'

'This has put the lid on things, you think?'

'To some extent, yes. But,' I said, glad to be able to drop a word of comfort, 'there is just a chance that, wind and weather permitting, the sun will 'ere long peep through the clouds. All depends on how the Wooster brain responds to the spurring it is going to get in the next half-hour or so.'

'What do you mean?'

'Rummy things have been happening, Nobby. You will recall how I tried the Fittleworth patent process for getting out of being engaged to Florence.'

'By kicking Edwin?'

'By, as you say, kicking Edwin. It has produced a bountiful harvest.'

'But you told me it hadn't worked.'

'Not in the way I had anticipated. But there has been an amazing by-product. Uncle Percy, informed of my activities, is all over me. For years, apparently, he has wanted to kick the young gumboil himself, but Florence has always stayed his foot.'

'I never knew that.'

'No doubt he has worn the mask. But the yearning was there, and it reached fever-point last night, when Edwin, sneaking up behind him, let him have it in the pants with his Scout's stick. So you can understand how he felt on learning that I had rushed in where he had feared to tread. It revolutionized his whole outlook. He shook my hand, gave me a cigar, pressed drink on me, and I am now his trusted friend and adviser. He thinks the world of me.'

'Yes, but –'

'You spoke?'

'I was only going to say that that's splendid and wonderful and marvellous, and I hope you will be very, very happy, but what I want is for him to think the world of Boko.'

'I am coming to that. Does the old relative ever speak to you of his affairs?'

'Only to tell me not to come bothering him now, because he's busy.'

'Then you wouldn't have heard of an American tycoon named J. Chichester Clam, with whom he has got to have a secret meeting in order to complete an important deal. Mysterious commercial stuff. He has asked me to think out some way of arranging this meeting. If I do, you will be on velvet.'

'How do you make that out?'

'Well, dash it, already I am practically Uncle Percy's ewe lamb. That will make me still ewer. He will be able to deny me nothing. I shall be in a position to melt his heart –'

'Oh, golly, yes. I see now.'

' – and get you and Boko fixed up. Then you show Florence that letter of mine, and that will get me fixed up.'

'But, Bertie, this is stupendous.'

'Yes, the prospects are of the rosiest, provided –'

'Provided what?'

'Well, provided I can think of a way of arranging this secret meeting, which at the moment of going to press I'm absolutely dashed if I can.'

'There are millions of ways.'

'Name three.'

'Why, you could . . . No, I see what you mean . . . It is difficult. I know. Ask Jeeves.'

'We have asked Jeeves. He says he's baffled.'

'Baffled? Jeeves?'

'I know. It came as a great shock to me. Chap was full of fish, too.'

'Then what are you going to do?'

'I told Uncle Percy I would brood.'

'Perhaps Boko would have something to suggest.'

Here, I was obliged to be firm.

'I bet he would,' I said, 'and I bet it would be something which would land us so deeply in the soup that it would require a dredging outfit to get us out again. I love Boko like a brother, but what I always feel about the dear old bird is that it's wisest not to stir him.'

She agreed with this, admitting that if there was a way of making things worse than they were Boko would unquestionably find it.

'I'm going to see him,' she said suddenly, after taking time out for a few moments in order to knit the brow.

'Boko?'

'Jeeves. I don't believe all this stuff about him being baffled.'

'He said he was.'

'I don't care. I don't believe it. Have you ever known Jeeves to be baffled?'

'Very seldom.'

'Well, then,' she said, and legged it for the staff quarters, leaving me to pass from the hall – I rather

think with bowed head – and move out into the open.
Here for a space I pondered.

How long I pondered, I cannot say. When the bean is
tensely occupied, it is difficult to keep tab on the
passage of time. I am unable to state, therefore, whether
it was ten minutes later or more like twenty when I
emerged from a profound reverie to discover that Jeeves
was in my midst. I had had no inkling of his approach,
but then one very often hasn't. He has a way of suddenly
materializing at one's side like one of those Indian
blokes who shoot their astral bodies to and fro, going
into thin air in Rangoon and re-assembling the parts in
Calcutta. I think it's done with mirrors.

Nobby was also there, looking pretty dashed pleased
with herself.

'I told you so,' she said.

'Eh?'

'About Jeeves being baffled. I knew there must be
some mistake. He isn't baffled at all.'

I stared at the man, astonished. True, he was looking
in rare intellectual form, what with his head sticking
out at the back and all the acumen gleaming from his
eyes, but he had stated so definitely to Uncle Percy and
self that he had been laid a stymie.

'Not baffled?'

'No. He was only fooling. He's got a terrific idea.'

'How much does he know of recent developments?'

'I've just been bringing him up to date.'

'You have been apprised of the failure of the
Fittleworth system, Jeeves?'

'Yes, sir. And also of your *rapprochement* with his
lordship.'

'My what with his lordship?'

'*Rapprochement*, sir. A French expression. I confess
that I experienced no little surprise on finding you on
such excellent terms, but Miss Hopwood's explanation
has rendered everything perfectly clear.'

'And you really have a scheme for bringing Uncle Percy and Clam together?'

'Yes, sir. I must confess that in our recent interview I intentionally misled his lordship. Realizing how vital it was to the interests of Mr Fittleworth and Miss Hopwood that you should be in a position to use your influence on their behalf, I thought it better that the suggestion should appear to emanate from you.'

'So that you can become more than ever the ewe lamb,' explained Nobby.

I nodded. His meaning had not escaped me. If you analysed it, it was the old Bacon and Shakespeare gag. Bacon, as you no doubt remember, wrote Shakespeare's stuff for him and then, possibly because he owed the latter money or it may be from sheer good nature, allowed him to take the credit for it. I mentioned this to Jeeves, and he said that perhaps an even closer parallel was that of Cyrano de Bergerac.

'The nature of the scheme which I have evolved, I should begin by saying, sir, renders the laying of it before his lordship a matter of some little delicacy, and it may be that a certain finesse will be required to induce him to fall in with it.'

'One of those schemes, is it?'

'Yes, sir. So, if I might make the suggestion, I think it would be best if you were to leave the matter in my hands.'

'You mean, let you sell it to him?'

'Precisely, sir. I would, of course, stress the fact that you were its originator and myself merely the go-between or emissary.'

'Just as you feel, Jeeves. You know best. And what is this scheme?'

'Briefly this, sir. I see no reason why his lordship and Mr Clam should not meet in perfect secrecy and safety at the fancy dress dance which is to take place to-night at the East Wibley Town Hall.'

I was absolutely staggered. I had clean forgotten that those East Wibley doings were scheduled for to-night. Which, when you reflect how keenly I had been looking forward to them, will give you some idea of the extent to which the fierce rush of life at Steeple Bumpleigh had disorganized my faculties.

'Isn't that a ball of fire?' said Nobby, enthusiastically.

I could not wholly subscribe to this.

'I spot a fatal flaw.'

'What do you mean, a flaw?'

'Well, try this on your pianola. Where, at such short notice, can Uncle Percy procure a costume? He can't go without one. Fancy dress, I take it, is obligatory. In other words, we come up against the snag the Wedding Guest ran into.'

'Which Wedding Guest? The one who beat his breast?'

'No, the chap in the parable, who was invited to a wedding but, having omitted to dress the part, got slung out on his ear like –'

I had been about to say 'like Boko from the precincts of Bumpleigh Hall', but refrained, fearing lest it might wound. But even without the addition my remorselessly logical words struck home.

'Oh, golly! I had forgotten about the upholstery. How do you get round that, Jeeves?'

'Quite simply, miss. I fear it will be necessary for you to lend his lordship your Sinbad the Sailor costume, sir.'

I uttered a stricken cry, like a cat to whom the suggestion has been made that she part with her new-born kitten.

'My God, Jeeves!'

'I fear so, sir.'

'But, dash it, that means I won't be able to attend the function.'

'I fear not, sir.'

'Well, why do you want to attend the rotten function?' demanded Nobby.

I gnawed the lower lip.

'You feel that this is absolutely essential, Jeeves? Think well.'

'Quite essential, sir. It may be a little difficult to persuade his lordship to take part in a frivolous affair of this nature, owing to his fear of what her ladyship would say, should she learn of it, and I am relying on the ginger whiskers which go with the costume to turn the scale. In placing the proposition before his lordship, I shall lay great stress on the completeness of the disguise which these will afford, preventing recognition by any acquaintance whom he may chance to encounter in the course of the festivities.'

I nodded. He was right. I decided to make the great sacrifice. The Woosters are seldom deaf to the voice of Reason, even if it involves draining the bitter cup.

'True, Jeeves. The keenest eye could not pierce those whiskers.'

'No, sir.'

'So be it, then. I will donate the costume.'

'Thank you, sir. Then I will be seeing his lordship immediately.'

'Heaven speed your efforts, Jeeves.'

'Thank you, sir.'

'Same here, Jeeves.'

'Thank you, miss.'

He shimmered off, and I turned to Nobby, with a sigh, saying that this was a blow and I would not attempt to conceal it. And once more she asked me why I was so keen on attending what she described as a footling country dance.

'Well, for one thing, I had set my heart on knocking East Wibley's eye out with that Sinbad. You've never seen me as Sinbad the Sailor, have you, Nobby?'

'No.'

'You haven't lived. But,' I proceeded, 'there is another

angle, and I wish it had floated into my mind before
Jeeves popped off, because I should like his views on it.
If Uncle Percy meets Chichester Clam at this orgy and
all goes well, he will, of course, be in malleable mood.
But the point is, do these malleable moods last? By the
following morning, may he not have simmered down? In
order to strike while the iron is hot, both I and Boko
ought to be there – I to seize the psychological moment
for approaching Uncle Percy on your behalf and Boko to
carry on from where I leave off.'

She saw what I meant.

'Yes, that wants thinking out.'

'If you don't mind, I'll pace up and down a bit.'

I did so, and was still hard at it, when Nobby's voice
hailed me, and I saw that Jeeves had returned from his
mission. Joining them at my best speed, I found him
looking modestly triumphant.

'His lordship has consented, sir.'

'Good. But –'

'I am to proceed to London without delay, in order to
see Mr Clam and secure his co-operation.'

'Quite. But –'

'Meanwhile, Miss Hopwood has drawn my attention
to the point which you have raised, sir, and I am in
cordial agreement with your view that both yourself and
Mr Fittleworth should be present at the dance. What I
would suggest, sir, is that Mr Fittleworth drives me to
the metropolis in his car, starting as soon as possible in
order that we may return in good time. While I am
interviewing Mr Clam, Mr Fittleworth can be
purchasing the necessary costumes. I think this meets
your difficulty, sir?'

I brooded for a moment. The scheme did, as he had
said, meet my difficulty. The only thing that was
bothering me was whether an essentially delicate matter
like the selection of fancy dress costumes could be left

safely in the hands of a bird like Boko. He was the sort of chap who might quite easily come back with a couple of Pierrots.

'Wouldn't it be better if I drove you to London?'

'No, sir. I think that you should remain, in order to keep his lordship's courage screwed to the sticking-place. His acceptance of the scheme was not obtained without considerable trouble. He would agree, and then he would glance at the portrait of her ladyship which hangs above the study door and demur once more. Left to himself, without constant exhortation and encouragement, I fear he might yet change his mind.'

I saw what he meant.

'Something in that, Jeeves. A bit jumpy, is he?'

'Extremely so, sir.'

I could not blame the old bird. I have already described my own emotions on catching the eye of that portrait of Aunt Agatha.

'Right ho, Jeeves.'

'Very good, sir. I would recommend constant allusions to the efficacy of the whiskers. As I had anticipated, it was they that turned the scale. Would Mr Fittleworth be at his residence now, miss? Then I will proceed thither at once.'

24

Jeeves's prediction that Uncle Percy would require constant exhortation and encouragement, to prevent him issuing an eleventh hour *nolle prosequi* and ducking out of the assignment he had undertaken, was abundantly fulfilled, and I must say I found the task of holding his hand and shooting pep into him a bit wearing. As the long day wore on, I began to understand why prize-fighters' managers, burdened with the job of bringing their men to the scratch, are always fairly careworn birds, with lined faces and dark circles under the eyes.

I could not but feel that it was ironical that the old relative should have spoken disparagingly of fawns as a class, sneering at their timidity in that rather lofty and superior manner, for he himself could have walked straight into a gathering of these animals, and no questions asked. There were moments, as he sat gazing at that portrait of Aunt Agatha over the study door, when he would have made even an unusually jumpy fawn look like Dangerous Dan McGrew.

Take it for all in all, therefore, it was a relief when, towards the quiet evenfall, the telephone rang and the following dialogue took place.

UNCLE PERCY: What? What? What-what-what? What? What? . . . Oh, hullo, Clam.

CLAM (off stage):   Quack, quack, quack, quack, quack, quack, quack, quack (about a minute and a half of this, in all).

UNCLE PERCY: Fine, good. Splendid. I'll look out for you, then.

'Clam,' he said, replacing the receiver. 'Says he's heart and soul in favour of the scheme, and is coming to the ball as Edward the Confessor.'

I nodded understandingly. I thought Clam's choice was good.

'A bearded bozo, was he not, this Edward?' I asked.

'To the eyebrows,' said Uncle Percy. 'Those were the days when the world was a solid mass of beavers. I shall keep my eye open for something that looks like a burst horsehair sofa, and that will be Clam.'

'Then you've really definitely and finally decided to attend the binge?'

'With bells on, my dear boy, with bells on. You might not think it, to look at me now, but there was a time when no Covent Garden ball was complete without me. I used to have the girls flocking round me like flies about a honey-pot. Between ourselves, it was owing to the fact that I got thrown out of a Covent Garden ball and taken to Vine Street Police Station in the company of a girl who, if memory serves me aright, was named Tottie that I escaped – that I had the misfortune not to marry your aunt thirty years earlier than I did.'

'Really?'

'I assure you. We had just got engaged at the time, and she broke it off within three minutes of reading my press notices in the evening papers. I was too late, of course, for the morning sheets, but the midday specials of the evening ones did me proud, and she was a little upset about it all. That is why I am so particularly anxious that no hint of to-night's doings shall reach her ears. Your aunt is a wonderful woman, Bertie . . . can't think what I should do without her . . . but – well, you know how it is.'

I said I knew how it was.

'So I trust that all will be well and that she will never learn of the dark deeds which have been done in her absence. I think I have the mechanics of the thing fairly well planned out. I shall sneak down the back stairs, muffled to the eyes in an overcoat, and tool over to East Wibley on my old push bicycle. It's only half a dozen miles. No flaws in that?'

'None that I can spot.'

'Of course, if Florence saw me –'

'She won't.'

'Or Edwin.'

'Not a chance.'

'Or Maple.'

I was distressed to note this resurgence of the old fawn complex just when everything had seemed hotsy-totsy, and addressed myself without delay to the task of putting a stopper on it. And eventually I succeeded. By the time I had finished pointing out that nothing was more unlikely than that Florence should be roaming the back stairs at such an hour, that Edwin was bound to take a day or two off from his spooring after the treatment I had administered that morning, and that Maple, if encountered, could readily be squared with a couple of quid, he bucked up enormously, and I left him trying out dance steps on the study floor.

Well, of course, you can't ginger up an uncle by marriage from shortly after breakfast to about five in the afternoon without paying the toll a bit. All this exhortation and encouragement had, as you may well imagine, taken it out of me not a little, inducing a limpness of the limbs and a sort of general feeling of stickiness. I don't say I was perspiring at every pore, but I felt in need of a thorough rinse: and, the river being at my very door, this was easy to obtain. A quarter of an hour later, I might have been observed breasting the waves, clad in a bathing suit from Boko's store.

In fact, I was observed, and by none other than G. D'Arcy Cheesewright. Doing the Australian crawl back to the bank after a refreshing plunge and holding on to a bush while I brushed the moisture from my eyes, I glanced up and saw him standing above me.

It was an embarrassing moment. I don't know when you feel less at ease than when encountering a bloke to whose *fiancée* you have just got engaged.

'Oh, hullo, Stilton,' I said. 'Coming in?'

'Not while you are polluting the water.'

'I'm just coming out.'

'Then I'll let it run a bit and perhaps it will be all right.'

His words alone would have been enough to inform a man of my quick intelligence that he was not unmixedly pro-Bertram, and as I climbed out and slid into the bath robe he gave me a look which drove the thing home. I have already, in another place, described at some length these looks of his, and I may say that this one was fully up to the sample he had given me outside Wee Nooke on the previous day.

However, if there is a chance that suavity will erase a situation, the Woosters always give it a buzz.

'Nice day,' I said. 'Pretty country, this.'

'Ruined by the people you meet.'

'Trippers, you mean?'

'No, I don't mean trippers. I refer to snakes in the grass.'

It would be absurd to say that his attitude was encouraging, but I persevered.

'Talking of grass,' I said, 'Boko was in that of Bumpleigh Hall this morning, and Uncle Percy trod on him.'

'I wish he had broken your neck.'

'I wasn't there.'

'I thought you said your uncle trod on you.'

'You don't listen, Stilton. I said he trod on Boko.'

'Oh Boko? Good Lord!' he cried, with honest heat.

'With a fellow like you around, he treads on Boko! What on earth was the use of treading on Boko?'

There was a pause, during which he tried to catch my eye and I tried to avoid his. Stilton's eye, even in repose, is nothing to write home about, being the sort of hard blue and rather bulging. In moments of emotion, it tends to protrude even farther, like that of an irascible snail, the general effect being rather displeasing.

Presently, he spoke again.

'I've just seen Florence.'

My embarrassment increased. I had been hoping that the topic might have been avoided. But Stilton is one of those rugged, forthright chaps who don't avoid topics.

'Oh, yes?' I said. 'Florence, eh?'

'She says she's going to marry you.'

I was liking this less and less.

'Oh, yes,' I said. 'Yes, I believe there is some idea of a union.'

'What do you mean, some idea? It's all fixed for September.'

'September?' I quavered, trembling from head to foot a bit. I hadn't had a notion that the curse was slated to come upon me so dashed quick.

'So she says,' he responded moodily. 'I'd like to break your neck. But I can't, because I'm in uniform.'

'Yes, there's that. One doesn't want one of these unpleasant police scandals does one?'

There was another pause. He was looking at me in a sort of yearning way.

'Gosh!' he murmured, almost dreamily. 'I wish there was something I could pinch you for!'

'Come, come, Stilton. Is this the tone?'

'I'd love to see you cowering in the dock, with me giving evidence against you.'

He was silent for a space, and I could see that he was still gloating over the vision he had conjured up. Then he asked me rather abruptly if I had finished with the river, and I said I had.

'Then in about five minutes or so I might take a chance and go in,' he said.

It was, as you may well imagine, in pretty fairly melancholy mood that I donned the bath robe and made my way back to the house. There's always something about the going phut of an old friendship that tends to lower the spirits. It was many years since this Cheesewright and I had started what I believe is known as plucking the gowans fine, and there had been a time when we had plucked them rather assiduously. But his attitude at the recent get-together had made it plain that the close season for gowans had now set in, and, as I say, it rather saddened me.

Shoving on the shirt and bags with an unshed tear in the eye, I trickled along to the sitting-room to see if Boko had returned from his mission to London. I found him sitting in an armchair with Nobby on his lap, seeming in admirable spirits.

'Come in, Bertie, come in,' he cried jovially. 'Jeeves is in the kitchen, brewing a dish of tea. You will join us in a cup?'

Inclining my head in assent to this suggestion, I addressed Nobby on a point of pre-eminent interest.

'Nobby,' I said, 'I have just seen Stilton, and he informs me that Florence has fixed the nuptials for a shockingly early date – viz. September. It is vital, therefore, that you lose no time in showing her that letter of mine.'

'If everything goes all right to-night, she will be skimming through it to-morrow morning over her early cup of tea.'

Relieved, I turned to Boko.

'Did you get the costumes?'

'Of course I got the costumes. What the dickens do you think I sweated up to London for? Two in all, one for self and one for you, the finest the Bros. Cohen could supply. Mine is a Cavalier. A rather sex-appealy wig goes with it. Yours –'

'Yes, what about mine?'

He hesitated a moment.

'You'll like yours. It's a Pierrot.'

I uttered a cry of chagrin. Boko, like all my circle, is well acquainted with my views on going to fancy dress dances as a Pierrot. I consider it roughly equivalent to shooting a sitting bird.

'Oh, is it?' I said, speaking with quiet firmness. 'Well, I'm jolly well going to have the Cavalier.'

'You can't, Bertie, old man. It wouldn't fit you. It was built for a shortish, squarish reveller like me. You are tall and slim and elegant. "Elegant" is the word?' he said, putting it up to Nobby.

'Just the word,' she assented.

'Another good adjective would be "willowy". Or "sylphlike". Gosh, I wish I had a figure like yours, Bertie. You don't know what you've got.'

'Yes, I do,' I riposted, coldly ignoring the salve. 'I've got a ruddy Pierrot costume. A Wooster going to a fancy dress ball as a Pierrot!' I said, and laughed shortly.

Boko shot Nobby off his knee and rose and began patting my shoulder. I suppose he could see that I was in dangerous mood.

'You need have no qualms about appearing in this Pierrot, Bertie,' he said soothingly. 'Where you have gone astray is in supposing that it is an ordinary Pierrot. Far from it. I doubt if, strictly speaking, you could call it a Pierrot at all. For one thing, it is mauve in colour. For another . . . But I'll show it to you, and I'll bet you go dancing about the house, clapping your hands.'

He reached for the suitcase which lay in the foreground, opened it, pulled out its contents and stared at them, aghast. So did I. So did Nobby. We all stared at them, aghast.

They consisted of what appeared to be a football suit. There was a pair of blue shorts, a pair of purple stockings and a crimson jersey.

Across the chest of the jersey, in large white letters, ran the legend 'BORSTAL ROVERS'.

25

It was some moments before any of us broke what I
believe is called the pregnant silence. Then Nobby
spoke.

'Do either of you see what I see?' she asked, in a sort
of hushed, awed voice.

My own was dull and toneless.

'If what you see is a gent's footballing outfit,' I replied,
'that is what is impressing itself on the Wooster retina.'

'With "Borstal Rovers" written across the jersey?'

'Right across the jersey.'

'In large white letters?'

'In very large white letters. I am waiting,' I said,
coldly, 'for an explanation, Fittleworth.'

Nobby uttered a passionate cry.

'I can give the explanation. Boko has gone and made
an ass of himself *again*!'

Cringing beneath her flaming eye, the wretched man
broke into a storm of protest.

'I haven't! I swear I haven't, darling!'

'Come, come, Boko,' I said, sternly. I had no wish to
grind the man into the dust, but he had the wages of sin
coming to him. 'A Cavalier costume and a mauve – if
your story is to be credited – Pierrot have changed, while
in your custody, into a football kit belonging apparently
to an athlete who turns out for the Borstal Rovers,
though I wouldn't have said offhand that there was such
a team. Someone has blundered, and all the evidence
points to you.'

Boko had tottered to a chair, and was sitting in it
with his head in his hands. He emitted a sudden yip.

'Catsmeat!' he cried. 'I see it all. It was that chump, Catsmeat. Before starting to return here,' he proceeded, looking up and looking quickly down again as his eye collided with Nobby's, 'I stopped in at the Drones to get one for the road. Catsmeat Potter-Pirbright was there. We fell into conversation, and it turned out that he, too, was going to a fancy dress binge to-night. We chatted for a while of this and that, and then he looked at his watch and found that he had only just time to catch his train, and buzzed off. What happened is obvious. Rendered cockeyed by haste, he took my suitcase in mistake for his own. And if you're going to make out that that was my fault,' said Boko, speaking now with some spirit, 'then all I can say is that there's no justice in the world and that it's a fat lot of use being as innocent as the driven snow.'

This appeal to our better feelings was not without its effect. Nobby flung herself into his arms, cooing over him to a considerable extent, and even I was compelled to admit that he had been more sinned against than sinning.

'Still, it's all right,' said Boko, now definitely chirpy once more. 'Catsmeat and I are about the same build, so I can wear this number. I would prefer, of course, not to have to flaunt myself before East Wibley as a member of the Borstal Rovers, but one realizes that this is not a time when one can pick and choose. Yes, I can take it.'

I mentioned a point which he appeared to have overlooked.

'And how about me? I've got to be there, too, to pave the way for you with Uncle Percy. A lot of solid talking will be required before it will be any use you approaching him. If I'm not at this East Wibley orgy, you might just as well stay at home.'

My words, as I had anticipated, produced a marked sensation. Nobby gave a sort of distraught hiccough, like a bull-pup choking on a rubber bone, and Boko confessed with a moody oath that he hadn't thought of that.

'Think of it now,' I said. 'Or, better,' I went on, as the door opened, 'ask Jeeves what his views on the matter are. You will probably have something to suggest, eh, Jeeves?'

'Sir?'

'A snag has arisen in our path, an Act of God having left us a costume short,' I explained, 'and we are frankly baffled.'

He placed the tea-tray on the table, and listened with respectful interest while we laid the facts before him.

'Might I take a short walk, sir,' he said, when we had finished, 'and think the problem over?'

'Certainly, Jeeves,' I replied, concealing a slight pang of disappointment, for I had hoped that he might have come across with an immediate solution. 'By all means take a short walk. You will find us here on your return.'

He oiled off, and we settled down to an informal debate, in which the note of hope was conspicuous by its a. It could scarcely escape the attention of three keen minds like ours that what looked like dishing us was the matter of time. It was now well past five o'clock, which rendered out of the question the idea of another quick dash to the metropolis and a second visit to the establishment of the Bros. Cohen. Zealous though they are in their self-chosen task of supplying the populace with clothing, there comes a moment when these merchants call it a day and put up the shutters. Not even by exceeding the speed limit all the way could a driver, starting from Steeple Bumpleigh now, reach the emporium in time to do business. Long 'ere he could arrive, the Bros. and their corps of assistants would have retired to their various residences and be relaxing over good books.

As for the chance of securing anything in the nature of a costume in Steeple Bumpleigh, that, it seemed to us, could be ruled out altogether. At the beginning of this chronicle, I gave a brief description of this hamlet, showing it to be rich in honeysuckle-covered cottages and apple-cheeked villagers, but that let it out. It had only one shop, that so ably conducted by Mrs Greenlees opposite the Jubilee watering-trough: and this, after it had supplied you with string, pink sweets, sides of bacon, tinned goods and *Old Moore's Almanac*, was a spent force.

Taking it for all in all, accordingly, the situation seemed pretty bleak. When I tell you that the best suggestion was the one advanced by Boko, that I should strip to a loincloth and smear myself with boot polish and go to the dance as a Zulu chief, you will see how little constructive progress had been made by the time the door opened and Jeeves was once more in our midst.

There is something about the mere sight of this number-nine-size-hatted man that seldom fails to jerk the beholder from despondency's depths in times of travail. Although Reason told us that he couldn't possibly have formulated a scheme for dragging home the gravy, we hailed him eagerly.

'Well?' I said.

'Well?' said Boko.

'Well?' said Nobby.

'Any luck, Jeeves?' I asked.

He inclined the coconut.

'Yes, sir. I am happy to say that I have been successful in finding a solution to the problem confronting you.'

'Gosh!' cried Nobby, stunned to the core.

'Egad!' cried Boko, the same.

'Well, I'm blowed!' I ejaculated, ibid. 'You have? I wouldn't have thought it possible. Would you, Boko?'

'I certainly wouldn't.'

'Or you, Nobby?'

'Not in a million years.'

'Well, there it is. That's Jeeves. Where others merely smite the brow and clutch the hair, he acts. Napoleon was the same.'

Boko shook his head.

'You can't class Napoleon with Jeeves.'

'Like putting up a fairish selling-plater against a classic yearling,' agreed Nobby.

'Napoleon had his moments,' I urged.

'On a very limited scale compared with Jeeves,' said Boko. 'I have nothing against Napoleon, but I cannot see him sauntering out into Steeple Bumpleigh at half-past five in the afternoon and coming back ten minutes later with a costume for a fancy dress ball. And this, you say, is what you have accomplished, Jeeves?'

'Yes, sir.'

'Well, I don't know how you feel about it, Bertie,' said Boko, 'but to me the thing looks like a ruddy miracle. Where is this costume, Jeeves?'

'I have placed it on the bed in Mr Wooster's room, sir.'

'But where on earth did you get it?'

'I found it, sir.'

'Found it? Just lying around, do you mean?'

'Yes, sir. On the bank of the river.'

I don't know why it was, unless possibly because we Woosters are a bit quicker than other men, but at these words a sudden horrible suspicion shot through me like a dose of salts, numbing the nerve centres and turning the blood to ice.

'Jeeves,' I faltered, 'this thing . . . this what-you-may-call-it . . . this costume of which you speak . . . what is it?'

'A policeman's uniform, sir.'

I collapsed into a chair as if the lower limbs had been mown off with a scythe. The s. had been well founded.

'It has occurred to me since that it may possibly have been the property of Mr Cheesewright, sir. I observed him disporting himself in the water not far away.'

I rose from the chair. It wasn't an easy thing to do, but I managed it.

'Jeeves,' I said, or perhaps it would be *mot juster* to say I thundered, 'you will go and restore that dashed uniform to its bally owner instanter!'

Boko and Nobby, who had been slapping each other's backs in the foreground, halted in mid-slap and stared at me, Boko as if he couldn't believe his ears, Nobby as if she couldn't believe hers.

'Restore it?' cried Nobby.

'To its bally owner?' gasped Boko. 'I simply fail to follow you, Bertie.'

'Me, too,' said Nobby. 'If you had been an Israelite in the wilderness, you wouldn't have passed up your plateful of manna, would you?'

'Exactly,' said Boko. 'Here, at the eleventh hour, just when the total downfall of all our hopes and dreams seemed to stare us in the eyeball because we were unable to lay our hooks on a fancy dress costume, an admirable costume has been sent from Heaven, as you might say, and you appear to be suggesting that we shall give it the go-by. You can't realize what you are saying. Reflect, Bertie. Consider.'

I preserved my iron front.

'That uniform,' I said, 'goes back to its proprietor by special messenger at the earliest possible date. My dear Boko, my good Nobby, have you the slightest conception of the bitterly anti-Wooster sentiments which prevail in Stilton's bosom? The man specifically stated to me not half an hour ago that his dearest wish was to catch Bertram bending. Let him discover that I have been pinching his uniforms, and I can hope for no mercy. Three months in the second division will be the best I can expect.'

Nobby started to say something about three months soon passing, but Boko shushed her.

'Why on earth should he discover anything of the sort?' he said. 'You aren't proposing to parade Steeple Bumpleigh day in and day out in this uniform. You're only going to wear it to-night.'

I corrected this view.

'I am not going to wear it to-night.'

'Oh, aren't you?' cried Nobby. 'Well, then, I'm jolly well not going to show that letter of yours to Florence.'

'Good girl,' said Boko. 'Well spoken, young light of my life. Laugh that off, Bertie.'

I made no endeavour to do so. Her words had chilled the spine. I don't suppose there is a man living who is swifter than Bertram Wooster to perceive when someone has got him by the short hairs, and it was clear to me that this was what had happened now. However fearful the perils that confronted me if I accepted Jeeves's loathsome gift, they must be faced.

A moment's struggle for utterance, and I bowed the onion and right-hoed.

'Splendid fellow!' said Boko. 'I knew you would see the light.'

'Bertie's always so reasonable,' said Nobby.

'Clear-thinking chap. Very level-headed,' agreed Boko. 'Then we're all set, eh? You come to the ball – of which in such a costume you can scarcely fail to be the belle – and you lurk till you have ascertained that old Worplesdon has had a satisfactory conference with Clam. If all has gone well, you buttonhole him and give me a build up. As soon as he is in melting mood, you give me the high sign, and I carry on from there, while you come home and turn in with an easy mind. I doubt if the whole thing – your part of it – will take more than half an hour. And now I think I had better be stepping along and taking Stilton a raincoat. No doubt he has a spare uniform at his residence, but one would like to get him there without causing comment. We can't have chaps roaming the countryside in the nude. All right for the Riviera, no doubt, but thank God we have a stricter code in Steeple Bumpleigh.'

He pushed off, taking Nobby with him, and I turned to Jeeves, who during these exchanges had been standing completely motionless, looking like a stuffed owl, his habit on occasions when he is among those present but has not been invited to join in the chit-chat.

'Jeeves,' I said.

'Sir?' he responded, coming to life in a deferential sort of way.

I did not mince my words.

'Well, Jeeves,' I said, and my face was hard and cold, 'you appreciate the set-up, I trust? Thanks to you, I am as properly up against it as I can remember being in the course of a not uneventful career. My position, as I see it, is roughly that of one who has removed a favourite cub from the custody of a rather more than usually short-tempered tigress, and is obliged to carry it on his person in the animal's immediate neighbourhood. I am not a weak man, Jeeves, but when I think of what will happen if Stilton cops me while I am draped in that uniform, it makes my knotted and combined locks . . . what was that gag of yours?'

'Part, sir, and each particular hair –'

'Stand on end, wasn't it?'

'Yes, sir. Like quills upon the fretful porpentine.'

'That's right. And that brings me back to it. What the dickens is a porpentine?'

'A porcupine, sir.'

'Oh, a *porcupine*? Why didn't you say that at first? It's been worrying me all day. Well, that, as I say, is the posish, Jeeves, and it is you who have brought it about.'

'I acted from the best motives, sir. It seemed to me that at all costs it was essential that you take part in to-night's festivities.'

I saw his point. If there's one thing the Woosters are, it's fairminded. We writhe, but we are just.

'Yes,' I assented with a moody nod, 'I suppose you meant well. And no doubt, in a sense, you did the right and judicious thing. But you can't get away from it that mine is a fearful predicament. One false step, and Stilton will be on the back of my neck, shouting for Justices of the Peace to come and sentence me to a long spell in the cooler. And, apart from that, has it occurred to you that this Cheesewright is about forty inches more round the chest and eight inches more round the head than me? Clad in his uniform, and especially wearing his helmet, I shall look like a Keystone Kop. Why, dash it, I'd rather go to this binge as the meanest Pierrot. Still, I suppose my bally preferences don't count.'

'I fear not, sir. For know, rash youth – if you will pardon me, sir – the expression is Mr Bernard Shaw's, not my own . . . For know, rash youth, that in this star crost world Fate drives us all to find our chiefest good in what we can, and not in what we would.'

Again, I saw his point.

'Quite,' I responded. 'Yes, I suppose the bullet must be bitten. Right ho, Jeeves,' I said, summoning to my aid all the splendid Wooster fortitude, 'lead me to it.'

26

It had been Boko's idea that he and I should make the journey to East Wibley in his car, he at the wheel, I at his side, so that if there were any minor details to be settled which we had overlooked, we could get them ironed out before arrival, thus achieving a perfect preparedness and avoiding any chance of last minute stymies.

To this suggestion, though admitting its basic soundness, I demurred. In fact, when I say I demurred, I ought to put it stronger. I more or less recoiled in horror. I had been Boko's passenger on a previous occasion, and it was not an experience one would wish to repeat. Put an author in the driver's seat of a car, and his natural goofiness seems to become intensified. Not only did Boko persistently overtake on blind corners, but he did it with a dreamy, faraway look in his eyes, telling one the plot of his next novel the while and not infrequently removing both hands from the wheel in order to drive home some dramatic point with gestures.

Another reason why I preferred to travel in the Wooster two-seater was that I was naturally anxious to get home and out of that uniform as speedily as possible. And, of course, it would be necessary, if all went well, for Boko to linger on and talk turkey to Uncle Percy.

My qualms regarding spending the evening in Stilton's plumage had in no way diminished with the passage of time. I still viewed the ordeal with concern.

Boko, returning from his errand of mercy to the zealous officer, had reported that the latter had seemed a bit upset about it all and inclined to suspect me of being

the motivating force behind the outrage. To this, Boko
had rather cleverly replied by saying that it was far more
likely to have been young Edwin who had done the
horrid deed. There comes a moment, he had pointed out,
in the life of every Boy Scout when he suddenly feels fed
up with doing acts of kindness and allows his human
side to get uppermost. On such occasions, the sight of a
policeman's uniform lying on the river bank would, he
maintained, call to such a Scout like deep calling to deep
and prove practically irresistible. He told me he thought
he had lulled Stilton's suspicions, all right.

This, of course, was all very well, as far as it went, but
I could not conceal it from myself that if Stilton were to
see me wearing the uniform, his suspicions would pretty
damn' soon come unlulled. He might or might not have
what it takes to make a man a master-mind of Scotland
Yard, but he unquestionably had sufficient intelligence,
should such a contingency occur, to put two and two
together, as the expression is. I mean to say, a policeman
who has had his uniform pinched and later in the day
comes on someone swathed in it is practically bound to
fall into a certain train of thought.

'No, Boko,' I said. 'I proceed to the tryst under my
own steam, and I come away the moment I have
completed my share in the proceedings, driving like the
wind.'

And so it was arranged.

Well, of course, it being so essential for me to get to
the scene of operations in good time, you might have
known what would happen. At about the half-way mark,
the old two-seater suddenly faded out, coming to a
placid standstill in prettily wooded country miles from
anywhere. And as I don't know the first thing about
fixing a car, my talents being limited to twisting the
wheel and tooting the tooter, I had to wait there till the
United States Marines arrived.

These took the shape – at about a quarter to twelve –

of a kindly bird in a lorry who, on being hailed, put everything right with a careless twiddle of the fingers so rapidly that he had occasion to spit only twice from start to finish. I thanked him, flung him a purse of gold and proceeded on my way, fetching up at journey's end just as the local clocks were striking midnight.

The interior of the East Wibley Town Hall presented a gay and fairylike appearance. Coloured lanterns hung from the roof, there was a good deal of smilax here and there, and on all sides the eye detected fair women and brave men. One of the latter, a footballer in the striking colours of the Borstal Rovers, detached himself from the throng and arrested my progress, full of recriminations.

'Bertie, you outstanding louse,' said Boko, for it was he, 'where the devil have you been? I was expecting you hours ago.'

I explained the reasons for my delay, and he said peevishly that I was just the sort of chap whose car would break down when every moment was precious, adding that it was a lucky thing that it hadn't been me they sent to bring the good news from Aix to Ghent, because, if it had been, Ghent would have got it first in the Sunday papers.

'It's going to be touch and go, Bertie,' he proceeded. 'A wholly unforeseen situation has arisen. Old Worplesdon has gone to earth in the bar and is lowering the stuff by the pailful.'

'But that's fine,' I said. 'The significance of his actions has probably escaped you, but I can read between the lines. It means that he has seen Clam and that everything is satisfactorily fixed up.'

He clicked his tongue impatiently.

'Of course it does. But the frightful danger is that at any moment he may pass completely out, and then where are we?'

I saw what he meant, and it was as if a hand of ice had been placed on my heart. No wonder he had used the words, 'frightful danger'. The peril was hideous. Our whole plan of strategy called for an Uncle Percy in whom the neap tide of the milk of human kindness was at its height. A blind and speechless Uncle P., stacked up against the wall in a corner of the bar like an umbrella in an umbrella stand, would defeat all our aims.

'Go to him without a second's delay,' said Boko, urgently. 'Pray Heaven it may not be too late!'

The words had scarcely left his lips before I was skimming barwards like a greyhound released from the slips. And it was with profound relief that I saw that I was in time. Uncle Percy had not passed out. He was still up and doing, playing the genial host to a platoon of friends and admirers who had plainly come to look on him in the light of a public drinking fountain.

I was just starting to head in his direction, when the band struck up another tune and his pals swallowed theirs quick and streamed out, leaving the old relative leaning back in his chair with his feet on the table. I lost no time in stepping up and fraternizing.

'What ho, Uncle Percy,' I said.

'Ah, Bertie,' he replied. He shut one eye and scrutinized me narrowly. 'I am right,' he queried, 'in supposing that that is Bertram Wooster rattling about inside that helmet?'

'It is,' I replied shortly. The uniform and helmet were proving ever roomier than I had feared they would be, and I was about fed up with them. The almost universal merriment which had greeted me, as I passed through the crowd of revellers, had been hard to bear. The Woosters are not accustomed to getting the horse's laugh when they lend their presence to fancy dress dances.

'It doesn't fit. It's too large. You should change your hatter, or your armourer, or whatever it is. Still, be that as it may, tiddly-om-pom-pom. Sit down and have some of this disgusting champagne, Bertie. I'll join you.'

I thought it best to speak the word in season.

'Haven't you had enough, Uncle Percy?'

He weighed this.

'If what you mean by that question is, am I stinko,' he replied, 'in a broad, general sense you are right. I *am* stinko. But everything is relative, Bertie . . . You, for instance, are my relative, and I am your relative . . . and the point I want to make is that I am not one bit as stinko as I'm going to be later on. This is a night for unstinted rejoicing, my dear boy, and if you think I am not going to rejoice – and unstintedly, at that – then I reply "Watch me!" That is all I say. Watch me!'

The spectacle of an uncle, even if only an uncle by marriage, going down for the third time in a sea of dance champagne can never be an agreeable one. But though I mourned as a nephew, I'm bound to say I found myself pretty bucked in my capacity of ambassador for Boko. Pie-eyed, even plastered, this man might be, but there was no mistaking his geniality. It was like something out of Dickens, and I saw that he was going to be clay in my hands.

'I've seen Clam,' he proceeded.

'You have?'

'With the naked eye. And I refuse to believe that Edward the Confessor really looked like that. Nobody presenting such an obscene appearance as J. Chichester Clam could possibly have held the throne of England for five minutes. Lynching parties would have been organized, knights sent out to cope with the nuisance with battleaxes.'

'Is everything all right?'

'Everything's fine, except that I am beginning to see two of you. And one was ample.'

'I mean, you've had your conference?'

'Oh, our conference? Yes, we had that, and I don't mind telling you, if you can hear me from inside that helmet, that I put it all over him. When he looks at that agreement we sketched out on the back of the wine list – an agreement, I may mention, legally witnessed by the chap behind the bar and impossible to get out of – he'll realize that he's practically given me his bally shipping line. That is why I say – and with all the emphasis at my disposal – tiddly-om-pom-pom. Fill your glass, Bertie. Don't spare the vitriol.'

I felt that the word of praise would not be amiss. However mellowed a man may be, it never hurts to mellow him a bit more by giving him the old oil.

'Smooth work, Uncle Percy.'

'You may well say so, my boy.'

'There can't be many fellows about with brains like yours.'

'There aren't.'

'Very creditable to you, the whole thing. I mean, considering your condition.'

'You allude to my being tight? Quite, quite. But I wasn't tight when I was dealing with Clam. Though my shoes were. I seem,' he said, his lips contorted by a spasm of pain, 'to have come out in a pair of shoes about eleven sizes too small, and they're nipping me like nobody's business. I'm going to look for a quiet spot where I can take them off for a bit.'

I drew my breath in sharply. I had seen the way. I suppose this is how great generals win battles, by suddenly spotting the right course to pursue and immediately pulling up their socks and snapping into it.

You see, what I had been alive to all along had been the danger that this man, as soon as I switched the conversation to the subject of Boko, would turn on his heel and stalk off, leaving me flat. Catch him with his shoes off, and this problem would not arise. An uncle by marriage with only socks on finds it dashed difficult to turn on his heel, especially if he's sitting in a car. And it was into a car that I proposed to decant this Percy.

'What you want,' I said, 'is to go and sit in a car.'

'I haven't got a car. I tooled over on my push bike, and a hell of a sweat it was, taxing the unaccustomed calf muscles like billy-o.'

'I'll find a car.'

'Not that rotten little two-seater of yours, I trust? I shall require space. I want to stretch my legs out and relax. The calves are still throbbing.'

'No, this is a bigger, better car altogether. The property of a friend of mine.'

'Will he object to my taking my shoes off?'

'Not a bit.'

'Excellent. Lead the way, then, my boy. Before starting, however, I had better procure another quart of this gooseberry cider and take it along.'

'If you think it advisable.'

'Not merely advisable. Imperative. One doesn't want to lose a moment.'

I had no difficulty in spotting Boko's car. It was a thing about the size of a young tank, which he had bought second-hand in his less oofy days and refused to part with because its admirable solidity served him so well in the give and take of traffic. He told me once that it brushed ordinary sports models aside like flies, and that his money would be on it even in the event of a collision with an omnibus.

I ushered the old relative into its cavernous depths, and he removed the shoes. Not till he was safely reclining on his spine, twiddling his toes out of the window, so that the cool night air could play on them, did I start to bring up the big item on the agenda paper.

'So you slipped it across Clam, did you, Uncle Percy?' I said. 'Splendid. Capital. And after accomplishing so notable a business triumph you are, I take it, feeling pretty benevolent towards your fellow men?'

'I love them all,' he said handsomely. 'I look on the entire human species with a kindly and indulgent eye.'

'Well, that's fine.'

'Always excepting, of course, the foe of that species, the hellhound Fittleworth.'

This wasn't so good.

'Would you make exceptions, Uncle Percy? On a night like this?'

'Oh this or any other night, and also by day. Fittleworth! Invites me to lunch –'

'I know. He told me.'

' – and wantonly causes spiders to emerge from the salt cellar.'

'I know. But –'

'Roams my grounds, officiously locking my business associates in potting sheds –'

'I know. Quite. But –'

'And, to top it all off, lurks in my grass like a ruddy grasshopper, so that I can't stir a step without treading on him. When I reflect that I have not dissected Fittleworth, limb by limb, and danced on his remains, my moderation astounds me. Don't talk to me about Fittleworth.'

'But that's just what I want to talk about. I want to plead his cause. You are aware, Uncle Percy,' I said, bunging a bit of a tremolo into the old voice, 'that he loves young Nobby.'

'So I have been informed, dash his cheek.'

'It would be an ideal match. You and he may not always have seen eye to eye in such matters as spiders in salt cellars, but you can't get away from it that he is one of the hottest of England's younger littérateurs. He earns more per annum than a Cabinet Minister.'

'He ought to be ashamed of himself, if he didn't. Have you ever met a Cabinet Minister? I know dozens, and not one of them that wouldn't be grossly overpaid at thirty shillings a week.'

'He could support Nobby in the style to which she is accustomed.'

'No, he couldn't. Ask me why not.'

'Why not?'

'Because I'm jolly well not going to let him.'

'But he loves, Uncle Percy.'

'Has he got an Uncle Percy?'

I saw that unless prompt steps were taken, we should be getting muddled.

'When I say He loves, Uncle Percy,' I explained, 'I don't mean he loves, verb transitive, Uncle Percy, accusative. I mean he loves, comma, Uncle Percy, exclamation mark.'

Even while uttering the words, I had had a fear lest I might be making the thing a shade too complex for one in the relative's condition. And so it proved.

'Bertie,' he said, gravely, 'I should have watched you more carefully. You're tighter than I am.'

'No, no.'

'Then just go over that observation of yours again slowly. I would be the last man to dispute that my faculties are a little blurred, but –'

'I only said, that he loved, and shoved in an "Uncle Percy" at the end of my remarks.'

'Addressing me, you mean?'

'Yes.'

'In the vocative, as it were?'

'That's right.'

'Now we've got it straight. And where does it get us? Just where we were before. You say he loves my ward, Zenobia. I reply, "All right, let him, and I hope he has a fine day for it. But I'm dashed if he's going to marry her". I take my position as guardian of that girl pretty seriously. You might say I regard it as a sacred trust. When confiding her to my care, I remember, her poor old father, as fine a fellow as ever stepped, though too fond of pink gin, clasped my hand and said, "Watch her like a hawk, Percy, old boy, or she'll go marrying some bally blot on the landscape". And I said, "Roddy, old man" – his name was Roderick – "just slip a clause in the lease, saying that she's got to get my consent first, and you need have no further uneasiness". And what happens? First thing you know, up pops probably the worst blot any landscape was ever afflicted with. But he finds me ready, my boy. He finds me ready and prepared. There is my authority in black and white, and I intend to exercise it.'

'But her father wasn't thinking of a chap like Boko.'

'There are limits to every man's imagination.'

'Boko's a frightfully good egg.'

'He is nothing of the kind. Good egg, forsooth! Tell me a single thing this Fittleworth has ever done that entitles him to consideration and respect.'

I thought for a moment. And when the Woosters think for a moment, they generally spear something good.

'It may be news to you,' I said, 'that he once kicked Edwin.'

This got home. His mouth opened, and his feet twitched, as if stirred by a passing zephyr.

'Is this true?'

'Ask Florence. Ask the knives and boots boy.'

'Well, I'm dashed.'

He sat for a while, deep in thought. I could see that revelation had made a deep impression.

'I confess,' he said at length, raising the bottle to his lips and swallowing about a third of its contents, 'that what you tell me causes me to look on the fellow with a somewhat kindlier eye. Yes, to some extent, I admit, it has modified my views regarding him. It just shows that there is good in all of us.'

'Then on consideration –'

He shook his head.

'No, Bertie, I cannot consent to this match. Look at it from my point of view. The fellow lives at my very doors. Give him an excuse like being married to my ward, and he would always be popping in. Every time I took a stroll in my garden, I should be watching my step in case he happened to be hiding in the grass. Every time he came to lunch, my eyes would be riveted on the salt cellar. No nervous system could stand it.'

I saw the talking point.

'But you haven't heard the latest, Uncle Percy. Boko leaves next month for Hollywood. Do you realize that America is three thousand miles away, and that Hollywood is three thousand miles on the other side of America?'

He started.

'Is it?'

'Absolutely.'

He sat for a moment twiddling his fingers.

'I make that six thousand miles.'

'That's right.'

'Six thousand miles,' he said, rolling the words round his tongue. 'Why, this alters everything. You think Zenobia loves him?'

'Devotedly.'

'Odd. Strange. And his financial position is as sound as you suggest?'

'Sounder. Editors scream like frightened children when his agent looks in to talk terms for a new contract.'

'And about Hollywood. You're sure your figures are right? Six thousand miles?'

'A bit more, if anything.'

'Well, then, really, dash it, in that case –'

I saw that the iron was hot, and that the moment had come for Boko to strike it.

'I'll send him to you,' I said, 'and you can have a talk and rough out the arrangements. No need for you to move. This is his car. By Jove, Uncle Percy, you'll be thankful for this later on, when you realize what a bit of a goose you're handing two young hearts in springtime.'

'Tiddly-om-pom-pom,' said the relative, waving a cordial toe and once more applying his lips to the bot.

I did not let the g. grow under the feet. Hastening back to the ballroom, I sorted Boko out from the revellers, and sent him off with many a hearty 'Tails up' and 'God speed'. Then, unleashing the two-seater, I drove home, thankful that a sticky bit of business had been safely concluded.

My first act, on reaching journey's end, was, of course, to tear off the uniform. Having crept to the river bank and consigned it to the dark waters, which might or might not eventually cast it up some distant shore whence it would be returned to its owner, I whizzed back to my room and darted into bed.

It was not immediately that the tired eyelids closed in sleep, for some hidden hand had placed a hedgehog between the sheets – practically, you might say, a fretful porpentine. Assuming this to be Boko's handiwork, I was strongly inclined to transfer it to his couch. Reflecting, however, that while this would teach him a much needed lesson it would be a bit tough on the porpentine, I took the latter out into the garden and loosed it into the grass.

Then, the day's work done, I turned in and soon sank into a dreamless slumber.

27

The sun was high in the heavens, or fairly high, when I awoke next morning. From behind the closed door of Boko's sleeping apartment there proceeded a rhythmic sound like the sawing of wood, indicating that he had not yet sprung from his bed. I would have liked to waken him and ask if all was well, but refrained. No doubt, I felt, he had returned at a late hour and needed an extra bit of what I have heard Jeeves call tired Nature's sweet restorer. I donned the bathing suit and bath robe, and started off for the river, and I hadn't more than shoved my nose outside the garden gate when along came Nobby on her bicycle.

It would have been plain even to the most casual observer that Nobby was in the pink. Her eyes were shining like twin stars as the expression is, and she greeted me with one of the heartiest pip-pips that ever proceeded from female throat.

'Hullo, Bertie,' she cried. 'I say, Bertie, isn't everything supercolossal!'

'I think so,' I replied. 'I hope so. I left Uncle Percy in malleable mood, and Boko was just going to confer with him. All should have gone well.'

'Then you haven't heard? Didn't Boko tell you?'

'I haven't seen him yet. Our waking moments have not synchronized. When he got back, I was asleep, and when I got up, he was asleep.'

'Oh, I see. Well, he came round in the small hours and threw gravel at my window and made his report. Everything went like a breeze.'

'It did?'

'According to Boko, the thing was a love feast. Uncle Percy sent him back to the bar for another bottle of champagne, and they split it like a couple of sailors on shore leave.'

'And he's given his consent?'

'Definitely, Boko says. He's so grateful to you for all you have done, Bertie. So am I. I could kiss you.'

'Just as you wish,' I assented civilly, and she did so. Then she legged it for the house, and I proceeded on my way to the river.

My mood, as I clove its crystal waters, was, as you may imagine, pretty uplifted. Nobby's story had left no room for doubt that happy endings had come popping up like rabbits. I had forgotten to ask her when she was going to show that letter to Florence, but no doubt this would be done in the course of the morning, releasing me from my honourable obligations. And, as for her and Boko, it was well within the bounds of possibility that before nightfall they would be united in the bonds of holy wedlock. Boko had made no secret of the fact that for many a day past he had had the licence tucked away in the drawer of his desk, ready to do its stuff the moment the starter's pistol went.

In addition to this, Stilton's uniform was floating on its way to the sea, and absolutely nothing to prove that it and Bertram had ever been in any way connected. It was just possible that some inkling of the truth might come to the promising young copper, causing him to regard me, when we next met, with sullen suspicion and even to go as far as to grind his teeth: but as for his assembling a telling weight of evidence which would land me in the dock and subsequently in the lowest dungeon beneath the castle moat, not a hope.

It was, accordingly, with no uncertain feeling that this was the maddest, merriest day of all the glad new year that I returned to the house, where genial smells from the dining-room greeted the nostrils and caused me

to dress like a streak. Entering the food zone a few
moments later, I found Boko restoring his tissues, with
Nobby sitting on the end of the table, drinking in his
every word.

'Ah, Bertie,' said Boko. 'Good morning, Bertie. Now
you're here, I'd better start again.'

He did so, and for some minutes held me spellbound.
Even though I had heard the outline of the plot from
Nobby and so knew how it all came out in the end, I
hung upon his lips from start to finish.

'You didn't get his consent in writing?' I asked, as he
concluded.

'Well, no,' he admitted. 'It never occurred to me. But
if what is in your mind is that he may try to back out of
it, don't worry. You have no conception, Bertie, literally
no conception of the chumminess which exists between
us. Hands were shaken, and backs slapped. He was all
over me like a bedspread. Well, to give you some idea, he
said he wished he had a son like me.'

'Well, considering he's got a son like Edwin, that isn't
saying much.'

'Don't be a wet blanket, Bertie. Don't try to cast a
gloom on this wonderful morning. Another thing he said
was that he hoped I would be very successful in
Hollywood and would remain working there for many
years – in fact, indefinitely. One sees what he meant, of
course. Like others, he has long chafed at the rottenness
of motion pictures and is relying on me to raise the
standard.'

'You will, angel,' said Nobby.

'You betcher,' said Boko, swilling coffee.

The meal proceeded on its pleasant course. A less
kindly man than Bertram Wooster might have struck a
jarring note by bringing up the matter of that porpentine
in my bed, but I refrained from this. Instead, I asked
what became of Uncle Percy at the close of the
proceedings.

'I suppose he pushed home on his push bike,' said Boko. 'What did you do with Stilton's uniform?'

I explained that I had committed it to the deep, and he said I could not have made a wiser move. And he was just starting to be dashed funny about my last night's outer crust, when I stopped him with an imperious gesture.

Out of the corner of my eye, I had seen something large and blue turning in at the garden gate. A moment later, there came the sound of feet crunching on gravel, and the *timbre* and volume of the noise was such that only regulation official boots could have caused it. I was not surprised when in due season the torso and helmeted head of Stilton were framed in the open window. And more profoundly than ever I congratulated myself on the shrewdness and foresight which had led me to bung that uniform into the river.

'Ah, Stilton,' I said, and, what is more, I said it airily. The keenest ear could not have detected that the conscience was not as clean as a whistle. One prefers, of course, on all occasions to be stainless and above reproach, but, failing that, the next best thing is unquestionably to have got rid of the body.

Boko, who is always a perfect host, bade the newcomer a cheery good morning, and asked him to keep his mouth open and he would throw a sardine into it. But apparently the latter had already breakfasted, for he declined the invitation with a petulant jerk of the head.

'Ho!' he said.

Touching for a moment on this matter of policemen and the word 'Ho'. I have an idea that the first thing they teach the young recruit on joining the Force is how to utter this ejaculation. I've never met a rozzer yet who didn't say it, and they all say it in just the same way. Inevitably one is led to assume a course of schooling.

'So there you are, you blasted Wooster!'

Speculating, as I had done from time to time since the previous evening, on the probable demeanour of this painstaking young officer when next he should catch sight of me, I had never anticipated that it would be elfin. I had budgeted for the dark frown, the flushed face and the hard and bulging eye. And there they all were, precisely as foreshadowed, and they found me ready to cope with them.

I preserved my aplomb.

'Yes, here I am,' I responded, buttering a nonchalant slice of toast. 'Where else would I be, my dear Stilton? This, thanks to Boko's princely hospitality, is where I am living.'

'Ho!' said Stilton. 'Well, you won't be living here much longer, because you're bally well coming along with me.'

Boko looked at me, and raised his eyebrows. I looked at Boko, and raised my eyebrows. Nobby looked at us both, and raised her eyebrows. Then we looked at Stilton, and all raised our eyebrows. It was one of those big eyebrow-raising mornings.

'Coming along with you? Surely, Stilton,' said Boko, 'you do not use that expression in a technical sense?'

'Yes, I do.'

'You have come to arrest Bertie?'

'Yes, I have.'

'What for?'

'Pinching my uniform.'

Nobby turned to me in girlish astonishment.

'Have you been pinching Stilton's uniform, Bertie?'

'Certainly not.'

'How lucky.'

'Extremely fortunate.'

'Because I suppose you could get about three months for a thing like that.'

'Besides the shame of it all,' I pointed out. 'If I ever

feel the temptation to commit this rash act, I must fight against it. Not that I imagine I shall.'

'Pretty unlikely,' Nobby agreed. 'I mean, what on earth would you want a policeman's uniform for?'

'Exactly,' I said. 'You have touched the matter with a needle.'

'Done what?'

'One of Jeeves's gags,' I explained. '*Rem* something. Latin stuff.'

Boko, who had been frowning thoughtfully, went more deeply into the matter.

'I believe I know what's on Stilton's mind,' he said. 'I don't think I told you, but yesterday, while he was bathing, somebody snitched his uniform, which he had left lying on the bank. Did I mention it?'

'Not to my recollection,' said Nobby.

'Nor to mine,' I said, shaking the bean.

'Odd,' said Boko. 'I suppose it slipped my mind.'

'Things do,' said Nobby.

'Frequently,' I agreed.

'Well, that's what happened, and one can't blame him for wanting to bring the criminal to justice. But why he has got this extraordinary idea that it was Bertie who was responsible for the foul outrage is more than I can understand. I told you yesterday, Stilton, that the hidden hand was almost certainly young Edwin's.'

'Yes, and I've just been tackling him about it. He denies it categorically.'

'And you accept his word?'

'Yes, I do. He has an alibi.'

'Well, you perfect chump,' cried Nobby, 'don't you know that that dishes him? Haven't you ever read any detective stories? Ask Lord Peter Wimsey what an alibi amounts to.'

'Or Monsieur Poirot,' I suggested.

'Yes. Or Reggie Fortune, or Inspector French, or Nero

Wolfe. I can't understand a man of your intelligence falling for that alibi stuff.'

'Incredible,' I said. 'The oldest trick in the game.'

'Trot along and bust it, is my advice, Stilton,' said Boko.

One might have expected a cop to wilt beneath all this, but it speedily became plain that the Cheesewrights were made of sterner stuff.

'If you want to know why I accept young Edwin's alibi,' said Stilton, allowing his eyes to bulge a bit farther from the parent sockets, 'it's because it's supported by the vicar, the vicar's wife, the curate, the curate's sister, the doctor, the doctor's aunt, a scoutmaster, fifteen assorted tradesmen and forty-seven Boy Scouts. It appears that the doctor was giving a lecture on First Aid in the village hall yesterday evening, and Edwin was the chap who went on the platform and was illustrated on. At the moment when my uniform was pinched, he was lying on a table, swathed in bandages, showing what you have to do to a bloke with a fractured thigh bone.'

This, I admit, spiked our guns to no little extent. Nobby did say that it might have been an accomplice cunningly disguised to look like Edwin, but you could see that it was simply a suggestion.

'Yes,' said Boko, at length, 'that does seem to let Edwin out. But I still don't see where you get this extraordinary idea that Bertie is the culprit.'

'I'll tell you that, too,' said Stilton, plainly resolved to keep nothing from us. 'Edwin, questioned, had an amazing story to relate. He stated that, going to accused's bedroom later in the evening to put a hedgehog in his bed – '

'Ha!' I exclaimed, and gave Boko a penitent look, remorseful that even in thought I should have wronged my kind host.

' – he saw the uniform there. And I met a chap this

morning who had been an extra waiter at the fancy dress ball at East Wibley last night, and he informs me that there was a loathsome-looking object taking part in the festivities, dressed in a policeman's uniform six sizes too large for him. I am ready to step along, Wooster, if you are.'

It seemed to me a fair cop, as I believe the expression is, and I saw nothing to be gained by postponing the inevitable. I rose, and wiped the lips with the napkin, like a French aristocrat informed that the tumbrel is at the door.

Boko's hat, however, was still in the ring.

'Just a minute, Stilton,' he said. 'Not so fast, officer. Have you a warrant?'

The question seemed to discompose Stilton.

'Why, I . . . Er, no.'

'Must have a warrant,' said Boko. 'You can't make a summary arrest on a serious charge like this.'

The momentary weakness passed. Stilton was himself again.

'I don't believe it,' he said stoutly. 'I think you're talking through your hat. Still, I'll go to the station and ask the sergeant.'

He vanished, and Boko became brisk and efficient.

'You'll have to leg it, Bertie,' he said, 'and without a second's delay. Get your car, drive to London and go abroad. They won't be watching the ports yet. Better look in on the Cohen Bros. *en route* and buy a false moustache.'

It isn't often that I would care to allow this borderline case's counsel to rule my actions, but on this occasion it seemed to me that his advice was good. I had been thinking along the same lines myself. Oh, as a matter of fact, I had just been saying to myself at that very moment, for the wings of a dove. Briefly requesting him to get hold of Jeeves and tell him to follow with the personal effects, I streaked for the garage.

And I was just about to fling wide the gates, when there suddenly came from the other side of the door the sound of a hoarse voice, and I paused, astounded. Unless the ears had deceived me, there was a human soul inside the edifice.

It spoke again, and what enabled me to get abreast and identify the thorax from which it proceeded was the fact that one caught the name 'Fittleworth', preceded by a number of qualifying adjectives of a rugged and rather Elizabethan nature. In a flash, I got the whole set-up.

Driving away from the East Wibley Town Hall at the conclusion of the recent festivities, Boko must inadvertently have taken Uncle Percy with him. He had sped homewards with a song on his lips, and all unknown to him, overlooked while getting a spot of tired Nature's sweet restorer in the back of the car, the old relative had come along for the ride.

28

I drew in the breath with a startled whoosh, and for some moments stood rooted to the s., the brow furrowed, the eyes bulging. To say that this thing had come upon me like a sock behind the ear from a stuffed eelskin would be in no wise to overstate the facts. As I stood there with my ear against the door, listening to what was filtering through the woodwork, it is not too much to say that melancholy marked me for its own.

Consider the posish, I mean. The one thing that was of the essence was that Boko should keep this man a thing of sweetness and light, and it was absurd to suppose that this could be done by locking him up all night in garages in the costume of Sinbad the Sailor. A man of generous spirit, like Uncle Percy, inevitably chafes at such treatment.

He was chafing now. I could hear him. The tone of his observations left no room for misunderstanding. They were not the *obiter dicta* of one who, when released, would laugh heartily at the amusing little misunderstanding, but rather of a man whose earnest endeavour it would be to skin the person responsible for his incarceration.

Indeed, it was upon this very point that he had now begun to touch. And not only was he resolved to skin Boko. He stressed in unmistakable terms his intention of doing it lingeringly and with a blunt knife. In short, it was abundantly clear that, however beautiful might have been the friendship which had been started overnight between his host and himself, it had now taken a bad toss and definitely come unstuck.

I found myself frankly unable to cope with the situation. It was one of those which seemed to call imperiously for a word or two of advice from Jeeves. And I was just regretting that he was not there, when a gentle cough in my rear told me that he was. It was as if some sort of telepathy, if that's the word I want, had warned him that the young master had lost his grip and could do with twopennyworth of feudal assistance.

'Jeeves!' I cried, and clutched him by the coat sleeve, like a lost child hooking on to its mother. When I had finished pouring my tale into his receptive ear, it was plain that he had not failed to grasp the nub.

'Most disturbing, sir,' he said.

'Most,' I responded.

I refrained from wounding him with any word of censure and rebuke, but I could not but feel, as I have so frequently felt before, that a spot of leaping about and eyeball-rolling would have been more in keeping with the gravity of the situation. If Jeeves has a fault, as I think I have already mentioned, it is that he is too prone merely to tut at times when you would prefer to see his knotted and combined locks do a bit of parting.

'His lordship, you gather, sir, is incensed?'

I could answer that one.

'Yes, Jeeves. His remarks, as far as I was able to catch them, were unquestionably those of a man a good deal steamed up. What is the Death of the Thousand Cuts?'

'It is a penal sentence in vogue in Chinese police courts for minor offences. Roughly equivalent to our fourteen days with the option of a fine. Why do you ask, sir?'

'Uncle Percy happened to mention it in passing. It's one of the things he is planning to do to Boko when they get together. Good Lord, Jeeves!' I exclaimed.

'Sir?'

The reason I had exclaimed as above was that this mention of police courts and penal sentences had

suddenly reminded me of my own position. For a brief
space, the mind, occupied with this business of uncles in
garages, had slid away from the fact that I was a fugitive
from a chain gang.

'You haven't heard the latest. Stilton. He has found
out about that uniform and has gone off to get warrants
and things.'

'Indeed, sir?'

'Yes. Young Edwin, creeping into my room last night
in order to insinuate a hedgehog into my bed, saw the
thing lying there, and went and squealed to Stilton, the
degraded little copper's nark. Only by making an
immediate getaway can I hope to escape undergoing the
utmost rigours of the Law. You see the frightful
dilemma I'm on the horns of. My car's in the garage. To
get it, I shall have to open the door. And opening the
door involves having Uncle Percy come popping out like
a cork out of a bottle.'

'You shrink from an encounter with his lordship, sir?'

'Yes, Jeeves. I shrink from an encounter with his
lordship. Oh, I know what you are going to say. You are
about to point out that it was Boko who lodged him in
the coop, not me.'

'Precisely, sir. You are not armed so strong in honesty
that his lordship's displeasure will pass by you as the
idle wind, which you respect not.'

'I dare say. But have you ever removed a wounded
puma from a trap?'

'No, sir. I have not had that experience.'

'Well, anyone will tell you that on such occasions the
animal does not pause to pick and choose. It just goes
baldheaded for the nearest innocent bystander in sight.'

'I appreciate your point, sir. It might be better if you
were to return to the house and allow me to extricate
his lordship.'

His nobility stunned me.

'Would you, Jeeves?'

'Certainly, sir.'

'Pretty white of you.'

'Not at all, sir.'

'You could turn the key, shout "All clear", and then run like a rabbit.'

'I would prefer to linger on the scene, sir, in the hope of doing something to smooth his lordship's wounded feelings.'

'With honeyed words, you mean?'

'Precisely, sir.'

I drew a deep breath.

'You wouldn't consider at least climbing a tree?'

'No, sir.'

I drew another one.

'Well, all right, if you say so. You know best. Carry on, then, Jeeves.'

'Very good, sir. I will bring your car to the front door, so that you will be enabled to make an immediate start. I will follow later in the day with the suitcases.'

It was some slight consolation to me in this dark hour to reflect, as I tooled back to the house, that the news I was bearing would, if he were still eating sardines, cause those sardines to turn to ashes in Boko's mouth. I am not a vindictive man, but I was feeling in no amiable frame of mind towards this literary screwball. I mean, it's all very well for a chap to plead that he's an author and expect on the strength of that to get away with conduct which would qualify the ordinary man for a one-way ticket to Colney Hatch, but even an author, I felt – and I think with justice – ought to have had the sense to glance through his car before he locked it up for the night, to make sure there weren't any shipping magnates dozing in the back seat.

As it happened, he was past the sardines phase. He was lolling in his chair in quiet enjoyment of the after-breakfast pipe, while Nobby, at his side, did the

crossword puzzle in the morning paper. At the sight of
Bertram, both expressed surprise.

'Why, hullo!' said Nobby.

'Haven't you gone yet?' said Boko.

'No, I haven't,' I replied, and laughed a hard, mirthless
one.

It caused Boko to frown disapprovingly.

'What's the idea of coming here and trilling with
laughter?' he asked austerely. 'You must try to get it
into your head, my lad, that this is not the time for that
sort of thing. Don't you realize your position? Unless
you're across the Channel by nightfall, you haven't a
hope. Where's your car?'

'In the garage.'

'Then get it out of the garage.'

'I can't,' I said, letting him have it right in the gizzard.
'Uncle Percy's there.'

And in a few crisp words I slipped him the lowdown.

I had anticipated that my statement would get in
amongst him a bit, and this expectation was fulfilled.
Man and boy, I have seen a good many lower jaws fall,
but never one that shot down with such a sudden swoop
as his. It was surprising that the thing didn't come off its
hinges.

'But how was he in my car? He can't have been in my
car. Why didn't I notice him?'

This, of course, was susceptible of a ready explanation.

'Because you're a fathead.'

Nobby, who since the initial spilling of the beans had
been sitting bolt upright in her chair with gleaming eyes,
making little gulping noises and chewing the lower lip
with pearly teeth, endorsed this.

'Fathead,' she concurred, speaking in a strange,
strangled voice, 'is right. Of all –'

Preoccupied though Boko was, there must have
penetrated to his consciousness some inkling of what

the harvest would be, were she permitted to get going and really start hauling up her slacks. He strove to head her off with a tortured gesture.

'Just a minute, darling.'

'Of all the –'

'Yes, yes.'

'Of all the gibbering –'

'Quite, quite. But half a second, angel. Bertie and I are threshing out an important point. Let me just try to envisage what happened after you left last night, Bertie. Here is the sequence, as I recall it. I had my talk with old Worplesdon, and, as I told you, secured a guardian's blessing: and then – yes, then I went back to the ballroom to tread the measure for a while.'

'Of all the gibbering, half-witted –'

'Exactly, exactly. But don't interrupt the flow of my thoughts, precious. I'm trying to get this thing straight. I danced, a saraband or two, and then looked in at the bar for a moment. I wanted to get a snootful and muse over my happiness. And I was doing this, when it suddenly occurred to me that Nobby was probably tossing sleeplessly on her pillow, dying to hear how everything had come out, and I felt that I must get home immediately and go and bung gravel at her window. I raced back to the car, accordingly, sprang to the wheel and drove off. I see now why I didn't notice old Worplesdon. Obviously, the man by that time had passed out and was lying on the floor. Well, dash it, a chap in my frame of mind, all joy and ecstasy and excitement, with his soul full to the brim of tender thoughts of the girl he loved, couldn't be expected to go over the floor of his car with a magnifying-glass, on the chance that there might be Worplesdons there. Naturally, not observing him, I assumed that he had gone off on his push bike. Would you have had me borrow a couple of bloodhounds and search the *tonneau* from end to end? I'm sure you understand everything now, darling, and will be the first to withdraw the adjective "gibbering". Oh, I am not angry,' said Boko, 'in fact, not even surprised that in the heat of the moment you should have spoken as you did. Just so long as you realize that I am innocent, blameless . . .'

At this juncture there was a confused noise without, and Uncle Percy crossed the threshold, moving well. A moment later, Jeeves shimmered in his wake.

Having become so accustomed during our hobnobbings of the previous day to seeing this uncle by marriage in genial and comradely mood, I had almost forgotten how like the Assyrian swooping down on the fold he could look, when deeply stirred. And that he was so now rather leaped to the eye. The ginger whiskers which go with the costume of Sinbad the Sailor obscured his countenance to a great extent, rendering it difficult to note the full play of expression on the features, but one was able to observe his eyes, and that was enough to be going on with. Fixed on Boko with an unwinking glare, they had the effect of causing that unhappy purveyor of wholesome literature for the masses to recoil at least a dozen feet. And he would undoubtedly have gone farther, had he not fetched up against the wall.

Jeeves had spoken of his intention of trying to smooth the ruffled Worplesdon feelings with honeyed words. Whether he hadn't been allowed to get one in edgeways, or whether he had tried a few and they hadn't been honeyed enough, I was not in a position to say. But the fact was patent that the above feelings were still as ruffled as dammit, and that Hampshire contained at this moment no hotter-under-the-collar shipping magnate.

Proof of this was given by his opening speech, which consisted of the word 'What', repeated over and over again as if fired from a machine-gun. It was always this uncle's practice, as I have mentioned, to what-what-what rather freely in moments of emotion, and he did not deviate from it on this occasion.

'What?' he said, in part, continuing to focus the eye on Boko. 'What-what-what-what-what-what-what-what?'

Here he paused, as if for a reply, and I think Boko did the wrong thing by asking him if he would like a sardine. The question, seeming to touch an exposed nerve, caused a sheet of flame to shoot from his eyes.

'Sardine?' he said, with a bitter intonation. 'Sardine? Sardine? Sardine?'

'You'll feel better, when you've had some breakfast,' said Nobby, pulling a quick ministering-angel-thou.

Uncle Percy opposed this view.

'I shall not. The only thing that can make me feel better is to thrash that pie-faced young wart-hog Fittleworth within an inch of his life. Bertie, get me a horsewhip.'

I pursed the lips dubiously.

'I don't believe we have one,' I said. 'Are there any horsewhips on the premises, Boko?'

'No, no horsewhips,' the latter responded, now trying to get through the wall.

Uncle Percy snorted.

'What a house! Jeeves.'

'M'lord?'

'Go over to the Hall and bring me my horsewhip with the ivory handle.'

'Yes, m'lord.'

'I think it's in my study. If not, hunt about for it.'

'Very good, m'lord. No doubt her ladyship will be able to inform me of the instrument's whereabouts.'

He spoke so casually that it was perhaps three seconds by the stop-watch before Uncle Percy got the gist. When he did, he started, like one jabbed in the fleshy parts with a sudden bradawl.

'Her . . . what?'

'Her ladyship, m'lord.'

'Her ladyship?'

'Yes, m'lord.'

Uncle Percy had crumpled like a wet sock. He sank into a chair, and clutched the marmalade jar, as if for support. His eyes popped out of his head, and waved about on their stalks.

'But her ladyship –'

' – returned unexpectedly late last night, m'lord.'

29

I don't know if the name of Lot's wife is familiar to you, and if you were told about her rather remarkable finish. I may not have got the facts right, but the story, as I heard it, was that she was advised not to look round at something or other or she would turn into a pillar of salt, so, naturally imagining that they were simply pulling her leg, she looked round, and – *bing* – a pillar of salt. And the reason I mention this now is that the very same thing seemed to have happened to Uncle Percy. Crouching there with his fingers riveted to the marmalade jar, he appeared to have turned into a pillar of salt. If it hadn't been that the ginger whiskers were quivering gently, you would have said that life had ceased to animate the rigid limbs.

'It appears that Master Thomas is now out of danger, m'lord, and no longer has need of her ladyship's ministrations.'

The whiskers continued to quiver, and I didn't blame them. I knew just how the old relative must be feeling, for, as I have already indicated, he had made no secret when chatting with me of his apprehensions concerning the shape of things to come, should Aunt Agatha ever learn that he had been attending fancy dress dances in her absence.

The poignant drama of it all had not escaped Nobby, either.

'Golly, Uncle Percy,' she said, a womanly pity in her voice that became her well, 'this is a bit awkward, is it not? You'll have to devote a minute or two, when you see her, to explaining why you were out all night, won't you?'

Her words had the effect of bringing the unhappy man out of his trance or coma as if she had touched off a stick of dynamite under him. He moved, he stirred, he seemed to feel the rush of life along his keel.

'Jeeves,' he said hoarsely.

'M'lord?'

'Jeeves.'

'M'lord?'

Uncle Percy shoved out his tongue about an inch, moistening the lips with the tip of it. It was plain that he was finding it no easy matter to get speech over the larynx.

'Her ladyship, Jeeves . . . Tell me . . . Is she . . . Has she . . . Is she by any chance aware of my absence?'

'Yes, m'lord. She was apprised of it by the head housemaid. I left them in conference. "You tell me his lordship's bed *has not been slept in*?" her ladyship was saying. Her agitation was most pronounced.'

I caught Uncle Percy's eye. It had swivelled round at me with a dumb, pleading look in it, as if saying that suggestions would be welcomed.

'How would it be,' I said – well, one had to say something, 'if you told her the truth?'

'The truth?' he repeated dazedly, and you could see he thought the idea a novel one.

'That you went to the ball to confer with Clam.'

He shook his head.

'I could never convince your aunt that I had gone to a fancy dress ball from purely business motives. Women are so prone to think the worst.'

'Something in that.'

'And it's no good trying to make them see reason, because they talk so damn' quick. No,' said Uncle Percy, 'this is the end. I can only set my teeth and take my medicine like an English gentleman.'

'Unless, of course, Jeeves has something to suggest.'

This perked him up for an instant. Then the drawn,

haggard look came back into his face, and he shook the lemon again, slowly and despondently.

'Impossible. The situation is beyond Jeeves.'

'No situation is beyond Jeeves,' I said, with quiet rebuke. 'In fact,' I went on, scrutinizing the man closely, 'I believe something is fermenting now inside that spacious bean. Am I wrong, Jeeves, in supposing that I can see the light of inspiration in your eye?'

'No, sir. You are quite correct. I think that I may perhaps be able to offer a satisfactory solution of his lordship's difficulty.'

Uncle Percy inhaled sharply. An awed look came into the unoccupied areas of his face. I heard him murmur something under his breath about fish.

'You mean that, Jeeves?'

'Yes, m'lord.'

'Then let us have it,' I said, feeling rather like some impresario of performing fleas who watches the star member of his troupe advance to the footlights. 'What is this solution of which you speak?'

'Well, sir, it occurred to me that as his lordship has, as I understand, given his consent to the union of Mr Fittleworth and Miss Hopwood –'

Uncle Percy uttered an animal cry.

'I haven't! Or, if I did, I've withdrawn it.'

'Very good, m'lord. In that case, I have nothing to suggest.'

There was a silence. One could sense the struggle proceeding in Uncle Percy's bosom. I saw him look at Boko, and quiver. Then a strong shudder passed through the frame, and I knew he was recalling what Jeeves had said about Aunt Agatha's agitation being most pronounced. When Aunt Agatha's agitation is pronounced, she has a way of drawing her eyebrows together and making her nose look like an eagle's beak. Strong men have quailed at the spectacle, repeatedly.

'May as well hear what you've got to say, I suppose,'
he said, at length.

'Quite,' I agreed. 'No harm in having a – what, Jeeves?'

'Academic discussion, sir.'

'Thank you, Jeeves.'

'Not at all, sir.'

'Carry on, then.'

'Very good, sir. It merely occurred to me that, had his
lordship consented to the union, nothing would have
been more natural than that he should have visited Mr
Fittleworth at his house for the purpose of talking the
matter over and making arrangements for the wedding.
Immersed in this absorbing subject, his lordship would
quite understandably have lost count of time –'

I yipped intelligently. I had got the set-up.

'And when he looked at his watch and found how late
it was –'

'Precisely, sir. When his lordship looked at his watch
and found how late it was, Mr Fittleworth hospitably
suggested that he should pass the remainder of the night
beneath his roof. His lordship agreed that this would be
the most convenient course, and so it was arranged.'

I looked at Uncle Percy, confidently expecting the
salvo of applause, and was amazed to find him shaking
the bean once more.

'It wouldn't work,' he said.

'Why on earth not? It's a pip.'

He kept on oscillating the lozenge.

'No, Bertie, the scheme is not practical. Your aunt,
my dear boy, is a suspicious woman. She probes beneath
the surface and asks questions. And the first one she
would ask on this occasion would be, Why, merely in
order to discuss wedding arrangements with my ward's
future husband, did I dress up as Sindbad the Sailor? You
can see for yourself how awkward that question would
be, and how difficult to answer.'

The point was well taken.

'A snag, Jeeves. Can you get round it?'

'Quite easily, sir. Before returning to the Hall, his lordship could borrow a suit of clothes from you, sir.'

'Off course he could. Clad in the herring-bone tweed which is in the cupboard in my bedroom, Uncle Percy, you could look Aunt Agatha in the eye without a tremor.'

I dare say you have frequently, when strolling in your garden, seen a parched flower beneath a refreshing downpour. It was of such a flower that Uncle Percy now irresistibly reminded me. He seemed to swell and burgeon, as it were, and the strained eyes lost that resemblance to the under side of a dead fish which had been so noticeable since the beginning of this sequence.

'Good Lord!' he exclaimed. 'You're quite right. So I could. Jeeves,' he went on, emotionally, 'you must have that brain of yours pickled and presented to some national museum.'

'Very good, m'lord.'

'When you've done with it, of course. Come on, Bertie, action, action! Ho for the herring-bone tweed!'

'This way, Uncle Percy,' I said, and we started for the door, to find our path barred by Boko. He was looking a bit green about the gills, but firm and resolute.

'Just a minute,' said Boko. 'Not so jolly fast, if you don't mind. How about that guardian's blessing? Do I cop?'

'Of course you do, old bird,' I said soothingly. 'That's all budgeted for in the estimates, Uncle Percy?'

'Eh? What?'

'The guardian's b. You're dishing that out?'

Once more there was that silent struggle. Then he nodded sombrely.

'It seems unavoidable.'

'It is unavoidable.'

'Then I won't try to avoid it.'

'Okay, Boko, you're all set.'

'Good,' said Boko. 'I'll just have that in writing, if you don't mind, my dear Worplesdon. I don't want to carp or criticize, but there's been a lot of in-and-out running about this business to present date, and one would welcome a few words in black and white. You will find pen and ink on the table in the corner. Sing out, my dear Worplesdon, if the nib doesn't suit you, and I will provide you with another.'

Uncle Percy went to the table in the corner, and took pen in hand. It would be too much to say that his demeanour, as he did so, was rollicking. I fancy that up to this moment he had been entertaining a faint hope that, if his luck held, he might somehow derive the benefits from Jeeves's scheme without having to sit in on its drawbacks. However, as I say, he took pen in hand and, having scribbled for a minute or so, handed the result to Boko, who read it through and handed it to Nobby, who read it through and tucked it away with a satisfied 'Okay-doke' in some safe deposit in the recesses of her costume.

She had scarcely done so, when heavy, official footsteps sounded without, and Stilton came clumping in.

You will scarcely believe me, but it is a fact that I had been so tensely gripped by the drama of the last quarter of an hour that the Stilton angle had been completely expunged from my mind, and it was only now, as I watched him heave to, that the thought of the Wooster personal peril came back to me. The first thing he did on entering the room was to give me one of those looks of his, and it chilled my insides like a quart of ice cream.

I had a shot at an airy 'Ah, there you are, Stilton', but my heart was not in it, and it elicited no response except a short 'Ho!' Having got off this 'Ho!' which, as I have explained, was in the nature of a sort of signature tune, he addressed himself to Boko.

'You were right about that warrant,' he said. 'The

sergeant says I've got to have one. I've brought it along.
It has to be signed by a Justice of the Peace.' Here, for
the first time, he appeared to become aware of Uncle
Percy's identity, which, of course, had been shrouded
from him by the whiskers. 'Why, hullo, Lord
Worplesdon,' he said, 'you're just the man I was looking
for. If you will shove your name on the dotted line, we
can go ahead. So you went to that fancy dress ball last
night?' he said, giving him the eye.

I think he had merely intended to be chatty and to
show a kindly interest, as it were, in the relative's
affairs, but he had said the wrong thing. Uncle Percy
stiffened haughtily.

'What do you mean, I went to the fancy dress ball last
night? I did nothing of the kind, and I shall be glad if you
will refrain from making loose statements of that
description. Went to the fancy dress ball, indeed! What
fancy dress ball? Where? It is news to me that there has
been a fancy dress ball.'

His generous indignation seemed to take Stilton
aback.

'Oh, sorry,' he said. 'I just thought . . . The costume, I
mean.'

'And what about the costume? If my ward and her
future husband are planning an evening of amateur
theatricals and asked me as a personal favour to put on
the costume of Sindbad the Sailor, to see if I was the
type for the part, is it so singular that I should
good-humouredly have acceded to their wishes? And is
it any business of yours? Does it entitle you to jump to
idiotic conclusions about fancy dress balls? Have I got to
explain every simple little action of mine to every
flatfooted copper who comes along and can't keep his
infernal nose out of my business?'

These were not easy questions to answer, and the best
Stilton could do was to shuffle his feet and say 'Oh, ah.'

'Well, anyway,' he said, after a rather painful pause,

changing the subject and getting back to the *res*, 'would you mind signing this warrant?'

'Warrant? What warrant? What's it all about? What's all this nonsense about warrants?'

There was a sound in the background like a distant sheep coughing gently on a mountainside. Jeeves sailing into action.

'If I might explain, your lordship. It appears that in the course of yesterday afternoon the officer's uniform was purloined as he bathed in the river. He accuses Mr Wooster of the crime.'

'Mr Wooster? Bertie? My nephew?'

'Yes, m'lord. To me, a most bizarre theory. One seeks in vain for a motive which could plausibly have led Mr Wooster to perpetrate such an outrage. The constable, I understand, alleges that Mr Wooster desired the uniform in order to be able to attend the fancy dress ball.'

This seemed to interest Uncle Percy.

'There really was a fancy dress ball, was there?'

'Yes, m'lord. At the neighbouring town of East Wibley.'

'Odd. I never heard about it.'

'A very minor affair, m'lord, I gather. Not at all the sort of entertainment in which a gentleman of Mr Wooster's position would condescend to participate.'

'Of course not. I wouldn't have gone to it myself. Just one of those potty little country affairs, eh?'

'Precisely, m'lord. Nobody, knowing Mr Wooster, would suppose for a moment that he would waste his sweetness on such desert air.'

'Eh?'

'A quotation, m'lord. The poet Gray.'

'Ah. But you say the officer sticks to it that he did?'

'Yes, m'lord. It is fortunate, therefore, that your lordship passed the night in this house, and so is able to testify that Mr Wooster never left the premises.'

'Dashed fortunate. Settles the whole thing.'

263

I never know, when I am telling a story where a couple of fellows are talking and a third fellow is trying to shove his oar in, whether to interpolate the last named's gulps and gurgles in the run of the dialogue or to wait till it's all over and then chalk up these gulps and gurgles to their utterer's score. I think it works out smoother the second way, and that is why, in recording the above exchanges, I have left out Stilton's attempts to chip in. All through this Jeeves-Worplesdon exchange of ideas he had been trying to catch the Speaker's eye, only to be 'Tchah'-ed and 'Be quiet, officer'-ed by Uncle Percy. A lull in the conversation having occurred at the word 'thing', he was now able to speak his piece.

'I tell you the accused Wooster did pinch my uniform!' he cried, his eyes bulging more than ever and his cheeks a pretty scarlet.

'It was seen on his bed by the witness Edwin.'

Things were going so well that I felt equal to raising the eyebrows and coming through with a light, amused laugh.

'Edwin, Uncle Percy! One smiles, does one not?'

The relative backed me up nobly.

'Smiles? Certainly one smiles. Like the dickens. Are you trying to tell me,' he said, letting Stilton have the eye in no uncertain measure, 'that this preposterous accusation of yours is based on the unsupported word of my son Edwin? I can scarcely credit it. Can you, Jeeves?'

'Most extraordinary, m'lord. But possibly the officer is not aware that Mr Wooster inflicted a personal assault upon Master Edwin yesterday, and so does not realize how biased any statement on the part of the young gentleman regarding Mr Wooster must inevitably be.'

'Don't make excuses for him. The man's a fool. And I should like to say,' said Uncle Percy, swelling like a balloon and starting to give Stilton the strong remarks from the bench, 'that we have had in my opinion far too much of late of these wild and irresponsible accusations

Joy in the Morning

on the part of the police. A deplorable spirit is creeping into the Force, and as long as I remain a Justice of the Peace I shall omit no word or act to express my strongest disapproval of it. I shall stamp it out, root and branch, and see to it that the liberty of the subject is not placed in jeopardy by officers of the Law who so far forget their – yes, dash it, their sacred obligations as to bring trumped-up charges right and left in a selfish desire to secure promotion. I have nothing further to add except to express my profound regret that you should have been subjected to this monstrous persecution, Bertie.'

'Quite all right, Uncle Percy.'

'It is not all right. It is outrageous. I advise you in future, officer, to be careful, very careful. And as for that warrant of yours, you can take it and stick it . . . However, that is neither here nor there.'

It was good stuff. Indeed, I can't remember ever having heard better, except once, when I was a stripling and Aunt Agatha was ticking me off for breaking a valuable china vase with my catapult. I confidently expected Stilton to cower beneath it like a worm in a thunderstorm. But he didn't. It was plain that he burned, not with shame and remorse but with the baffled fury of the man who, while not quite abreast of the run of the scenario, realizes that dirty work is afoot at the crossroads and that something swift is being slipped across him.

'Ho!' he said, and paused for a moment to wrestle with his feelings. Then, with generous emotion: 'It's a bally conspiracy,' he cried. 'It's a lowdown, hornswoggling plot to defeat the ends of justice. For the last time, Lord Worplesdon, will you sign this warrant?'

Nothing could have been more dignified than Uncle Percy's demeanour. He drew himself up, and his voice was quiet and cold.

'I have already indicated what you can do with that warrant. I think, officer, that it would be well if you were to go and sleep it off. For the kindest interpretation which I can place upon your extraordinary behaviour is that you are intoxicated. Bertie, show the constable the door.'

I showed Stilton the door, and he took a sort of dazed look at it, as if it was the first time he had seen the bally thing. Then he navigated slowly through, and disappeared, not even pausing to say 'Ho' over his shoulder. The impression I received was that his haughty spirit was at last crushed. Presently we heard the sound of his violin cases tramping away down the garden path.

'And now, my boy,' said Uncle Percy, as the last echoes died away, 'for the herring-bone tweed. Also a bath and a shave and a cup of strong black coffee with perhaps the merest suspicion of brandy in it. And perhaps it would be as well, when I am ready to start for the Hall, if you were to accompany me, to add your testimony to mine regarding my spending last night under this roof. You will not falter, will you? You will support my statement, will you not, in a strong resonant voice, carrying conviction in every syllable? Nothing on these occasions creates so unfortunate an impression as the pause for thought, the hesitating utterance, the nervous twiddling of the fingers. Above all things, remember not to stand on one leg. Right, my boy. Let us go.'

I escorted him to my room, dug out the suit, showed him the bathroom and left him to it. When I got back to the dining-room, Boko had gone, but Nobby was still there, chatting with Jeeves. She greeted me warmly.

'Boko's gone to fetch his car,' she said. 'We're going to run up to London and get married. Wonderful how everything has come out, isn't it? I thought Uncle Percy was terrific.'

'Most impressive,' I agreed.

'And what words that tongue could utter could

give even a sketchy idea of how one feels about you,
Jeeves.'

'I am deeply gratified, miss, if I have been able to give
satisfaction.'

'I've said it before, and I'll say it again – there's
nobody like you.'

'Thank you very much, miss.'

I think this might have gone on for some time, for
Nobby was plainly filled to the back teeth with girlish
enthusiasm, but at this point I interrupted. I would be
the last man ever to deprive Jeeves of his meed of praise,
but I had a question of compelling interest to put.

'Have you shown Florence that letter of mine,
Nobby?' I asked.

A sudden cloud came over her eager map, and she
made a clicking noise.

'I knew there was something I had forgotten. Oh,
Bertie, I'm so sorry.'

'Sorry?' I said, filled with a nameless fear.

'I've been meaning to tell you. When I got up this
morning, I couldn't find that letter anywhere, and I was
looking for it, when Edwin came along and told me he
had done an act of kindness last night by tidying my
room. I think he must have destroyed the letter. He
generally does destroy all correspondence when he tidies
rooms. I'm most awfully sorry, but I expect you'll find
some other way of coping with Florence. Ask Jeeves.
He's sure to think of something. Ah,' she said, as a
booming voice came from the great open spaces, 'there's
Boko calling me. Good-bye, Bertie. Good-bye, Jeeves. I
must rush.'

She was gone with the wind, and I turned to Jeeves
with a pale, set face.

'Yes, sir.'

'Can you think of a course to pursue?'

'No, sir.'

'You are baffled?'

'For the moment, sir, unquestionable. I fear that Miss Hopwood overestimated my potentialities.'

'Come, come, Jeeves. It is not like you to be a . . . what's the word . . . it's on the tip of my tongue.'

'Defeatist, sir?'

'That's right. It is not like you to be a defeatist. Don't give it up. Go and brood in the kitchen. There may be some fish there. Did you notice any, when you were there yesterday?'

'Only a tin of anchovy paste, sir.'

My heart sank a bit. Anchovy paste is a slender reed on which to lean in a major crisis. Still, it was fish within the meaning of the act, and no doubt contained its quota of phosphorus.

'Go and wade into it.'

'Very good, sir.'

'Don't spare the stuff. Dig it out with a spoon,' I said, and dismissed him with a moody gesture.

Moody was the word which would have described my aspect, as a few moments later I left the house and proceeded to the garden, feeling in need of a bit of air. I had kept up a brave front, but I had little real hope that anchovy paste would bring home the bacon. As I stood at the garden gate, staring sombrely before me, I was at a pretty low ebb.

I mean to say, I had been banking everything on that letter. I had counted on it to destroy the Wooster glamour in Florence's eyes. And, lacking it, I couldn't see how she was going to be persuaded that I was not a king among men. Not for the first time, I found myself musing bitterly on young Edwin, the *fons et origo* – a Latin expression – of all my troubles.

And I was just regretting that we were not in China, where it would have been a simple matter to frame up something against the child, thus putting him in line for the Death of the Thousand Cuts, when my reverie was

interrupted by the ting of a bicycle bell, and Stilton
came wheeling up.

After what had passed, of course, it was not agreeable
to be closeted with this vindictive copper, and I am not
ashamed to say that I backed a pace. In fact, I would
probably have gone on backing, had he not reached out
a hand like a ham and grabbed me by the slack of my
coat.

'Stand still, you blasted object,' he said. 'I have
something to say to you.'

'You couldn't write?'

'No, I could not write. Don't wriggle. Listen.'

I could see that the man was wrestling with some
strong emotion, and could only hope that it was not
homicidal. The eyes were glittering, and the face
flushed.

'Listen,' he said again. 'You know that engagement of
yours?'

'To Florence?'

'To Florence. It's off.'

'Off?'

'Off,' said Stilton.

A sharp exclamation passed my lips. I clutched at the
gate for support. The sun, which a moment before had
gone behind a cloud, suddenly came shooting out like a
rabbit and started shining like the dickens. On every
side, it seemed to me, birds began to tootle their songs of
joy. It will give you some rough indication of my
feelings when I tell you that not only did all Nature
become beautiful, but even for an instant Stilton.

Through a sort of pink mist, I heard myself asking
faintly what he meant. The question caused him to
frown with some impatience.

'You can understand words of one syllable, can't you?
I tell you your engagement is off. Florence is going to
marry me. I met her, as I came away from this pest

house, and had it out with her. After that revolting
exhibition of fraud and skulduggery in there, I had
decided to resign from the Force, and I told her so. It
removed the only barrier there had ever been between
us. Questioned, she broke down and came clean,
admitting that she had always loved me, and had got
engaged to you merely to score off me for something I
had said about modern enlightened thought. I withdrew
the remark, and she fell into my arms. She seemed
not to like the idea of breaking the news to you, so I
said I would do it. "And if young blasted Wooster has
anything to say", I told her, "I will twist his head off and
ram it down his throat". Have you anything to say,
Wooster?'

I paused for a moment to listen to the tootling birds.
Then I raised the map, and allowed the beaming sun to
play on it.

'Not a thing,' I assured him.

'You realize the position? She has returned you to
store. No ruddy wedding bells for you.'

'Quite.'

'Good. You will be leaving here fairly soon, I take it?'

'Almost at once.'

'Good,' said Stilton, and sprang on his bicycle as if it
had been a mettlesome charger.

Nor did I linger. I did the distance from the gate to
the kitchen in about three seconds flat. From the
window of the bathroom, as I passed, there came the
voice of Uncle Percy as he sluiced the frame. He was
singing some gay air. A sea chanty, probably, which he
had learned from Clam or one of the captains in his
employment.

Jeeves was pacing the kitchen floor, deep in thought.
He looked round, as I entered, and his manner was
apologetic.

'It appears, sir, I regret to say, that there is no anchovy
paste. It was finished yesterday.'

I didn't actually slap him on the back, but I gave him the dickens of a beaming smile.

'Never mind the anchovy paste, Jeeves. It will not be required. I've just seen Stilton. A reconciliation has taken place between him and Lady Florence, and they are once more headed for the altar rails. So, there being nothing to keep us in Steeple Bumpleigh, let's go.'

'Very good, sir. The car is at the door.'

I paused.

'Oh, but, dash it, we can't.'

'Sir?'

'I've just remembered I promised Uncle Percy to go to the Hall with him and help him cope with Aunt Agatha.'

'Her ladyship is not at the Hall, sir.'

'What! But you said she was.'

'Yes, sir. I fear I was guilty of subterfuge. I regretted the necessity, but it seemed to me essential in the best interests of all concerned.'

I goggled at the man.

'Egad, Jeeves!'

'Yes, sir.'

Faintly from the distance there came the sound of Uncle Percy working through his chanty.

'How would it be,' I suggested, 'to zoom off immediately, without waiting to pack?'

'I was about to suggest such a course myself, sir.'

'It would enable one to avoid tedious explanations.'

'Precisely, sir.'

'Then shift ho, Jeeves,' I said.

It was as we were about half-way between Steeple Bumpleigh and the old metrop, that I mentioned that there was an expression on the tip of my tongue which seemed to me to sum up the nub of the recent proceedings.

'Or, rather, when I say an expression, I mean a saying. A wheeze. A gag. What I believe is called a saw. Something about Joy . . .'

But we went into all that before, didn't we?

The P G Wodehouse Society (UK)

The P G Wodehouse Society (UK) was formed in 1997 and exists to promote the enjoyment of the works of the greatest humorist of the twentieth century.

The Society publishes a quarterly magazine, *Wooster Sauce*, which features articles, reviews, archive material and current news. It also publishes an occasional newsletter in the *By The Way* series which relates a single matter of Wodehousean interest. Members are rewarded in their second and subsequent years by receiving a specially produced text of a Wodehouse magazine story which has never been collected into one of his books.

A variety of Society events are arranged for members including regular meetings at a London club, a golf day, a cricket match, a Society dinner, and walks round Bertie Wooster's London. Meetings are also arranged in other parts of the country.

Membership enquiries

Membership of the Society is available to applicants from all parts of the world. The cost of a year's membership in 1998 was £15. Enquiries and requests for an application form should be addressed in writing to the Membership Secretary, Helen Murphy, at 16 Herbert Street, Plaistow, London E13 8BE, or write to the Editor of *Wooster Sauce*, Tony Ring, at 34 Longfield Road, Great Missenden, Bucks HP16 0EG.

You can visit their website at:
http://www.eclipse.co.uk/wodehouse

refresh yourself at penguin.co.uk

Visit penguin.co.uk for exclusive information and interviews with
bestselling authors, fantastic give-aways and the
inside track on all our books, from the Penguin Classics
to the latest bestsellers.

BE FIRST ⬇

first chapters, first editions, first novels

EXCLUSIVES ⬇

author chats, video interviews, biographies, special
features

EVERYONE'S A WINNER ⬇

give-aways, competitions, quizzes, ecards

READERS GROUPS ⬇

exciting features to support existing groups and
create new ones

NEWS ⬇

author events, bestsellers, awards, what's new

EBOOKS ⬇

books that click – download an ePenguin today

BROWSE AND BUY ⬇

thousands of books to investigate – search, try
and buy the perfect gift online – or treat yourself!

ABOUT US ⬇

job vacancies, advice for writers and company
history

Get Closer To Penguin . . . www.penguin.co.uk